Sam could feel Sara's heart thundering like a skittish colt; its vibration could be felt even through the thickness of her down coat. Anger for the years they had lost came out in the way he kissed her. The springtime scent and womanly feel of her only managed to remind him of all they'd lost, of all he wanted to find. _This isn't enough_, he thought. _I can never have enough of her._

"Call me when you wake up," he said, kissing her as the cab pulled up directly in front of the Carberry. "I want to be the first voice you hear in the morning."

"Call me tonight," she answered quickly, as the doorman hurried toward the taxi. "I want to be the last voice you hear before you sleep."

Then, suddenly, just before the door swung open and she was ushered back into reality, Sara leaned toward Sam and kissed him once more, committing his scent and touch to memory.

"Soon," she said, touching his mouth with one finger.

"Very soon," he answered.

BARBARA BRETTON

STARFIRE

MIRA BOOKS

ISBN 1-55166-066-0

STARFIRE

For Peerquith, as promised,
and
for the Graduate,
because he asked…

I love you both.

1

Sara Chance handed the salesclerk her American Express card and waited. So far the woman hadn't batted one false eyelash at the sight of the face that had made media headlines, but Sara knew it was just a matter of time.

The woman glanced at the gold plastic card, seemed to hesitate one slight moment, then put the card on the machine with the carboned sales check and slid the roller over both, imprinting Sara's name and number clearly in black ink.

Any second now, Sara thought. There would be the double take, the flicker of eyes darting from name to face and back again, then the full realization that the woman whose face had haunted the world from the cover of every major newspaper and magazine was indeed standing right there.

Sara began the countdown: five, four, three, two—

"Excuse me, but aren't you the widow of Maxwell Chance?" The woman's hands were curved nervously around the American Express card, and Sara could see the grooves her crimson nails were making in the flesh of her palm.

Sara reached for the card and nodded her head. There was no point in denying what was plainly before them both in black and white. "Yes, I am." *Don't ask questions,* she thought. *Don't tell me how you don't believe a thing you read.*

The salesclerk, forgetting she had to wrap the tiny ebony cigarette lighter Sara had just bought for Deanna, her personal assistant, turned toward the back of the boutique. "Edna!" Her voice, Manhattan chic and beautifully modulated just moments ago, had risen to a decibel level suitable for the New Jersey Meadowlands Arena during halftime. "Hurry out here! Maxwell Ch—"

Sara's strong slim hand grasped the woman's forearm securely, cutting off the announcement. "Please," she said, keeping her voice low and calm and hoping the other woman would follow suit, "I'll be happy to sign an autograph for you if you'd like, but I would appreciate your helping me to stay anonymous here."

The salesclerk's ruby-lipsticked mouth formed an O of surprise at the request, as if Sara had just asked her to fly to the moon unaided. Sara Chance had as much of an opportunity for anonymity as Jacqueline Onassis, and maybe less, thanks to her eye-catching head of dark frothy curls that soared up and around her face.

Edna had now joined the first salesclerk, Marie, and Sara shifted from foot to foot, praying they would get on with business so she could escape before someone else in the small boutique noticed who she was.

"Now I'm not much of a music fan myself," Edna said, clutching at Sara's hand, "but when Maxwell Chance died— well, I took it nearly as hard as my daughter. He was such a special man."

Sara sighed and settled down for a long siege. "Yes, he was," she said, not lying. "His talent was special indeed." Even now, two years after his death, the legend of Maxwell Chance continued to grow.

Marie, who had finally remembered to wrap the cigarette lighter, stopped fiddling with tissue and ribbon and looked back at Sara, her gray eyes almost misty. "You really showed the press, didn't you? They were so hard on you when you married Maxwell, but you won them over when he died. I remember seeing the photos of you at the funeral—you looked so beautiful."

"Like a queen," Edna said.

"Like a queen," Marie repeated, continuing with her wrapping.

I can't handle this, Sara thought. The urge to make a run for the door of the boutique was growing dangerously strong. She had been both demon and darling of the public and found one extreme to be as ultimately damaging as the other.

She was glad she was going to be out of town for the second anniversary of Max's death. With the anniversary so close at hand now, the press had once again picked up on Sara and were making her attempts at living a normal life nearly impossible. Their renewed interest in her had sparked a stream of abusive letters that for the past month had caused Sara to stick close to home. Deanna had said the letters were nothing to worry about, but they haunted Sara and made her very aware of her vulnerabilities.

"I'm sorry to rush you," Sara said to Marie, "but I am in a bit of a hurry and..." She let her words trail off gently, hoping the saleswoman would understand.

Marie glanced around at the customers, who were beginning to fill the small boutique. She caught Sara's eye and winked, the up-down movement of her thick false lashes so comical that Sara had to suppress a very untimely giggle.

"You like your privacy, don't you, dear?" Marie asked as she slipped the package into a tiny shopping bag of slick red paper and handed it to Sara. "It must be hard with a face as pretty as a picture to get around unnoticed."

The last thing Sara wanted was to talk about either her looks or her lack of privacy, but courtesy was as much a part of her makeup as her blue eyes or dark hair. "Well," she began slowly, "when your face has been on as many front pages as mine has, everyone does think he or she knows you personally." The back of her neck prickled. She knew someone had zeroed in on her from across the aisle. She began to edge toward the door, praying Marie wouldn't pursue the topic any further. "Thank you so much," she said, tucking the shopping bag under her arm. "You did a beautiful wrapping job."

Marie brushed her compliment away with one multi-ringed hand. "It was a pleasure to do something for you. Especially after all the happiness your dear husband gave the world."

Out of nowhere the urge to cry hit Sara, and she prayed she'd make it out into the main shopping area before tears started. They expected so much, these people to whom celebrities were minor deities, and Sara was painfully aware of the reality behind the glamour. Personal boundaries shrink inward; private lives disappear. She had learned all of that during her marriage, and it was a lesson she remembered well. She hurried toward the door, ignoring the startled look of an older man who obviously recognized her face but was unsure of her identity. She had almost made it through when Marie's voice rang out loud and clear. "Mrs. Chance! You forgot your receipt!"

Sara, however, didn't turn around. She strode past the open doors of other tiny, obscenely expensive shops in the Trump Tower. Crazy thoughts of how many years an average person would have to work to afford just one perfect square of the imported Carrara marble that covered floors and walls in the decadently beautiful building danced in her mind as she hurried through the crowd. Crazy thoughts of how many lifetimes her late parents would have had to work to afford just one of the luxuries she, as both Max's widow and wife, had at her disposal taunted her as she stepped onto the ridged metal stair of the escalator. The sound of the splashing waterfall cascading its way down the marble wall behind her mingled with the unmistakable smell of money, and the combination made her acutely aware of the inequities of life.

Maybe that was why the American dream so often contained within it the elements of tragedy. And maybe that was also why Maxwell Chance—and everyone who had surrounded him—still fascinated the press. Rainbows didn't always lead to a pot of gold. People liked to be reminded of that fact.

Sam Berenger ran his fingertips lightly along the glowing top of the antique mahogany Empire table and grinned at the older man who stood before him.

"Better raise your insurance coverage, Leonard," he said, unable to resist the sensual pleasure of well-polished wood. "These expandable dining tables are rare enough, but ones with makers' marks on them like this piece are practically nonexistent."

Leonard Klein adjusted his glasses and inspected the brass fittings with a careful eye. "Frankly, Samuel, I think you have a workshop hidden somewhere in your apartment where you turn out incredible reproductions." He looked over at the younger man, who was running a thumb along the molded edge of the top of the table. "I've looked fifteen years to find an Empire table, and you found it for me in three months." He reached into the jacket pocket of his silk suit and withdrew a discreet white envelope and extended it toward Sam. "A small gesture of my appreciation, Samuel."

Sam shook his head and pushed the sleeves of his thick beige sweater up over well-muscled forearms. "I appreciate the gesture, Leonard, but you've paid my fee already." He grinned. "Despite my objections."

"But Samuel, Margaret and I want to—"

Sam raised one hand and extended it, palm out, toward the older man. "We're friends, Leonard. I can't take it."

"Then at least let me give it to your favorite charity. You have no idea how much this piece means to Margaret and me."

Sam's face was wide open and guileless; his emotions were as readable as if they were printed on his forehead. He bowed slightly toward his friend and former mentor. "Cancer Care, and I thank you very much, Leonard."

Leonard finally drew his eyes away from his newest acquisition and clapped the younger man on the back—the bittersweet gesture of one who remembered how it felt to be young and strong and filled with ideals. "How about a toast to future dealings?"

Sam's thick, well-shaped eyebrows arched, and he glanced at the grandfather's clock across the room, which stood tall and stately in a puddle of morning sun. "It's a little early for me, Leonard," he said easily, "but don't let me stop you."

Leonard glanced at the bottles standing at attention on top of the bar across the room and shrugged. "You young people don't know the value of a well-aged whiskey. Appreciation of good Scotch has gone the way of high-topped shoes and the five-cent cigar."

Judging from the slightly bloodshot appearance of Leonard's brown eyes, Sam felt sure that Leonard was maintaining the tradition of whiskey appreciation quite well on his own. Sam hated to see the insidious way wealth and position had of insulating men and women from the smaller, more lasting pleasures in life.

"So have you started going to the health club?" Sam asked as they crossed the gleaming parquet floor to the foyer.

Leonard chuckled and absently patted his waistline, which was beginning to show the accumulation of fifty-five years. "You sound like my doctor, Samuel."

"Not a doctor." Sam rested his hand on the older man's shoulder for a moment. "A friend." He grinned and tilted his head back toward the inside of the sprawling twelve-room apartment. "You could try jogging in there," he said, his deep voice filled with laughter. "You could do a mile between the master bedroom and the bath alone."

Leonard lit up a cigar and drew in deeply. "Margaret says we should have stayed in the old apartment on Madison Avenue, but—" He shook his head absently. "Why in hell have I been working my butt off for forty years if I can't give my wife the best?"

Sam had no answer. An apartment in the new Trump Tower building in midtown Manhattan was the latest in status symbols among the ultrarich, and Sam would be hard put to find fault with either the architecture, the location or the neighbors. Yet there was something lacking in Leonard now—a certain joy that Sam had watched disappear as the other man's fortunes had grown. Leonard seemed happier ten years ago when he first hired Sam to do construction work on a series of small shops and galleries he was renovating along Third Avenue.

Then there had been time for the beer and pizza after a long day, for Sunday dinners, with Margaret hovering over Sam, pushing extra helpings on him the same way his mother used to. Now it seemed as if Leonard himself—not just his firm—had been gobbled up in the corporate take-over that had left him an extremely wealthy man but, Sam suspected, a much poorer one, as well.

"So," Leonard said, breaking the silence, "when do you move into your new place?"

Sam groaned. "I wish to hell I knew. I get bounced out of my old one December fifteenth, and I still haven't any idea when the new house in Maine will be ready."

"You know Margaret's going to miss you, with you way up in the wilderness."

Sam smiled. That was Leonard's way of saying that he, too, would miss Sam.

"It's only for a year," Sam said, pushing up the sleeves on his heavy beige sweater. "It was too good an opportunity to miss."

Sam had been offered the chance to study with Karl Bergmann, a premier craftsman in wood. Bergmann was growing old, and his sight was failing, and he had chosen Sam, through reputation, to be the recipient of his eighty-plus years of knowledge and expertise.

"Damned stupid way to do business," Leonard grumbled between puffs on his cigar. He zeroed in again on the real estate problem. "Where will you live if it's not ready?"

Sam shrugged his wide shoulders. "Beats me, Leonard. I'll probably rent a hotel room somewhere and wait it out.

I have too many valuable pieces to ship them up to New England and put them in storage.''

"You'll keep everything in a hotel room?" Leonard sounded as if he couldn't quite believe his ears.

"What other choice is there? It's either that or drag everything up north and wait in a hotel up there."

Leonard dismissed both ideas with a wave of his hand. "Ridiculous," he said. "Margaret and I are heading down to Palm Beach two weeks from tomorrow. Take this place."

"Leonard, I—"

"I don't want to hear it." Leonard's voice was all business. "You'd be doing us a favor. You think we like leaving the apartment vacant so soon after we move in? Move in for as long as you need—give this damned drafty warehouse a lived-in look, will you, please?"

"You're a tough man, Leonard." Sam reached out and shook the older man's hand warmly. "Do I have anything to say about this?"

"Hell, no." Leonard grinned, his newly capped teeth shining white and even in the dim light of the foyer. "Call me tonight and we'll talk about the arrangements."

Sam was still smiling when he exited the private elevator that serviced Leonard's apartment and headed for the escalator that would take him to the mezzanine. There was a pricey confectionery shop there he'd noticed last week that was said to have the best chocolates in town. Leonard might find it hard to accept thanks for the offer of the apartment, but chocolate truffles? That was another story.

Sara caught a glimpse of herself in the highly polished surface of a column as she rode the escalator down to the lobby. No good. Her collar had slipped, and without her cap on she might as well just announce to the crowd that she was there. Swiftly, she adjusted the collar of her bright blue down coat up around her throat and the lower part of her face. She pulled a cheerful woolen hat knitted in shades of red and cream from her pocket and tugged it down over her head until just a few dark curls bounced over her eyebrows.

Much better. Now she looked as anonymous as any other shopper. She was feeling so secure in her recaptured anonymity that she thought she was mistaken when a male voice called out, "Sara! Wait up!"

But no. He called her name again. There was something about that man's voice—a certain emphasis on the "r" in her name, a particular combination of words—that triggered a memory she couldn't quite bring to the front of her mind. The escalator next to hers was zipping its way up to the mezzanine, and she forced herself not to steal a quick look at the owner of the voice. Keep your head down, she told herself. The last thing she needed was another one of those "Brave Widow Out on the Town" stories that had been popping up in New York newspapers of late. She focused her eyes on the stair below and tried not to draw any more attention her way.

"Sara! Up here."

On the escalator step below, a young mother, toddler firmly grasped with one hand and infant suspended against her breast in a sling-type carrier, looked curiously around, then turned and glanced up the opposite escalator.

She grinned at Sara, who held her breath. "You should see him," the woman said. "Makes me almost wish I were Sara."

Sara nodded and forced a small grin, wishing that the building's engineer, in his infinite wisdom, had made escalators that moved much faster. Deanna was right; she never should have come shopping on her own. It was too close to the anniversary. She was too much on the public's mind. She turned her head slightly to the right. Why hadn't she called in her order or sent Neal or—but it was such a sunny morning, and she had been feeling that maybe, just maybe, she could find a way to break free of the clutches of fame just this once.

That oddly familiar voice called out her name again. She was only two-thirds of the way to street level. A trickle of perspiration began to slide its way down her back as a distinct memory of the crowds that had clutched and grabbed at her after Max's funeral made her shiver.

She had to do something. When she was just ten feet away from the lobby and freedom, Sara excused her way past the young mother, elbowed quickly around a business man who was checking his appointment book, then flew down the remaining folding steps.

Even if the persistent fan jumped immediately onto the down escalator to follow her, she was sure that given the crowds and the blessed slowness of the contraption, she could be out on Fifth Avenue and gone before he knew what hit him. She tucked her red shopping bag under her arm, adjusted the shoulder bag slung across her body, then, head ducked forward like a wide receiver racing for a touchdown, began moving toward the door. She had gone no more than five feet when a voice, very loud and very clear, rang out, "Paisley! Wait up!"

Paisley. Her maiden name. The one fact about her life that had not interested even the most avid of reporters. She had often thought they chose to believe she sprang to life fully grown in the arms of Maxwell Chance. Paisley—the name that went with a lifetime she had nearly forgotten. She stopped; she couldn't have moved even if she'd wanted to. Curiosity held her captive.

The lobby was filled with late-autumn sunlight that bounced off the slick marble and glass surfaces, and her eyes narrowed against the glare. The grand piano that later on would delight passersby with the sounds of Gershwin and Cole Porter was still covered. A group of schoolchildren were clustered on her right, staring up at an exceptionally tall doorman who wore his red uniform with the dignified air of a palace guard. She couldn't distinguish any faces, and she wished she had taken time to insert her contact lenses before she left the apartment. It would be nice to know whom she was dealing with.

Then, suddenly, her eyes were drawn back in the direction of the escalators, and she saw a man of medium height, dressed in dark brown slacks, boots and a bulky beige ragg wool sweater stretched across wide, strong shoulders, heading toward her. Even with her myopic vision, she could see that his wide-boned, handsome face was lit with a grin that seemed nearly incandescent.

"Sam?" Her heart bounced against her ribs. It just wasn't possible—it had been years since she'd seen him. But one look at his walk and she was certain. She had never seen anyone east of Omaha walk with that particular open-range stride of Sam Berenger.

"Stop squinting at me, Paisley," the man said as he came closer, his arms extended toward her. "Will you never have your glasses when you need them?"

"Oh, it *is* you, Sam. I can't believe it. I—" Her words were muffled against the soft wool of his sweater as he enveloped her in an embrace, her pocketbook and shopping bag crunching between them. Fear rose up and out of her body like smoke from an open window as she breathed in Sam's clean scent of soap and water, so refreshing after the cloying smells of money and power that permeated the Trump Tower. "What are you doing here? I can't believe bumping into you again after so long. How—"

He pushed her a fraction away from him and looked down, his eyes sparking in the sunlight. "Don't you know Manhattan is just a collection of small towns, Paisley? Sooner or later you bump into everyone."

She laughed, and he tugged her woolen cap lower over her forehead with a gesture so affectionate—so normal—that she wanted to kiss him.

"Samuel Berenger, where have you been all my life?" Raising on her toes, she kissed his cheek, relishing the texture and warmth of his skin beneath her lips.

He tilted his head slightly, and she could see amusement and concern battle for dominance on his face. "Right here, Paisley," he said. "I've always been here."

His words, gentle as they were, reminded her of things that might have been.

"We have a lot to catch up on, Sara."

"Almost five years," she said, adjusting her hat and pulling her collar back up around her face. She was torn. She wanted to escape the Trump Tower, but she didn't want to lose Sam. Not again. She'd even risk a photo in the *News* or *Post* just to hang on to Sam a moment longer. She motioned over her shoulder toward the small dining area near the foot of the indoor waterfall. "Shall we have coffee?"

"And pay three dollars a cup?" He slipped one hand beneath her elbow and propelled her toward the door. "Come on. I know a little place around the corner where we can sit all morning and no one will hustle us out."

She looked up at him, at those oddly beautiful eyes of his—the irises were a swirl of blue and green rimmed with a dark gold—and grinned. "Anything like the Venus Coffee Shop where we used to have lunch in the old days?"

"Exactly like it, except there's no Vinny to bring us extra cream cheese for our onion bagels."

And just like that a rush of memories of a less complicated time filled Sara. Had she ever really been that young—or was the word "naive"—to believe that Sara Paisley could make her own distinct mark on the world? She was thankful they were separated for a moment by the cubicles of the revolving door so she could regain her bearings, remember that it was no longer the past and she was no longer Sara Paisley but the widow of Maxwell Chance.

Seconds later Sam exited the revolving door and propelled them down Fifth Avenue. The tall, elegant buildings sheltered them from the wind, but the air was still quite cold for late November. Sara shivered and burrowed her way deeper into her down-filled coat and glanced up at Sam, who wore just a bulky sweater.

"My blood freezes just looking at you," she said as he guided her down the street, weaving a path through strolling sightseers and parcel-bearing messengers. "You midwesterners are a sturdy lot."

He laughed, and a lock of golden-flecked brown hair flopped over his forehead. He scraped it back with his right hand. "Woman, this feels like springtime to me. Tell me about being cold when it gets closer to zero."

She groaned and rolled her eyes. "Don't even talk about it getting any colder. I start shivering in October, and I don't thaw until June."

"Sara, Sara." He shook his head playfully. "Still meant for beaches and palm trees, aren't you? What in hell are you doing north of the equator?"

"I've been asking myself the same thing."

They turned east on Fifty-sixth Street and waited for the light at the corner of Madison Avenue. Long, sleek limousines, big yellow cabs and tiny sports cars jockeyed for pole position on the crowded street, all anxious to be first off the line at the green light. Sara and Sam had to break into a run to reach the opposite corner before the Don't Walk sign flashed on.

A black Mercedes sedan swung around the corner, cutting dangerously close to the curb. Sara stopped to adjust her cap, and Sam had to grab her by the elbow and propel her forward and away from the speeding car.

"My hero!" she said. "Was that man on a search-and-destroy mission?"

"No, just an off-duty cabdriver out for a ride."

She raised an eyebrow. "A cabbie with a Mercedes?"

He shrugged. "Have you seen the rates lately?"

"Remember the days when we could hop a cab and zoom from the Village to the Upper East Side for less than five dollars?" Sara asked as they resumed walking toward the elusive coffee shop.

"I can go you one better," he answered. "I can remember when pizza cost a quarter a slice."

"Better be careful, Berenger," she said with a laugh. "Your age is showing." The truth was, she had noticed the fine lines beginning around his eyes and the deeper lines at the edges of his mouth where his easy smile had already left its mark.

Traffic was particularly noisy on Park Avenue, and they fell into a companionable silence. Sam linked her arm through his "— so you can't get away from me—" and to Sara it felt as easy and natural as breathing. Street-corner Santa Clauses shivered, and she felt warmed by the way Sam still seemed unable to walk by one without depositing some of his change in the enormous metal caldrons.

"You're a nice man," she said as they hurried across Lexington Avenue, dodging and weaving their way through a maze of taxicabs. "I'm glad some things never change."

He looked down at her, and the odd gold rim that framed his irises seemed particularly beautiful to her in the winter sunlight. "A cryptic remark, Paisley. Don't think I'm not going to ask for an explanation once we're settled down with a cup of coffee."

"Don't think I'm not going to try to come up with a damned good one by then," she countered, pleased she could still make him laugh.

Sara found herself nearly breaking into a run to keep up with Sam as they walked toward Third Avenue. "Are you sure you remember where this coffee shop is?" she asked, feigning exhaustion.

"One more block, Paisley. Surely your old bones can make it."

She recognized a challenge when she heard one and began to accelerate her pace until she was nearly pulling Sam along by the hand. Suddenly, she wasn't cold any longer. The wind was a sweet slap against her cheeks, and she felt free and easy in a way she hadn't felt for years. She was actually disappointed when Sam pulled her to a stop in front of a tiny coffee shop with a green awning that looked as if it had withstood one decade of wear too many.

"Chez Niko's," he said, holding the door open and motioning her inside.

It was the kind of luncheonette she knew well from her working days: an all-American coffee shop that specialized in Greek food with a Spanish accent, the type of restaurant exclusive to Manhattan. In the second it took for Sara's eyes to adjust to the dimness of the luncheonette, Sam had found them a booth in the rear and shepherded her back there. She slipped off her down coat, folded it and placed it on the bench next to her. Sam had already taken his seat facing toward the inside of the coffee shop, and she realized he was sensitive to her need for what privacy she could manage.

Sam motioned for the waiter, a dark-haired man with cigarette permanently plastered to his lips who obviously looked upon his job as an enormous trial.

"Two black coffees and—" He looked at Sara. "Do you still like baklava?" She nodded, remembering the flaky pastry with delight. "Bring us two pieces." He handed the waiter the ripped plastic menu, then turned back to Sara.

"You have no idea how long it's been since I've had baklava," she said, fiddling with her glass of water. "The honey, the butter—" She laughed. "I'm gaining weight just talking about it."

Sam tilted his head to one side and looked at her slim, small-boned form. "You could use a few pounds, Paisley. Don't they feed you right these days?"

"It's a different world I'm in now, Sam. They feast on lettuce leaves and sushi. Every now and then I think about calling out for a Whopper with heavy pickles and onion, but I can just hear 'Eyewitness News'—'Sara Chance seen at Burger King. Is Max's widow down on her luck? Film at eleven.'" They both laughed, and she continued. "Anyway, I'm afraid Neal and Deanna would have apoplexy if I did."

"Neal and Deanna?" Sam's deep voice was casual, but Sara could detect a slight tone of above-average curiosity.

"Deanna is my assistant and Neal was Max's—I mean he's my financial consultant." She paused. "Actually, Deanna seems to be doing most of the work these days." Damn it, why did the subject have to come up? Reality tugged at her heart, and she resented it. Reality was the world of fame and fortune and fear. She wanted none of it. She wanted to pretend she was twenty-two again and she and Sam were grabbing a quick lunch before returning to work. Impulsively, she reached across the small table and rested her hand on Sam's. "I know that sounds insufferably elitist, Sam. It's just that Max had a lot of business interests and I simply couldn't take care of everything myself." She grinned. "Too much a right-brain type, I guess." She made a broad gesture with her hands. "There's the wildlife foundation Deanna handles, and there's StopHunger." Sam said nothing. She stopped and looked at him. "Why do I sound like I'm apologizing?"

"Good question, Paisley. I was thinking about asking you the same thing."

"I have a wonderful idea," she said, sitting back on the lumpy vinyl-covered seat so the waiter could drop knives and forks and paper napkins at their places. "Go to the supermarket. You can find out anything you need to know about Sara Chance in the *Globe* or the *Enquirer*. What I'd really like to do is talk about the old days with a dear friend." She ripped open a packet of sugar and dumped it into her cup of black coffee. "Are you still a carpenter, Sam?"

"Still in the union," he said, swallowing a piece of the sweet Greek pastry, "but I don't do too much building any longer. Just for my own pleasure."

Sara held the coffee cup between both hands, letting its heat warm her. "What do you do?"

"I track down and restore antique furniture. In fact, I'll be going up to Maine soon to study." He looked at her. "Did you happen to catch that exhibit of colonial cradles and beds at the Metropolitan last year?" Sara nodded. "I did the restoration on most of them and set up the showing."

Her blue eyes widened. "I envy you," she said, breaking off a piece of baklava and toying with it. "It must be marvelous to feel you're using your talents to the best of your ability."

"Cryptic remark number two." He watched her closely for a moment. "Nothing is said without a reason, Paisley. Do you need a nonpartisan shoulder to lean on?"

"No, no." She popped a piece of pastry in her mouth and took her time chewing. "One thing I'm surrounded with are shoulders to lean upon." She wiped a drop of honey from the side of her mouth with the edge of her napkin. "Sometimes I think they would arrange to have someone else get my colds for me if I'd let them."

"So the term 'idle rich' has some validity?"

She rolled her eyes. "More than you know."

In that moment Sam realized just how far the past five years had taken Sara away from the world they had once shared, and he felt a sense of loss sweep over him that was even greater than the loss he had felt when she married Maxwell Chance.

"I suppose limousines and Swiss bank accounts aren't all they're cracked up to be?" His voice held a tinge of sarcasm he couldn't control.

Sara looked up from her coffee. "I don't own a limousine, Sam, and if we have money in a Swiss account, I'm not aware of it." She drained her cup and put it down on the saucer with a loud clunk. "Most of Max's estate has been put into charitable foundations."

"I'm sorry, Sara." He had never learned to hide his feelings. The world had always been reflected in his eyes and still was. "I don't know why I said that."

I know why, she thought, and she suspected Sam did, as well. The same deep emotional pull that had existed between them five years ago was still present, coloring their words with unspoken but well-remembered longings. The rapport they had enjoyed for the past hour turned into an uneasy silence that settled around their shoulders like heavy fog. She reached down next to her and retrieved her coat. *You really can't go back,* she thought.

Across the table, Sam frowned. "Do you have to leave so soon?"

"It's after eleven," she said, reading the time upside down from his large, leather-strapped watch. "I suppose I really should be going."

"Do you have an appointment somewhere?"

She looked at him. "No. It's just that I told Deanna I'd be back for lunch."

"Do you have to punch a time clock back at your apartment?"

He was grinning at her, and she had to grin back. "No, I don't, Mr. Berenger."

"One more cup," he said, motioning again for the waiter to return with the coffeepot. "Let me tell you what Sally and Danielle have been up to lately."

She leaned back against her seat. "You've kept in touch with them after all these years?" Sara had worked with the two women in the Obelisk Gallery.

"My work keeps me in contact with all the galleries in the Northeast." He poured some sugar into his cup, then pushed the container toward Sara, who shook her head. "Besides, I've always felt old friends were the best friends."

"Is that a dig at me, Sam?"

"No," he said, not smiling. "Just the truth."

Again the silence fell between them, protecting them from emotions better left unexplored. Sara drummed the table-top with her fingers as Sam stirred his coffee more times than could possibly be necessary. Finally, she could stand it no longer.

"I know I should have called you afterward, Sam." Her words were so low that he had to lean across the chipped plastic table to hear them. "You have no idea how many times I wrote you."

"The mail *is* slow these days," he said. His voice barely masked his remembered pain.

A pained, sad smile drifted across her face. "I never mailed them, Sam. What could I tell you that you hadn't already seen in the newspapers?"

You could have told me why, he thought. "You didn't owe me any explanations, Paisley," he said. "The fact remained that I wasn't free to offer you anything at all."

When Sam and Sara first met, he had been in the middle of a painful divorce suit and had been reluctant to bring Sara into his life and expose her to an ugly court case. So he had opted for friendship when they both needed love and ultimately had wound up with neither.

I would have waited for you, she thought, moving a piece of baklava around on her plate with the bent tines of her fork. *If you had just told me you wanted me to...* "Are you—" she stopped and cleared her throat. "Did the divorce ever come through? I mean, I'm sure you must be divorced by now." *Are you remarried?* She pictured a beautiful dark-haired wife and an infant with gold-rimmed eyes.

"The divorce was final eighteen months after you..." His voice trailed off.

Sara picked up his thought. "After I married Maxwell."

She saw a flash of unexpected anger in his beautiful eyes. "Yes."

The name separated them as completely as if an Iron Curtain had been dropped down the middle of the small table, and this time she knew there would be no easy way to recapture the rapport they had enjoyed for a brief while.

"Well," she said, slipping her arms into the sleeves of her puffy blue coat, "this time I'd really better get going." She forced a smile, well-practiced after five years in the public eye. "Deanna might send a rescue squad out to look for me."

His shoulders sagged for a moment, but Sam dissembled quickly. He grabbed the check, glanced at it, then threw a five-dollar bill down on the table. "Let's go."

Seconds later they were out on the street, facing each other, neither one sure what the next move should be. The street was crowded for it was nearly lunchtime, and pedestrians repeatedly jostled them and muttered curses in languages Sara had never heard. They stepped into the doorway of a luggage shop.

"Better put your hat on," Sam said, pulling it out of her right pocket. "It's cold."

She took the red-and-cream knit cap from him and pulled it carelessly over her thick mane of dark curls. The cold she was feeling seemed to be working its way from the very inside of her heart outward. "I thought you didn't feel the cold, Sam."

His breath wreathed his face. "I don't usually." His voice was husky. "I must be getting old."

Oh, Sam, she thought, looking away at the white-and-orange courier van that was maneuvering into a parking space at the curb. She wanted to touch his cheek, feel his warmth, but the kiss she had given him so spontaneously before was locked now behind years of separate living. She extended her hand.

He didn't shake it. Instead, he reached into his back pocket, pulled out a business card, then pressed it into her palm. The heavy gold wedding band on her finger picked up the sunlight and flung it back in his face. "I work out of my home," he said, his eyes fused to hers. "If you need me for anything at all—even just to reminisce—call me, Sara."

She nodded, curling her fingers around the crisp white card. "Sam, I—"

Her words were cut off when Sam, unable to dissemble any longer, closed the yawning space between them and covered her mouth with his own.

2

She smelled of springtime. Sam's first sensation was of the sweet smell of violets blossoming all around him as he kissed Sara. The scent was delicate, nostalgic, evocative of sunshine and warm days filled with the promise of delights yet to come. The Manhattan street receded as if into another dimension of reality, and Sam was unaware of the curious glances of passersby and the bleating horns of traffic moving slowly toward Third Avenue. Sara was his only reality. He had to make this moment last for a very long time.

For Sara the years slid away, and suddenly she understood all about the circular nature of time. Once she had pictured time as a great high wall made of stone, the years piling one atop the other until you could barely see the place from which you started. However, in this moment, with Sam's mouth—warm and sweet with honey—on hers, she was Sara Paisley again, and time was a stream that flowed around her, bringing her back to the source.

Illusions, however, are prey to reality. Before she could think or react in any way at all to Sam's impulsive kiss, he moved away. The sun was in her eyes, and she found it difficult to read the expression on his face.

"Sam?" She took a tentative step forward, her right hand reaching out to make contact with him once more, but he took another step back. Her breathing was tight and shallow, as if her chest had been snugly bound.

"Turn around and leave."

His voice was low and controlled, and a sense of pain mingled with fear came over her.

"Sam, please. What kind of joke is—"

"You've been spotted," he broke in. A false stranger's smile was secured on his face. "A photographer from the *Post* just came out of the jewelry store on the corner, and he's watching you."

Her instant reaction was to turn around, but Sam's low "No" kept her in check. Nervously, she fiddled with her knit cap, pulling it down lower on her forehead. "What should I do?" she asked. She felt as vulnerable as a soldier behind enemy lines. Memories of the mob scene at Max's funeral were never far from her thoughts.

"Just nod and smile at me as if we're having a casual conversation."

Sara forced a pleasant, carefree look on her face. "I deserve an Oscar for this performance," she said, her voice shaky.

Sam's laugh this time was natural and full. "Perfect. Now shake my hand and walk down toward Second Avenue. Don't turn back. I'll get rid of him."

He extended his hand. She hesitated. There was so much they had yet to say, so many things left unresolved between them.

"Now, Sara."

She shook his hand, savoring the brief contact of skin on skin. Then he pulled her forward as he walked past, and she found herself moving quickly down the long block east to Second Avenue. A scuffle erupted behind her, and curiosity made her break stride for a second. She wanted to turn around to see what had happened, but then she heard Sam's voice, loud and clear, say, "Listen, pal, I'm real sorry. I'll pay for any broken lenses," and she knew exactly what had occurred. He had obviously "bumped" into the paparazzo, creating a diversion during which Sara could disappear.

She stopped near a public phone at the corner of Second Avenue. Their coded conversation in the coffee shop kept running through her brain, and she tried to decipher the messages they had given each other.

What she wanted to do was turn left on Second Avenue, race up Fifty-seventh Street and waylay Sam as he walked back toward Fifth; but the crowds were heavy and the glances too curious. A cold wind slashed up the street and made her shiver. Sam was a dream, she thought, one that had disappeared a long time ago.

This was reality.

So she made a left on Second Avenue, and instead of running to Sam as she hadn't five years ago, she stepped into the street and raised her arm to hail a cab to take her home.

The photographer was young and lean and hungry, and Sam had knocked into him just as he was setting his Nikon for a shot. The kid's hands fumbled, and something had fallen from his grip and splintered on the sidewalk with the sound of breaking glass.

"Listen, pal, I'm real sorry," Sam said honestly, for the look of disappointment and anger on the boy's face was keen. "I'll pay for any broken lenses."

"The hell with that," the photographer snapped. "You made me miss a shot at Max Chance's widow, for heaven's sake. I've been trying to get a shot of her for a month now." He narrowed his brown eyes and glared at Sam. "You look familiar. Who are you? How come you know her?"

"The woman in the blue coat?" Sam sounded casual, unperturbed. "That wasn't Sara Chance."

"Like hell it wasn't. I'd know her face anywhere." The photographer bent down to pick up the shards of a shattered filter, and Sam stepped between him and the view of East Fifty-sixth Street where Sara had been.

Sam saw her stop by the Plexiglas telephone enclosure at the corner of Fifty-sixth and Second, had seen the familiar way her eyes crinkled as she tried to bring him into focus. Sam angled his body in a way that he hoped blocked Sara from the young photographer's view and hemmed and hawed and apologized until he saw her turn the corner and disappear.

So that was it. Sara had entered and exited his life once again, but in their hour together he had discovered that for him nothing at all had changed. Neither time nor distance had altered his feelings for her.

A deep sigh escaped his body, and his apologies stopped short. He pressed a twenty-dollar bill into the photographer's hand, and jamming his fists into the pockets of his brown pants, Sam lowered his head against the wind and headed back toward the Trump Tower.

Not Sara Chance?

The hell she wasn't.

Jack Farrell pocketed the twenty-dollar bill and watched the man push his way through the midtown crowd and disappear around the corner. Jack never forgot a face, and it had been the man's wide-boned open face and sandy hair that had first caught his attention. He'd seen the man before, and not too long ago at that. Finding Sara had just been a lucky break.

He patted the Nikon that was slung around his neck and took a last glance down the block where the woman with the mane of glossy black curls had disappeared.

Not Sara Chance?

Not very likely.

And he had the pictures to prove it.

Sara breathed a silent prayer of thanks that she had gotten the only cabdriver in the city of New York who wasn't interested in conversation. He was a young dark-haired man whose punk hairstyle stood up in an arrangement that seemed to defy all known laws of physics. He slid back the bulletproof panel between them only long enough to mumble, "Where to?" and hear, "Carberry Towers," before he slammed it shut so he could be alone with his New Wave music.

He headed toward East Fifty-seventh Street, which would take him up to Fifth Avenue, and Sara stole a quick glance backward, almost as if she expected to see Sam standing on the corner, watching.

Something unexpected had happened. An imaginary boundary that had always existed between them had crumbled, and its suddenness had taken them both by surprise. She could still feel his lips on hers, taste the sweetness of his mouth, but she couldn't bring herself to examine exactly what it was that had transpired. Each time she tried to zero in on the heart of the matter, her mind refused to be pinned down, and she found her eyes drawn to the traffic, to the people walking the city streets, to the driver's hands keeping time to the music that filtered through the partition in the cab.

She had Sam's address. She had his phone number. Sam was free now, and so was she. She had only to take the initiative. Sighing, she leaned her head back against the worn leather seat and closed her eyes, wondering why opportunities always presented themselves years too late.

Five years ago, when she was working at the gallery and Sam was involved in rebuilding the shops along that street, she would have followed him to the ends of the earth had he asked her to. Even though it was his wife who had found another and was seeking the divorce, he knew he was being watched by her detectives and that one ill-advised encounter with another woman would mean an ugly and public courtroom battle. So he and Sara had contented themselves with lunch dates with co-workers and long and aching interludes in the gallery where the tension between them made the air shiver with denied passion.

But why think about it? She had chosen another way of life when she married Maxwell. Why should she expect to be given another chance with Sam when she already knew there were no happy endings?

The taxi jerked to a halt outside the imposing wrought-iron entrance to the Carberry Towers, where she lived. The doorman, dressed in a hunter-green uniform festooned with yards of gold braid, raced from his post in front of the locked doors and regally helped Sara from the cab.

"Thank you, Larry," she said, smiling up at his lined face as they walked toward the building. A few diehard fans maintained their vigil behind a wooden barricade. Max's death hadn't diminished their loyalty. Unfortunately, since the blind items and out-and-out lies had begun popping up in the papers, not all of the fans were sympathetic. Deanna said one of them was probably responsible for the disturbing letters Sara had been receiving. An undercurrent of anger, of betrayal, had begun to tinge their vigils.

It was as if Sara had to earn the right to the big apartment at the Carberry by unnecessary devotion to a life-style that no longer existed. To a man who no longer existed. She ducked her head down and waited quietly while Larry fiddled with his keys.

"I'm glad to see you got a cab this morning, Mrs. C.," he said, unlocking the heavy glass door to the lobby and holding it open for Sara to pass through. "With the winter solstice approaching, it'll get harder and harder to do."

"I'll keep that in mind." Larry was an institution at the Carberry. An ersatz astronomer-cum-meteorologist, he was able to tie in any and all traffic foul-ups to corresponding weather disturbances. Sara had long ago learned to treat him with the greatest respect.

She nodded her way past the guard, who kept vigil over the neat rows of mailboxes in the alcove off the main lobby, and continued heading toward the elevator banks at the end of the inner lobby. Security cameras quietly scanned the public areas of the building. Sara often thought that it would be easier to scale the Berlin Wall than to slip unnoticed into the *sanctum sanctorum* of the Carberry Towers.

A white-haired old man, also in a dark green uniform, sat on a small chair near the elevator bank. At the sound of Sara's boots clicking across the black-and-white tiled floor, he put down his crossword puzzle and stood up. His Santa Clausesque belly strained the buttons of the jacket, and he tugged at it in vain.

"Morning, Mrs. Chance." He went to tip his hat, then noticed it was on the tabletop, not on his head. He grinned at Sara. "Getting a little forgetful." He punched the button to bring the elevator down to ground level for her.

Sara smiled at him. "Blame it on the weather, Hector."

Hector nodded. "You been talking to Larry, I can see. Last week he told me that when the thermometer dips, you lose half of your brainpower with every degree it goes below thirty."

"I'm sure he has the statistics to prove it," Sara said with a laugh.

The elevator door slid open, and Hector held it open for her. Sara pushed the button marked P and smiled at the man, who once again made to tip his nonexistent cap to her.

"Have a nice day, Mrs. Chance." His words were almost lost as the door slid shut and the elevator began its stately ascent.

Sara leaned against the wall and pulled off the woolen cap, running her hand through her thick curls. She often found it difficult to deal with the men and women who worked to make the Carberry a comfortable, secure place to live.

When Larry wanted to carry a bag for her, her instinct was to say, "I'll do it myself." When Hector made a show of ushering her into the elevator, she felt guilty. She was just Sara, after all, from a working-class neighborhood in Queens, daughter of a secretary and an auto mechanic.

It was at odd moments like these that she felt Max's absence most keenly. He had been born to wealth and so had taken easily to success and all its incumbent responsibilities. While Sara had found it easier to make a cup of tea for herself than to ring for the cook, Max had explained that by so doing, she was making their jobs seem less important and less secure, as well.

It had taken her over a year to realize that the life-style of the wealthy was patterned very closely after the life-style of an army. There was a definite chain of command; duties and obligations were clearly delineated, and the organism only ran smoothly if everyone followed the rules. And now she was the general's widow, the figurehead around whom everything now revolved.

She might not have a family to care for, but there were people who depended on her for jobs and people she depended on for a form of security and friendship that was hard to come by for a woman in the public eye.

The discreet sound of chimes signaled that the elevator had reached the penthouse floor. The car automatically moved a fraction up, then down, aligning itself even with the floor. The doors slid open with a soft whirring sound, and she stepped out onto the thick silvery-gray carpeting that made the long hallway resemble a lunar landscape.

Originally, the hall had opened onto two separate apartments Max had bought a year before she met him. One he decorated as a home for himself and ultimately for Sara; the other he broke up into an office and two small apartments where Neal Travis, Deanna Rollins and Deanna's brother, Paul, now lived and worked.

She unlocked the door and stepped into the foyer. The faint scent of lemon oil filled the air. The apartment was quiet except for the sounds of Mrs. Raines, the cook, preparing lunch in the kitchen. Nothing seemed out of order as Sara headed to her office, but she couldn't quite shake a peculiar feeling of unease. Every now and again the feeling settled itself on her shoulders, and it took great effort to shrug it off.

She stopped by the door to one of the many closets and, leaning against the wall, yanked off her leather boots and sighed with pleasure as her feet sank into the plush champagne-colored carpet. The carpet and thick interior walls of the apartment so effectively soundproofed the rooms that Max used to sneak up behind her when she was fiddling with her canvas and paints and cause her to leap up with a shriek when he planted a kiss along the side of her neck.

So the sound was overwhelming when an enormous sneeze ricocheted through her body, a great big theatrical "Ah choo!" that even superior acoustics couldn't mask.

"Sara?" A woman's voice, low and husky and flavored with traces of South Philadelphia streets, floated out of Sara's office. "Is that you?"

"Yes," Sara called out, sneezing again for punctuation. "Damn! I think I'm coming down with something." She entered the large and airy office, tossing her boots on the floor near a file cabinet. She prayed this wouldn't be one of Deanna's "off" days. Sara was feeling emotionally vulnerable after seeing Sam and doubted she could handle Deanna's sometimes sharp tongue.

Deanna Rollins, tall and sleek with red hair that glowed like molten lava, was kneeling by Sara's desk, retrieving a stack of legal-sized papers that were scattered on the floor. "Why do I always drop things as soon as I get them either alphabetized or in numerical order?"

"Murphy's Law," Sara answered, bending down to help Deanna pick up the papers. Thankfully, Deanna was in a cheerful frame of mind. In the two years Deanna had been working for her, Sara had grown able to judge the other woman's mood in seconds. Deanna had a mysterious background that neither her brother, Paul Rollins, nor Maxwell would ever elaborate on. Sara suspected it had something to do with drugs but had never asked questions when the other woman floated in and out of their lives. When Max was alive, Deanna hadn't seemed terribly important to Sara; now that he was dead, Deanna was too important to question. Sara had few enough friends to risk losing one. "I think there's a little gremlin who sits and waits until an office is in order, then says, 'Bombs away!'" She reached under the desk for a few outsized pieces of paper, but Deanna quickly grabbed them herself and tossed them on top of her pile.

"That's the last one." Deanna stood up. Her yellow jersey tunic fell effortlessly into place over brown trousers that were tucked into cuffed boots of honey-colored leather. Sara instantly felt seventy-five years old and hopelessly out of style. "Next time I'll have to staple them to the palms of my hands."

"Let's not get carried away." Sara picked up the red shopping bag and placed it on top of the curved oak desk that dominated the room. "I'm all in favor of efficiency, but that smacks of medieval torture."

Deanna laughed and peeked around Sara's back at the slick red bag. "You've been shopping—how wonderful! You must show me what you bought."

Sara quickly took the bag and placed it on the floor near her desk chair. "Oh, it's nothing much," she said, amused by Deanna's unabashed curiosity. "I just wandered over to the Trump and browsed around for a while."

Deanna's hazel eyes twinkled. When Deanna was in a good mood, her beauty was almost overwhelming. "The Trump? Judging by the size of the package, it can be only one of two things—jewels or chocolate."

Sara slid out of her down coat and tossed it on the end section of the oatmeal-shaded sofa in the corner of the room. "Jewels," she answered, hoping Deanna would leave before she managed to pry the truth out of Sara and ruin her birthday surprise. "I went in with my trusty shopping bag and told them to fill it up—diamonds, emeralds, hold the rubies."

Deanna's laugh was hearty. "I like your style, Sara."

"Such as it is." She had to remind herself she even had a style when Deanna was in the room. Sara was about to pick up the red shopping bag and take it to her room when something glittery caught her eye. "Deanna!" She hurried over and stared at a lovely pear-shaped diamond that hung from a fine platinum chain around the woman's throat. "This is beautiful. A present?"

"You bet it is. From me to me." The red-haired woman fingered the large stone. "It's something I've always wanted," she said with a slight smile, "and I decided to take matters into my own hands and get it. Call it a little pre-birthday present."

"It must have cost you a small fortune," Sara said, thinking of the lovely jewelry Max had given her that she hadn't even looked at since his death.

Deanna's eyes glittered like the diamond around her slender throat. "You'd be surprised," she answered. "It was much less than you'd think."

"Well, more power to you." Sara wondered how her gift of the cigarette lighter could begin to compare. "You only turn thirty-five once, right?"

Deanna's thin, elegant eyebrow arched. "Oh, no," she said, her cadence giving the words a droll sound. "I intend to keep on turning thirty-five until I do it right." She grinned. "It might take me five or six years at least."

The red-haired woman turned to leave, and Sara was about to freshen up for lunch when she remembered.

"Deanna! Just a second."

Deanna turned around, still smiling. "Yes?"

Sara motioned toward the sheaf of papers tucked neatly under the woman's left arm. "Was there something you wanted in here?"

For a second Deanna looked blank; then she slapped the heel of her right hand against her forehead and groaned. "How could I forget?" She walked toward Sara, shaking her head. "I came in here to ask you to initial these papers on the FAWN advertising budget."

"It's finally getting under way?" Neal had been working on the foundation for four years with no progress; it was only in the eighteen months since Deanna took over that any appreciable movement had occurred.

Deanna nodded. "Neal needs them by one o'clock to run them over to the bank so everything is settled before we leave tomorrow." She shook her head. "How stupid of me."

Sara smiled. "Don't worry about it. As Larry would say, it's the weather." She glanced through page after page of legalese, then picked up her fountain pen and began initialing the top right-hand corner of each page. "I don't know why I bother to even try," she said, handing the pages back to Deanna. "I don't understand one darned bit of it."

Deanna tapped the bottoms of the pages on the desk to align them, then turned the stack sideways and did the same thing. "You don't have to understand it," she said, flashing one of her best smiles at Sara. "That's what you over-pay us for." The tall redhead disappeared down the hallway.

Sara sighed and picked her coat up from the sofa and hung it in the closet. She envied Deanna the luxury of a job to go to, some solid, practical way to define the parameters of her existence. Initialing papers was the extent of Sara's duties. Her most pressing problem was where to hide Deanna's birthday present.

The living-room clock chimed twelve noon. Any moment Mrs. Raines would be setting the dining table for lunch. Sara hurried through the door that joined her office to her bedroom to put the package in her locked dresser drawer where she kept Max's more personal papers.

She kept the key under the carpet in the far corner of the bedroom near the windows—the one spot where she'd been able to pry up a tiny section without it being noticeable. Reaching around the chaise longue that faced the window, she slid her fingers under the carpet to retrieve the key, but it just managed to stay out of reach. The cleaning service must have repositioned the chaise. She managed to crawl behind it and, on hands and knees, again slid her fingers under the carpet. It took a little twisting and straining, but finally she got a grip on the small metal key and stood up. Next time she'd either nail the chaise to the floor or make darned sure she didn't push the key so far under the rug.

She unlocked the dresser drawer, slipped the present into a half-empty box of stationery, then closed and relocked it. From the hallway she heard Mrs. Raines call her to lunch, so she stashed the key in the front pocket of her dark gray corduroy pants and hurried to wash up.

There'd be plenty of time later to hide the key. One thing she had in abundance was time.

Jack Farrell's apartment was the perfect one for a photographer. It was so dark, so dismal, so overwhelmingly depressing, that even at high noon he could develop photos in the kitchen without pulling the blinds. Sunlight had as much chance of finding his windows as he had of winning the Pulitzer Prize.

Jack leaned against the edge of his sink and took a long gulp of Heineken. He wiped his mouth with the back of his hand and leaned carefully over the contact sheets that were spread on the countertop to dry.

He'd raced home from his encounter with Sara Chance and that man whose identity was lingering just on the edges of his memory and immediately processed his film, the results of which lay drying before him now. The first eight shots were ones he'd taken at a fire early that morning to bracket the roll of film he'd already used on it. Another shot was the back of Jackie Onassis as she hurried to work at Doubleday. Nothing that would win him any awards—or make him any money, for that matter. Jackie was yesterday's news. However, this one of Sara Chance looking into that man's face as if he were the sun and moon and everything else—that was a different story.

It was a good shot—candid, sharp, capturing that brief moment of private emotion before the subject becomes aware of the camera. It was everything the gossip columns—from *Time* to *People* to the *Enquirer*—loved.

Then why wasn't he on the phone hawking it right now?

Jack crushed the empty beer can and tossed it into the paper garbage bag, piled high with wrappers from Burger King and McDonald's and the local deli, that rested on the floor near the kitchen door.

Admit it, he told himself. It wasn't that the exposure was off or it needed cropping or anything else. It was the look in her eyes, that look of surprise and delight that held him back. He'd never given a moment's pause to thoughts of a subject's right to privacy; he believed with everyone else in the media that public figures had no right to demand private lives. Yet Sara's eyes, large and trusting, looked up at him from the contract sheet and made him feel uncomfortable about his profession for the first time in his life.

"Crap." He didn't have time for this sentimental garbage. He had to earn a living, didn't he? He picked up the

receiver on his wall phone and ran his finger down the list
of phone numbers scrawled in pencil on the wall next to it.
He had just finished punching in the exchange when he
slammed the phone back down and stared across the room
at the pictures drying on the counter.

It was just one picture, after all. One picture, which would
only manage to pay his phone bill or keep the electricity
from being turned off. Nothing that would shoot him up
into another tax bracket, for heaven's sake. It could wait.

He carefully picked up the strip of negative and the contact sheet, then carried them into the bedroom where his
enlarging equipment was set up. Maybe this time the story
wasn't so much in Sara, in her very marketable face. Maybe
this time the story was in the man who could make her look
that way.

From lunchtime on, the two apartments at the Carberry
bustled with activity, with everyone busy with preparations
for their getaway to the eastern end of Long Island where
they would observe the anniversary of Max's death in private. Sara had toyed with the idea of going out for another
walk, but Deanna told her the crowds in front of the Carberry had tripled since noon and she would be better off
staying put.

As the day wore on, Sara grew chilled and achy, and by
four o'clock she knew she was coming down with a whopper of a cold. She was about to slip out of her clothing and
into a hot bath when she felt her dresser key still in the
pocket of her trousers. She started the tub, then hurried into
her bedroom. She was on hands and knees, about to slide
the key under the loose end of the carpet, when a male voice
behind her said, "Sara? What in hell are you doing down
there?"

She was so startled that her head shot up and she cracked
it on the underside of a table next to the chaise.

"Oh, for goodness' sake, Paul!" She stood up, rubbing
the sore spot on her skull with one hand while she con-

cealed the key in the other. "Don't you have enough sense to knock before barging right in?"

His eyes were the same hazel as his sister Deanna's, but his were level, while at times hers sparkled with a near-manic zest. "The door was wide open," he said. "There seemed little point in it."

"Common courtesy, for one," she said, slipping the key back into her pants pocket. "Not to mention the fact you scared hell out of me."

He entered the room, carrying a manila folder that bulged with papers. "Perhaps you scare a little too easily."

"Perhaps," she answered coolly. Although that was probably Paul's attempt at humor, Sara felt a small tremor of alarm run through her. His eyes strayed toward the floor near the chaise longue. She feigned a cough and turned away, quickly checking that the loose portion of rug wasn't still turned back. "Did you want something, Paul?"

He hesitated a beat before he spoke. "The limousine service will be here at eleven tomorrow morning." He leafed through a few of the papers in his folder. "There's going to be a lot of press outside, so we'll be going out through the basement passageway into the utility room of the Brubaker next door and meet the car on Seventy-fourth Street."

"Is that much subterfuge necessary?" Although Sara was not fond of the press, she often found such maneuvers more difficult to pull off than a simple statement to reporters. "If we just leave earlier, we could avoid it all."

Paul crossed the room and looked out the window onto the courtyard below. "There's at least a hundred people out there right now," he said. "By tomorrow morning there could be a thousand. Do you want to face them, too?"

Sara could handle Maxwell's fans on a one-to-one basis, but since the awful spectacle of his funeral, when thousands stormed the grave site, she had become wary of crowds. "No, I don't."

"There's a girl." A quick smile flickered across his lean face.

She balanced on the edge of the sofa and played with the fringe on one of the scarlet throw pillows. "How can you be sure the reporters won't follow us all the way out to Quogue?"

"Are you planning on telling them you're going there?"

"Of course not," she answered.

"Then how will they know about it?"

"How do they know about anything?" she countered. "Reliable sources."

For a second his sober hazel eyes seemed to twinkle like his sister's. "Listen, Sara, the only way the press can find out we're heading for Quogue tomorrow is either if they're collectively psychic or one of us tells them." Again, his quick smile. "Are you planning on sending out any communiqués?"

"No." Three sneezes in quick succession zoomed through her, leaving her teary eyed and gasping for air.

"Fine," he said, ignoring another series of sneezes and a mean bout with some Kleenex. He quickly ran through a précis of some legal matters concerning the StopHunger Foundation that Sara barely heard through her clogged-up ear passages. Finally, he turned and headed for the door, and she sighed with relief, fantasizing how wonderful it would be when she sank into the warm scented tub that awaited her in the next room.

"By the way," he said, before he disappeared, "you really should do something about that cold. You sound awful."

He never knew how close he came to having Webster's Collegiate aimed at his head.

"Mr. Berenger?" The man's voice was smooth, cultured and a little annoyed. "Have you heard a word I said?"

Sam looked up from the top rail of the mahogany Queen Anne corner chair he was repairing. In the eight hours since he'd seen Sara, she hadn't been out of his mind. "No, I haven't," he said, tempering his words with a smile. "Not one word." He slid his hand along the cabriole leg of the chair, feeling for rough spots. "I signed a lease with you three years ago. You have no right to this apartment until December fifteenth."

"I'd been told you were a reasonable man, Mr. Berenger." The young man slid a small envelope from his breast pocket and opened it. Sam could see the color green quite clearly. "I'd been told you would understand the difficulty of our position here."

"First lesson—never believe what you hear." Sam stood up, stretching his tightly muscled arms toward the ceiling. The slim, dark-suited man took a step backward "I was fully prepared to move out December fifteenth. I still am. But December first? That's four days from now." He shook his head. "Can't do it."

The slim young man looked around the large living room that had been all but turned completely into a workshop for Sam. "You do your work here, don't you?"

Sam eyed him, then nodded. There was no point in saying he only did some of it there. Some or all—the place still looked like a carpenter's shop. He crossed his arms over his chest and waited for the next move, even though he had a pretty good idea what it would be.

"Let me read you something." The man slipped the money into his pants pocket and pulled out a thick sheaf of papers. He flipped them open, paged to a particular spot. "Clause 14c—The Tenant shall not use said premises in the pursuit of any profit-making venture without the express consent of the Owner in writing." He refolded the papers and looked over at Sam. "Have you obtained written consent?"

Check and mate, Sam thought, cursing under his breath. "We had a handshake arrangement," he said. "A verbal commitment."

The young attorney in front of him was unable to hold back a self-satisfied grin. "As you said before, Mr. Berenger, you can't believe everything you hear." He extended his hand, but Sam kept his arms folded across his chest. "We'd like the premises cleared by 4:00 p.m. on Tuesday Decem-

ber first.'' He grabbed his camel's hair coat from the claw-
footed rack near the entrance to the hall. "Mr. McCullough
said he would be happy to extend a twenty-four-hour grace
period, should you need it.''

"Tell Mr. McCullough he can take his twenty-four-hour
grace period and shove it.'' Sam's temper had been pushed
to the breaking point and beyond. Slow to anger, once he
exploded, he was a force to be reckoned with, and it was
apparent by the way the lawyer backed toward the door that
his anger was being felt. He stepped past the young man,
flung open the door to his apartment and waited for him to
leave before slamming the door shut. He hoped the sound
echoed in the guy's head for weeks.

Damn it to hell. The last thing he'd wanted to do—the last
thing he should have done—was lose his temper. He'd always felt explosions such as he'd just had were signs of
weakness, that once an opponent saw he could rile you, your
defeat was imminent. There was another, more civilized way
of going about things. The way he usually went about
things.

He retrieved his plane from the floor and bent down to
continue evening out the bottom of the leg he'd repaired on
the Queen Anne chair. However, his first movement was
clumsy and stiff, and he tossed the tool back down on the
sawdust-covered floor.

It was no use. Since seeing Sara again that morning, he'd
found it impossible to concentrate on anything but the look
in her blue eyes and the scent of violets that still seemed to
linger just out of his reach. Bits and pieces of forgotten
conversations with her from long ago would pop into his
mind; images of her, her dark curly hair piled on top of her
head, as she ate a strawberry ice cream cone in the middle
of a hot New York July.

It had been a summer of heat and fantasy, a painful time
when he hung suspended between the need to protect Sara
from his estranged wife's wrath and his own aching desire
to pull Sara into his arms. They had spent six months as
more than friends but less than lovers, with only the hope

of his divorce coming through to keep them sane. When Jennifer suddenly withdrew her request for divorce—a ploy to bring her straying boyfriend back to her, he later learned—Sara quit her job at the Obelisk and took a position in Rio de Janeiro that had been offered to her months earlier. That morning at the Trump Tower was the first time they'd seen one another in five years.

He had found it almost impossible to keep his mind on the dinner conversation and knew that Margaret had noticed his odd lack of attention. Leonard had tried to talk with him about taking over the penthouse, but Sam's attention span was abysmally short. He'd wanted to tell them about Sara, that he'd found her again, but some deep need to hold the secret close to his heart had prevailed. All it had taken was being near her once more, feeling her lips beneath his for the first time, to bring the memories flooding out of him like a riptide. *Call me, Sara,* he thought, staring at the phone across the room as if he could will it to ring. There hadn't been time to get her phone number; there hadn't been time enough for him to ask her if she even wanted him to have her phone number. There had just been those few seconds for him to press his business card into her hand—as if what had passed between them was of no more consequence than the exchange of information between acquaintances—shake her hand and take his leave.

Sam already knew she wasn't listed in the phone directory; he had checked once just after Maxwell Chance had been killed in the auto race in France. He had wanted to call Sara to let her know he was thinking of her, that he had always thought of her, every day since she'd left. Her address at the Carberry Towers was public knowledge, yet Sam had felt awkward about committing to paper the thoughts that had been with him for so long. Once he'd actually sat down and begun a short note of sympathy to her but ended up crumpling the ivory paper into a ball and flinging it across the room. The words "I need you" had seemingly written themselves, and he no longer had the right to say them to her. He'd never had that right.

He walked over to the phone, lifted the receiver and listened for the dial tone. It worked. He replaced it, then stood still for a long moment as if it could be coaxed to ring. He stripped off his faded blue work shirt and was about to head for the shower when the telephone finally rang, one long beautiful sound that sent adrenaline storming through his body as he picked it up.

"Hello, Sam Berenger speaking." A pause. His shoulders sagged slightly as he sat on the edge of the worktable and stared out the window at the evening sky. "Of course I have time to talk about the apartment, Leonard." He twisted the lever on the venetian blinds and closed out the stars. "All the time in the world."

The bath relaxed Sara so much that she dried off, put on a loose nightgown, then climbed into bed for a nap. She had planned to sleep only an hour or so, but the cold medicines she'd swallowed took effect, and she slept through dinner. By the time she awakened around eight, her apartment was empty. Mrs. Raines had left dinner carefully wrapped and ready to be popped into the microwave, but Sara's stomach threatened mutiny at the sight of the herbed chicken.

Instead, she swallowed the last two of her cold capsules with a glass of orange juice, fixed herself some buttered whole wheat toast, filled a carafe with coffee, then slipped into her office. The drapes were still open, and the city twinkled against the night sky. She looked down at the courtyard before she pulled the drapes closed. Paul was right. Even without her misplaced contact lenses, she was able to see the multiplying crowd of Maxwell's faithful who were gathering for their own anniversary vigil. Some had blankets spread out on the pavement; some held lit candles that flickered eerily in the shadowy darkness; some softly sang the songs he and his group Last Chance had made famous what seemed like a lifetime ago.

The sight of these people always touched her, but her affection was tinged with an unease that had nothing to do with their numbers. There was something basically wrong about their attachment to Maxwell, something tragic in their loyalty to a past that no longer existed. Many of them were fans who had spent the better part of five years waiting first for a glimpse of Max and now for a glimpse of his widow.

She yanked the drapes closed and turned back to the cheerfully sloppy room she called her office. She had made sure that the terribly chic, terribly neutral color scheme that dominated the rest of the apartment was broken up by slashes of ruby and emerald and turquoise. She allowed the cleaning service to keep the clutter and dust down to a minimum, but she let absolutely no one touch anything on her rolltop desk. Rolltops were supposed to be cluttered; the pigeonholes were supposed to be used, not decorated.

Sara was about to sit down and tackle the mountain of letters Deanna had deemed worthy of her personal attention when she noticed a piece of paper peeking out from under the desk. It was probably one of the papers Deanna had dropped earlier that morning, she thought as she leaned over and retrieved it.

She was about to stick it in a folder with a note for Deanna when she noticed Max's spiky, angular handwriting sprawled across the page.

"The idea refused to jell," she read, her eyes drawn to his words. "I spoke to Paul about getting me out of the contract, but no dice. I feel as if the idea is blocked behind a wall of time and it's up to me to break through and grab it."

Sara folded the sheet of paper and silently cursed her own lack of organization. How could she be so careless as to let this journal entry get away from the rest? It was important enough to be locked away in her dresser drawer with his personal letters. It was a pivotal notation; those few sentences had triggered *Wall of Time,* which became Max's biggest-selling album. She got up and went into her bedroom and unlocked her briefcase, stashing the notation with the others she was taking with her to Long Island.

She stared for the bedroom door when a noise stopped her. The sound of voices raised in song was like a soft, sad whisper in her ears as the waiting fans below harmonized on one of Max's compositions. Maybe it was her mood, but the song was deeply melancholy, and it reminded her of broken promises and shattered dreams.

You're just like they are, she thought suddenly, watching her reflection in the enormous beveled mirror that hung over her dressing table. *You edit his journals, you watch over his music, you tend the flame.* She was as defined by Maxwell and his memory as any of the poor souls outside who stood holding candles against the night. Paul Rollins and Deanna and Neal could walk away from Max's memory anytime they wished. For Sara it would be much harder. She shivered, and this time it was not from her cold.

Sam's business card was on her nightstand, under the latest thriller she was reading. She picked it up, squinted at the phone number and without hesitation punched the digits into her phone. Her heart was thumping so loudly that she found it hard to hear when it began ringing.

"Give me a break, Leonard!" There it was: Sam's voice, alive, filled with laughter, caressed her ear and warmed her body. "We just hung up ten seconds ago. You know I'd—"

"Sam?" She wanted to say more, but her throat went suddenly dry.

He was quiet for a moment, and she gripped the receiver so tightly that her fingers ached. "If you're not the woman I'm hoping you are, I'm really sorry," he said, "but it *is* you, isn't it, Sara?"

There was no mistaking the hope in his voice. She felt suddenly light-headed, love and desire washing over her. "It's Sara," she said, smiling alone in her room. "I wanted to thank you for coffee this morning."

Sam wanted to let out a whoop of pleasure that his family in Omaha could hear, but he restrained himself. *Don't scare her away,* he thought. It had taken them over five years to get to this point, and he'd be damned if he'd blow it now. "My pleasure," he answered easily, as if all he had offered her was coffee. "I'm just sorry it had to end so abruptly."

She could feel another sneeze tickling. She tried to fight it back. "Did you have any trouble with the photographer?

I heard something break and…" Her voice trailed off as she placed a finger beneath her nose in an attempt to forestall the inevitable.

"Only a filter broke, and I—" He stopped. "Sara, you sound odd." Suddenly, he wondered if perhaps she drank—or worse—to ease her loneliness. "Are you all right?"

"Of course, I am. I—" It was no use. A sneeze tore out of her body, followed by two more in quick succession. "I came down with a cold."

He was so relieved that he laughed.

"I don't think it's funny, Sam. I feel awful."

"Poor kid. Did you take anything for it?"

"Two cold capsules."

"Do they still make you dizzy?"

"Your memory is incredible. Yes, as a matter of fact, they do."

"Are you alone?" He cradled the phone closer to his ear, thinking of the mystery of a woman's body, of Sara.

She leaned back against her pillows and closed her eyes. "I am." But not really. A vision of Sam, more real than her life these past two years, was making her tremble with longing.

"I wish I were with you, Sara."

But you are, she thought. "I wish you were, too," she answered out loud. There. She'd said it. After all these years of trying to pretend, she had finally admitted how she felt about him. She waited for his reaction.

"Can you see me tomorrow? We need to talk."

"I can't."

"Sara, Sara, don't pull way from me again. There's so much we need to say to each other."

"We're going out to Quogue on the Island for a week. The anniversary—" she fumbled for words but found none. "You understand."

He didn't. "Don't go without seeing me."

"This is a difficult time, Sam. I just can't get away right now."

"Five minutes, Sara. Just give me five minutes before you leave." How could he tell her he had to see her eyes before he could believe she was real?

"Sam, listen, please. Try to understand. The apartment building is crawling with fans and press. It's just not possible for me to get out unnoticed."

"When will you be back?"

"A week, maybe ten days. We just want to wait for the publicity to die down."

"Will you see me then?" He felt as if his life was being measured by her words.

"Yes." The medicine was taking effect, and her words began to slur slightly. "I want to see you, Sam. I've missed you."

He closed his eyes for a moment against a vivid picture of her, vulnerable and lovely, in his arms. His gut wrenched with emotions that tilted crazily from desire to protectiveness and back again. "Go to sleep, Paisley." His voice was husky, a little raw. "Call me when you get back." *Call me, Sara.*

He was allowing her to decide when and how their relationship would proceed, and she silently thanked him for that. "I will, Sam. I promise you." A fierce longing swept across her, and she wished she were in his arms right then, breathing in his clean scent of goodness and life.

"Now get some sleep," he said, his voice gentle. "You're starting to sound a little rocky."

"You're a good man, Sam."

He grinned. "You've said that before, Paisley."

"It bears repeating."

"Sleep well, Sara." He wanted to caress her with his words.

"And you, Sam."

He hung up the phone, but his hand clasped the receiver for a moment, as if touch could be transmitted by wire. "I love you, Sara Paisley," he said out loud. This time he wasn't going to let her go.

3

Even Sam knew it was ridiculous, but the next morning he found himself sitting in Niko's, the same luncheonette he'd been to with Sara the day before. It wasn't as if he thought she'd be there waiting for him—after all, he knew she was on her way out to Long Island—but after all the years of not seeing her, a sleepless night had rendered him more emotional than rational. He ordered fried eggs and toast and let them grow cold on his plate while he drank black coffee and thought of another time and place.

The first time Sam saw Sara Paisley, he was standing in front of the Obelisk Gallery, and he felt as if someone had tilted the sidewalk beneath his feet.

"Sam Berenger?" she called. "From Klein Construction?"

He wiped his dusty hands on the legs of his jeans and walked toward her. "That's me."

"Leonard Klein just phoned." Her voice made him think of soft April rain. "I don't know how to break this to you after all your work—" she motioned toward the neat piles of lumber he'd stacked at the edge of the sidewalk "—but you can't start until Wednesday."

Sam groaned and dragged his hand through his thick brown hair. "This is an April Fools' joke, isn't it?" he asked. "Leonard's idea of fun?"

"Afraid not." She smiled, and it seemed as if all the spring sunshine had been captured there. "Something about the variance not being in order." She shrugged her narrow shoulders, and he loved the way her silky blouse rustled with the movement. "Besides," she continued, "it's April twenty-seventh. A bit late for an April Fools' joke, no?" She laughed at him, and he felt the sound slide easily around his heart.

He motioned toward the Obelisk. "You work there?"

She nodded. "Assistant to the assistant, but not for long." Her eyes were a dusky blue, and her gaze was direct. He'd forgotten what a nice trait that could be in a woman.

"Are you in line for a promotion?" he asked.

"Not exactly," she said. "I'm an artist. One day they'll be begging me for my paintings. The name Sara Paisley will be on every art connoisseur's lips."

"Well, Sara Paisley," he said, "it looks like we're going to be working together for the next few months. I'm Sam Berenger."

She extended her hand in greeting. His hand easily engulfed hers, but he had the sensation that it was he who was being captured. The scent of violets blossomed around him.

A police car stopped near the double-parked truck and beeped twice, the cop motioning for Sam to move the vehicle. Sam looked at Sara, then at the pile of construction materials he'd have to pile back on the truck. "You sure this isn't an April Fools' trick?" he asked as he moved toward the truck.

She shook her head, her dark curls fluttering over her forehead. "Sorry," she said. "No trick."

And in that moment he knew life had played the cruelest trick of all: giving him the woman he'd always dreamed of when he no longer had the right to dream. Technically, Sam Berenger was still a married man.

"Not this time." Sam's voice broke the early-morning quiet of the luncheonette.

"'Scuse me?" The waitress, balancing plates of scrambled eggs and French toast, stopped briefly by his table. "More coffee?"

Sam shook his head. He glanced at the bill and threw six singles down by his plate. Sara was in reach now, and he'd be damned if he'd let their chance for happiness together slip away.

The November wind was chill and damp as he left Niko's, but Sam didn't notice. All he could think of was the scent of violets and the way Sara had felt in his arms.

The inside of the rented limousine was plush and warm and smelled of Bailey's Irish Cream. Sara was curled in the corner of the rear seat, sipping warm lemon and honey, trying vainly to keep up with the chatter that bounced from Neal to Deanna and back again. She was feverish, achy and generally zonked from cold medicine, and it was all she could do to keep the threads of conversation from getting her all tangled up.

She coughed to clear her throat. "Now, why was it Paul couldn't come with us?" she asked for the third time.

Deanna grinned at Neal, who shook his head in a good-natured "I give up" manner. "My compulsive brother wasn't happy with the reports he did for StopHunger, so he decided to stay in town an extra two days to get things in order."

Sara nodded. "Oh, yes. I asked that before, didn't I?"

Deanna chuckled. "Repeatedly." She checked her watch. "It's time for more medicine."

Sara groaned. "Oh, no! If I take any more of that stuff, I won't be able to walk. Can't we just stop someplace and pick up my regular?"

"We're miles away from any drugstores." Deanna reached into her purse and took two capsules from an envelope and handed them to Sara. "Come on," she said, pressing them into her employer's hand. "If you don't take these every four hours, you'll never shake this bug."

"Really, Deanna, these things are worse than a triple martini for me. Couldn't we just—"

Deanna glanced at Neal, then back at Sara. "No, we couldn't. Now come on. If these things are good enough for me, they're good enough for you. Swallow."

"You're worse than a guard dog, Deanna." Sara took the two multicolored capsules from her, then swallowed them quickly with the lemon-and-honey mixture she'd been nursing. "I'll probably sleep the rest of the way out to Quogue."

Neal looked up from some balance sheets he'd been working on. "Best thing for you," he said. "How're you going to enjoy walking on the dunes if you're laid up with pneumonia?" When Maxwell was alive, Neal had been his shadow, the man who kept life's little aggravations from thwarting Maxwell's creativity. Now he seemed content to perform a somewhat similar function for Deanna. He was a relentlessly average man whose only outstanding feature was a head of thick curly blond hair that rivaled a Michelangelo.

Sara fluffed up the small pillow she'd brought with her and rested her cheek against it. "Of course you're right," she murmured, closing her eyes. "What would I ever do without you?"

Deanna looked across the small built-in table at Neal. "I hope you'll never have to."

Their easy chatter filled the limousine with a comforting sound, and Sara closed her eyes. She felt light-headed; a faint but not unpleasant buzzing seemed to be building inside her brain. How nice Neal and Deanna were. Who else was there to take care of her? Who else was there who cared? She was glad Paul wasn't with them; Paul, with his disapproving presence, the suppressed anger that always made her feel uneasy and gauche. He had frightened her the night before when he popped up in her room. She didn't like to be frightened . . . She just wanted to sleep . . . She wanted to sleep . . .

* * *

You can stop here and use the phone.... What about her...? She won't see anything.... Those pills will keep her under another hour.... You worry too much.... She never knew what hit her, did she...? I can make her do anything.... She might have fooled Maxwell, but...

I don't want to dream this, Sara thought. The voices were so familiar; it all seemed so real she could almost feel the limousine roll to a halt, could almost hear the door slam shut, the crackle of footsteps on gravel. *It's just a dream. I can wake up any time I want to. It's not real at all.* But the evil, the pervading sense of evil, was so intense that she couldn't wake up. She wanted to— Oh, please, but she wanted to wake up....

The sound came at Sara as if from the end of a very long tunnel. "Wake up," the woman's voice said. "I think you were having a nightmare."

Sara felt as if she'd just come off a three-day bender. Her throat was sore, her head ached, and the repeated doses of cold medicine blurred her vision. She sat up, pushed her hair off her face and groaned.

Deanna's face came fuzzily into view. "Here," she said, extending a cup toward Sara. "Have some water."

Sara shook her head. "Not unless there's some hemlock in it. I feel like death." Her voice was thick and indistinct.

"You sound like it, too." Deanna pushed the cup of water toward Sara again until she finally accepted it.

"What was in those capsules, anyway?" Sara managed between sips. "They're lethal."

Deanna chuckled. "It wasn't the capsules," she said easily. She leaned over and touched Sara's forehead. "You're running one hell of a fever, Sara. That's what it was."

Sara shivered and drew the blanket more closely around her and looked out the window. "Where are we?" she asked.

"Just a few minutes away from Quogue," Deanna said.

They had stopped for gasoline while Sara napped, and Neal had decided to sit up front with the driver. Now he slid back the privacy shield between the two sections of the limo and said, "Bad news, ladies. The press is waiting en masse at the gates."

Deanna uttered a mild expletive. "Isn't there some way we can elude them?"

Neal frowned and shook his head. "No way I can think of. That's the only entrance into the property, unless there's something I've missed." He looked at Sara for confirmation.

"That's the only way, Neal," she managed, her voice a hoarse whisper. "Max had wanted only one way on and off the property for security reasons. It seemed a good idea at the time."

Deanna patted her head. "It probably was a good idea at the time." She looked at her lover, Neal, and shrugged. "How could any of us know what life had in store?"

"I'm afraid we don't have any time for philosophizing, ladies," Neal said, cutting into Deanna's speech. "We have to make a few decisions. Do we just plow right on past them, or do we stop and make a statement?"

"Plow right past them." Deanna's words were quick and sure.

"No." Sara's voice was fading fast. "We have to stop, anyway, for one of us to punch in the code number at the gate. What makes you think the reporters are going to stand politely by while we do that?" She pointed toward a folded-up copy of one of the daily papers that bore the headline "The Life and Death of Maxwell Chance—Seven-Part Series Starts Today!" "We can't stop the talk, can we? Maybe if we give them a statement, they'll give us some privacy."

Deanna shrugged and looked out the window. Neal lit a cigarette and glared at Sara. "You don't mind if I think you're crazy, do you?"

"I don't mind at all," she answered. "If they want a story badly enough to follow us all the way out here—" she sighed "— well, we might as well make a short statement." She gestured toward the newspaper. "It beats getting coverage like this."

"It's up to you," Neal said as they pulled into the long driveway that swooped up to the main gate. "Let's just have it on record that I'm against the whole idea."

"Put me on record, as well," Deanna said. "I think you're giving the press credit for too much sensitivity."

Sara rummaged in her pocketbook for some folded Kleenex and blew her nose. "I'm not giving them credit for any sensitivity," she said. "I just think if we give them a statement right now they may leave us alone for the next few days."

Neal was whistling "Beautiful Dreamer" as he got out of the limo and walked over to the cluster of newspeople who had pens poised, cameras ready. Sara watched through the tinted glass as he spoke to them.

Deanna touched up her lipstick. "You know you don't have to do this," she said as she blotted a tiny smudge of coral from the corner of her mouth. "Widowhood does have some privileges."

Sara buttoned the top of her bright blue coat and pulled the collar up. "Maybe I don't want them anymore, Deanna. How long can I go on defining myself as the widow of Maxwell Chance?"

Deanna clicked shut her compact and met Sara's eyes. "It would be enough for some women."

Sara must have looked shocked, because Deanna laughed and patted her arm. "Don't look that way, honey. I was just playing devil's advocate to get you ready for the beasts out there."

Sara wanted to believe her. "You had me worried for a minute."

Neal approached the car and tapped on the window. Sara pushed a button, and the glass softly whirred down a fraction. "I set up a few ground rules," he said, his brown eyes locked on Sara's. "You'll give a brief statement, answer three questions—one each from the major networks—and then they respect your privacy for the rest of our stay."

Sara nodded, then winced as sinus pain sliced through her head.

"Are you sure you're ready, Sara?" he asked.

"As ready as I'll ever be."

He opened the door to the limousine and helped her out. She was a little unsteady on her feet both from her fever and from sitting so long, and he had to grip her tightly while she regained her bearings. "Come, fair maiden," he said sotto voce as they headed toward the phalanx of reporters who were descending on them. "The lions await."

"Hey, Farrell! How come you're not out there pounding the pavement today?"

Jack looked up from the dizzying pile of newspapers and tried to focus on the heavyset man who'd just come into the newspaper's morgue. "Got some research to do, Perez. Trying to match a name to a face."

It wasn't a total lie. He had been trying to thumb through some old photo stories of his to see if the man with Sara Chance matched any faces from the past, but his main reason for hanging around the paper that afternoon was to bump casually into Charlie Perez, one of the hottest celebrity photographers in New York City.

Charlie rested one foot on an empty chair and leaned on his thigh as he looked over Jack's shoulder. "Anything I can do to help?"

Jack shook his head. "I'm working on a hunch—nothing concrete."

Charlie lit a cigarette, then lowered himself into the chair next to Jack, sighing loudly as he settled his bulk down. "Don't waste your time on hunches, pal. They don't pay the bills."

"Don't I know it." Jack waited a moment before he spoke again. "Hey, you were out on the Sara Chance thing on the Island this afternoon, weren't you?" Perfect. Charlie would have no idea how many times Jack had rehearsed his words so they would have just the right touch of "I don't give a damn."

Charlie took a drag on his cigarette and nodded. "Yeah. I got that shot of her hanging on to that Travis guy's arm like he was the only railing on a sinking ship."

Jack flipped one newspaper closed and opened another. "Drugs?"

"That or booze. I mean, that woman was on another planet." Charlie ground out his cigarette, then stood up, pulling his creased trousers down around his legs.

Jack paged through another newspaper. He kept his eyes on the photos, because he knew the curiosity on his face would never escape Charlie Perez. "Couldn't it have been nerves or fatigue?"

Charlie snorted. "Like hell. When you been spending as much time in front of Regine's and all the other watering holes as I have, you get to recognize the signs pretty damned fast."

"She wasn't in front of Regine's, Charlie."

Charlie frowned. "You're coming on like a DA, Farrell. What gives? You got some bet going on this or something? I mean, we're not talking about Princess Grace here. This dame married a rock star, not the king of England."

Jack wanted to tell Charlie he was mixing his monarchies, but he bit his tongue. "Guilt by association?"

Charlie chuckled. "Maybe so. How come the interest?"

Jack closed the paper and tossed it on the growing pile. "Rent's due. A good picture of Sara Chance could set me up until Valentine's Day." He accepted a cigarette from Charlie. "How in hell did you know she was heading out to Quogue, anyway?"

Charlie flicked his lighter with this thumb and lit his cigarette, then Jack's. "Damnedest thing, actually." Smoke swirled out of his mouth and nostrils and wreathed his round face. "I got a call the night before telling me they'd be at the big house around two o'clock."

"Who called you?"

Charlie shrugged. "Have no idea."

"Man or woman?"

"Beats me. It was one of those gravelly voices that could be either/or."

"And you spread the word?"

"You got to be kidding!" Charlie took another drag on his cigarette. "Do you really think I'd give away an exclusive picture spread?" He shook his head. "Jesus! If I'd had rights to that whole set of shots, I'd be talking to you right now from Hawaii."

Jack couldn't feign interest in the papers any longer. "So how did they find out?"

"Phone calls, same as me. Whoever this joker was, he called every major daily, the wire services and a few of the hotter free-lancers in town."

"It's great to know where I stand in the scheme of things."

"How long you been at it?" Charlie asked. "Two years? Three?"

"A year and a half."

Charlie laughed and stubbed out his second cigarette. "And you're complaining? Tell me about it when you've been at it fifteen years and the big stories still pass you by." He patted Jack on the shoulder. "With all the gossip rags published today, all you'll have to do in a few years is worry how to shelter the money you're raking in."

Jack thought about his miserable sixth-floor walk-up apartment and snickered. "Are you sure those are Camels you been smoking?"

"There are enough celebrities in this town for all of us. So you missed out on the rock widow. You'll get another chance."

Jack groaned "Spare me the bad puns, Charlie."

"I wasn't trying to be funny, kid. She's still out in Quogue—you could drive out there and try to get an exclusive. I hear most of the other guys have left for the night."

"Thanks for the idea," he said, "but I can't think on an empty stomach."

Charlie looked at his watch. "Empty stomach? It's after nine!" He went to light another cigarette, then apparently thought better of it and stuck the package back in his coat pocket. "Why don't we go over to Spinelli's for a pizza and a few beers?"

Jack's stomach had been supplying percussion sounds for hours now, and pizza sounded just like the right antidote. Work, however, was a greater hunger. "I think I'll pass on it," he said finally. "I've been trying to knock off a few pounds."

Charlie rubbed his own ample belly and shrugged. "You already look like *Back to Bataan,* but if that's how you feel, so be it." He rapped his knuckles on the wooden table in salute and disappeared through the swinging door, leaving behind the faint scent of sweat and English Leather.

Jack's stomach growled again, and he sighed. It was going to be a long, long night.

"Damn it to hell." Neal slammed a copy of New York's major morning paper down on the breakfast table in front of Deanna. It was their first full day out in Quogue.

"Don't get so excited, Neal." Deanna's voice was low and lazy, faintly amused. "At least they spelled your name right."

Neal ignored her. His voice rose in agitation. "How the hell are we going to explain this?"

Even from where she stood in the doorway, Sara could see his even, regular features were flushed with anger. Her stomach twisted into a knot as she took a deep breath and entered the room. "Explain what?" she asked. Laryngitis had claimed most of her voice overnight, and all she had left was a hoarse whisper.

Deanna's hazel eyes darted to Neal, then to Sara. "We thought you'd sleep later," she said, jumping up to pour her employer a cup of coffee. "We'd hoped to have it all figured out by then."

"Here, take a look at what your pals in the press did to you." Neal picked up the top newspaper and tossed it at Sara. "I must have been a damned fool to go along with this stunt."

The photo was awful: her hair was disheveled, her eyes looked bleary and unfocused, and it was obvious from the way Neal gripped her by the shoulders that her balance wasn't the best.

She sank into the captain's chair at the head of the kitchen table and looked up at Neal. "I look drunk," she said, pointing at the grainy black-and-white photo, "or worse."

Deanna put a cup of café au lait down next to Sara and took her seat again. "Don't worry about it," she said, sipping from her own cup of black coffee. "You had a cold— no one expected Miss America."

"Don't try to shield her, Deanna. We're not worrying about Sara's looks here. We're worrying about her reputation."

"My reputation?" Sara wrapped her hands around the coffee cup and stared across the table at the blond man.

He grabbed the newspaper from her and flipped it open to page 3. "Read this."

Sara plucked her oversized glasses from the pocket of her red bathrobe, slipped them on and zeroed in on the feature story.

Has Grief Taken Its Toll on Max's Widow?
(See cover photo and centerfold.)

Sara Chance, beautiful young widow of the late singer/ songwriter Maxwell Chance, whose group Last Chance made rock satire an art form, arrived at her beach house in Quogue this afternoon showing the strain of grief as the second anniversary of her husband's death approaches. She was accompanied by Dina Rollins, her personal secretary, and Neal Travis.

Friday marks the second anniversary of Maxwell Chance's tragic death in a charity auto race outside of Paris. The world remembers the dignity and courage Sara Chance brought to his funeral despite the wild outpouring of grief that culminated in a mob scene at the grave site.

When asked by a reporter from WABC-TV news why she's retreated to the house in Quogue to mark the anniversary, Sara seemed to have difficulty finding the right words. In a slow and barely audible voice she said, "This is a private time for me, and I want it to remain so," and was then led back to the waiting limousine by Travis.

Al Hirschfeld, from Cable News/Long Island, said Mrs. Chance appeared fatigued and that may account for her seeming lack of coordination and slurred speech.

(For more on Max and Sara, turn to page 23: part II of "The Life and Times of Maxwell Chance.")

A sidebar advised readers to watch for an upcoming series entitled, "Celebrity Addictions: Why do stars turn to booze and dope when they seem to have everything?"

"My God!" She tossed the newspaper to the floor in disgust. "They make me sound like I'm either a drunk or a druggie. Can't we sue them?"

"For what? Spelling our names wrong?" Neal asked, his eyes darting toward Deanna for an instant while she fiddled with the top of the sugar bowl. "For saying you looked tired? For saying you had trouble standing upright?" He pointed toward the newspaper on the floor. "This picture is no lie, Sara. That's exactly how you looked yesterday."

Deanna stood up and faced the man she lived with. "Don't you think you're being a little hard on her, Neal? How was she supposed to know it would turn out this way?"

"Because it's a tough world out there, Deanna. The public chews up people like Sara and spits them out when they hit the bone. You were in public relations—this can't be news to you."

Sara stood up and carried her untouched cup of coffee over to the sink. The late-autumn sun streamed in, splashing across the ceramic tile floor in a pool of butterscotch. She leaned against the sink, fitting the small of her back into the curved edge. "Why can't we issue a statement or something? A denial, maybe."

Deanna picked up the newspaper Sara had tossed to the floor and stacked it on top of the other one on the kitchen table. Her hazel eyes seemed far away, and Sara could almost hear her thought processes at work. "I'm afraid Neal is right on this," she said finally, turning her chair around to face Sara. "Anything we say will sound like an admission of guilt." Her voice softened. "Think about it, Sara—Sara Chance wants you to know she wasn't drunk or under the influence of drugs yesterday. She was merely over-coughdropped, over-Contac'd and overtired." She turned her hands palms up in a gesture of resignation. "To borrow a phrase, 'The lady doth protest too much.'"

"It's not fair," Sara said, pulling a fresh Kleenex out of the pocket of her robe. "Even I think I sound like a lady with a lot of problems."

Neal took the newspapers, folded them, then tossed them overhand into the wastebasket on his left. "You'd be surprised what subliminal messages a crafty layout artist can get across. Why, I remember one—"

Sara's sneeze echoed throughout the room. Suddenly, she felt unbearably hot and horribly cold simultaneously. Big fat tears began to roll down her cheeks, and she was helpless to stop them.

Deanna stood up and put her hand on Sara's shoulder. "You look like death," she said bluntly. "You'd better get back to bed before they report you're on a suicide mission here."

"Oh, no," Sara said, reaching for another Kleenex. "What about Paul? He'll hit the roof when he sees this. What are we going to do?"

"He's already hit the roof and gone through it," Deanna said, turning her in the direction of the bedrooms. "It can be repaired."

Neal patted her hand awkwardly as she walked by. "Don't worry, Mrs. Sara," he teased, using her nickname from the early days of her marriage. "We'll keep big, bad Paul in line."

Deanna linked her arm through Neal's and smiled at Sara. With the November sun streaming through the window and catching the lights in her red hair, Deanna looked more beautiful than Sara had ever seen her. "Aren't we your best friends, after all?"

I've always believed you were, Sara thought as she slowly made her way through the cedar-paneled beach house toward her bedroom suite. She must be feverish—why else would she have such a feeling of being unprotected, of being prey to something she couldn't define?

None of it made any sense. Not her vague suspicions, not the thinly veiled innuendos in the newspapers and most of all, not the intensity of her feelings for Sam. In just those few minutes with Sam yesterday she had felt stronger, more cared for than ever in her life. How could she be so sure Sam would make it right when she had no idea at all if he would even want to see her again once he read the morning paper?

Has Grief Taken Its Toll on Max's Widow?

Sara Chance, beautiful young widow of the late singer/songwriter Maxwell Chance, whose—

Sam crumpled up the newspaper and tossed it back down on top of his workbench. "Why do I bother reading it again? I know every stinking word by heart." It seemed as if he'd read the story a thousand times since Leonard handed it to him an hour ago. He had the whole thing committed to memory: the pictures, the captions, the second installment of Max's life story.

Leonard Klein stood in the center of Sam's living room and wished he'd left the morning paper on Sam's doorstep where it belonged.

"It's speculative journalism," he said, watching the way the veins on the younger man's neck seemed to throb as he read the story. "Sleaze of the first order. No one believes that type of thing."

Sam arched an eyebrow in Leonard's direction. "Like hell they don't." His eyes again sought the newsprint in front of him: wonderful Maxwell, beautiful Sara, tragic accident—pat phrases perfect for tabloid psychology but totally useless when it came to explaining the fear that suddenly slid up his spine.

"Come on, Sam." Leonard stepped over the base of the Savonarola chair Sam was restoring. "You're no fool. You know about bottom-line journalism, don't you?"

"Economics over ethics. I know all about it." He kicked aside some papers that were scattered on the floor with the tip of his running shoe.

Leonard took a deep breath. "Is there any chance there's some truth to this story?"

Sam whirled around to face his friend and mentor. *"Et tu?"*

Leonard placed a comforting arm on Sam's shoulder. "I didn't know her as well as you, Sammy. It had to be asked."

"Sara was sick, Leonard. I spoke to her not thirty-six hours ago—she sounded awful."

Hadn't he mentioned how cold medicines always made her feel like someone who'd had a few whiskeys? And hadn't there also been one brief, ugly moment when he wondered if maybe—just maybe—she eased her pain with pills or booze?

"They don't know her, Sam. They don't have to be kind."

"They don't even have to be honest." Sam's voice was brittle with anger.

She was surrounded by money and widowhood and protectors who stood guard. Why wouldn't the press speculate? After all, speculation was their business. Did Jackie drink after JFK died? How is Prince Rainier holding up after losing Grace? Can Sara make it without Maxwell?

Like rubbernecking drivers at the scene of an accident who stare at the twisted metal and fresh blood and marvel that five seconds stood between them and disaster, readers could experience the same delicious shiver of safety that their world was still intact, that money and power and beauty could not insulate one from sorrow. In this one thing, they were equal to the mighty.

Leonard hesitated a moment, then fished out a wallet from the breast pocket of his topcoat. "I didn't come here planning to be the bearer of bad tidings," he said, extending the black leather wallet toward Sam. "Margaret found this in the sofa cushions after you left last night."

Sam accepted the wallet with a nod and jammed it into the back pocket of his jeans. "Thanks. I can just see me trying to cash a check without any ID." He made an effort to shake off the melancholia that had surrounded him. "Feel like some coffee?"

Leonard checked his watch and shook his head. "No, thanks. I've got an early lunch meeting, and besides, Margaret's been after me to cut down on caffeine." He grinned. "Says I'm making her nervous."

Sam walked the older man to the door. Leonard watched him for a moment, then gave him a quick embrace.

"If it's meant to be this time, it will work out," he said, referring to Sara.

Sam just shrugged. He felt exposed somehow, as if Leonard had been able to put words to all his nameless fears.

Leonard left, and Sam was left with silent images of Sara that flickered like old movies behind his eyelids.

"So you're going to let it happen again?" His words echoed in the high-ceilinged room. "You're going to let her slip past you again?" Sam was no fool, and he never made the same mistake a second time. He'd waited long enough.

He picked up the telephone and dialed Long Island information. No Chances in Quogue. No Paisleys. Could they have no telephone at all? He bent over and picked up the discarded newspaper, laying it on top of his workbench and smoothing out the creases.

He scanned the article again, feeling his blood pressure soar at the thinly veiled intimations of drugs and drinking.

The names Travis and Rollins popped out at him. He stopped reading and picked up the phone again.

Pay dirt.

Paul Rollins, 2 Job's Lane, Quogue. The operator rattled off the number, and Sam scribbled it on the scarred top of his workbench with a grease pencil.

He didn't even stop to frame a few comforting phrases to ease them over any possible rough spots in their conversation. He just dialed the 516 area code and the number and listened to the sound of his heartbeat and the phone that rang a hundred miles away.

Sara hadn't thought it possible to feel worse than she'd felt the night before, but she was wrong. Somehow seeing that damning picture of herself in the paper and reading the article had depleted all of her resources and left her drained.

When she got back to her bedroom she pulled the drapes closed, locking out the pale winter sunlight, and crawled under the covers to try and get warm.

She finally dozed off, and her dreams were vivid and distorted with her fever. Swirling masses of reds and oranges, Max's little sports car careening into the railing and spilling gasoline and blood, crowds and contorted faces with hands that pulled and grabbed at her, voices talking about medicines and mysteries, Sam's beautiful eyes hovering over her and somewhere the faint, persistent ring of a telephone that she was unable to rouse herself to answer.

It was early evening when she finally awoke. Her nightgown and sheets were drenched in sweat. Her fever had broken, and the shivering had stopped. She stripped off her nightgown and went into the bathroom to shower.

How wonderful it was to feel even semihuman again, she thought as she toweled herself dry and puffed on a cloud of dusting powder. She still felt sick and empty, but at least that terrible other-world feeling had passed and she could think clearly. She slipped on a fresh nightgown and her red robe. She realized the empty feeling was hunger, and she headed for the kitchen. Things would seem much better on a full stomach.

As she walked down the hallway, she heard the stereo softly playing from the den and the sounds of a fire crackling in the hearth and conversation from Deanna and Neal. She decided she'd rather eat before she tried being sociable. It had been a difficult day, and the wrong look from Deanna would be enough to unnerve her totally. She retreated to the kitchen.

Sara hadn't counted on Paul Rollins being there, hunched over a tuna sandwich and the *New York Times*.

He looked up at her as she entered the room. "Sleeping Beauty finally awakens."

"Hello, Paul." She opened the refrigerator. "When did you get out here?"

He leaned back in his chair and watched as she pulled out two eggs, juice and bread. "About an hour and a half ago." He took a sip of his coffee. "Do you feel like talking?"

She pulled an iron frying pan down from the wrought-iron holder overhead and placed it on the burner. "Do I have a choice?" Her voice still sounded husky and indistinct from her cold.

"No, you probably don't." He got up to pour more coffee from the automatic machine set up on the counter beneath the window. "Care for any?"

"I'm having tea." She broke two eggs into a glass bowl and mixed them with a fork. "Well, go ahead," she said as she turned the gas on and added a pat of butter to the frying pan. "Read me the riot act."

Paul leaned against the counter, sipping his black coffee. "Is that what you think I'm going to do?"

"Oh, yes," she said, adding the egg mixture to the sizzling butter. "That's exactly what I think you're going to do."

He placed one hand over his heart. "I'm deeply wounded, Sara. And after all we've meant to one another."

"I don't think you're being funny." She turned away from him and tended to her scrambled eggs. She could feel his eyes on her back.

"You forgot to start your toast."

"Thank you."

"You also forgot to turn on the teakettle."

"Thank you again," she said. "I appreciate having my shortcomings pointed out to me."

"You never were the organized type, were you, Sara? Too much the right-brain creative type."

She tossed the fork down on the stove with a clatter. "Damn it, Paul, if you have something to say, just say it."

"You're feeling irritable tonight."

"I'm feeling sick tonight. I'm in no mood for one of our verbal fencing matches. If you have something to tell me about that newspaper article, please do."

"It's not the newspaper article," he said. "It's articles."

She swallowed. "Such as?"

"All the major dailies in New York—"

"That's not so awful," she interrupted.

"—and every national wire service plus a few foreign."

"I suppose they sent it to Russia, Lapland and points north, as well."

"It's not a laughing matter, Sara."

She arched a brow at him "If you'll take note, Paul, I'm not laughing."

He put his coffee cup down on the counter. "Whatever prompted you to give that little interview yesterday?"

How could she explain that despite feeling sick and doped up from cold medicines, she had also been feeling a rush of confidence as a result of her conversation with Sam the night before? She had truly believed she would be able to begin the painful process of breaking away from myth and heading toward reality.

"Sara?"

The eggs had scorched and stuck like Krazy Glue to the bottom of the skillet. She scraped the mess into the garbage disposal. "I thought the only way to have some privacy here this week would be to give them what they wanted right off the bat." She went back to the stove and turned the water on for tea. "Chalk it up to bad judgment."

"Phenomenally bad judgment."

Sara bowed in his direction. "Phenomenally bad judgment, then." She reached up on top of the refrigerator where she kept tea bags in a glass apothecary jar. "We all make mistakes."

Paul stretched his long arms toward the ceiling, and one of his rare smiles cracked across his narrow face. "Yes, we do, but most of us don't have ours looking up at us from the front page of the *National Enquirer.*"

Sara groaned. "Not that one, too?"

Paul's smile broadened. "If it's good enough for the *Times* to print, you can be damned sure it's good enough for the *Enquirer.* They'll probably increase circulation for this issue."

"Don't look so amused," she said, putting a tea bag into her cup and adding the boiling water. "You're acting as if you have stock in the *Enquirer.*" She had expected angry accusations and harsh words. His attitude puzzled her. "What's with you tonight? I feel like I'm in the 'Twilight Zone.'"

"There's not a thing we can do to change it. Besides," he continued, rolling the sleeves of his white shirt up to his elbows, "there's a certain ironic symmetry to the whole situation."

She tossed the used tea bag into the garbage. "I'm afraid I fail to see it."

"Don't you find it amusing that the woman who guards her privacy like the Holy Grail is the same woman who put the reporters onto her trail?"

She stirred sugar slowly into her teacup, taking a deep breath to recover her equilibrium. "Explanation, please," she said, her voice thin but even.

He took a step closer to her, and she tensed until he reached past her for the coffeepot. "Does the name Sam Berenger sound familiar to you?"

It was crazy, but an instant, overpowering feeling of guilt overcame her like a blush. "Of course it does," she said easily. "I used to work with Sam." She had no reason on earth to feel guilty. "What about him?"

"He called about forty-five minutes ago."

"Sam called here?"

"I thought I heard that someplace before."

"Cut the sarcasm, please, Paul. Did he leave a message?"

He shrugged again as he took a long sip of his third cup of coffee. "Can't answer that. Deanna took the call."

They heard footsteps coming along the hall and looked up to find Deanna and Neal standing in the doorway to the kitchen.

"Deanna took what call?" Neal asked as they carried empty plates and wineglasses to the counter and Deanna began searching around for more Chablis.

"The one from Sara's mysterious friend Sam."

Deanna broke a piece of French bread from the loaf on the counter and popped it into her mouth. "He sounded quite concerned," she said. "Who is he?"

All three of them seemed to be hanging on Sara's next words, and she felt unexpectedly nervous. The memory of the nightmare she'd had in the limousine rose, and she pushed it back down. "I worked with him a number of years ago," she said, hoping they attributed her shaky voice to her cold. "At the Obelisk Gallery."

"Ah," Neal said with a smile. "Before Max."

"It might be hard for you to believe it, but I did have a life before marriage."

"Down, girl," Neal said. "That was a jest."

"Well, I didn't find it funny." What was the matter with her? She was supposed to be acting unconcerned, and instead she was flying off the handle at the slightest provocation.

Deanna broke off another piece of French bread. "Ease up on Sara. You know she's not feeling well." She looked at her brother and her lover. "Do me a favor and get some more wood from the back and rebuild the fire, would you?"

Paul shook his head. "It doesn't take two of us, Deanna."

"That's my brother," she said wryly. "Never knows how to take a hint gracefully."

Neal grabbed Paul's arm. "They want to be alone for some woman-to-woman talk. Let's split."

Grumbling something about needing another cup of coffee, Paul grudgingly followed Neal out of the kitchen.

"I can't figure him out," Deanna said after the two men left the room. "Paul can be either the brightest or the most obtuse man in the world—there's no middle ground with him. It's our lower-middle-class background." She put an arm around Sara, who had sat down at the kitchen table.

"It's more than that," Sara said. "I come from the same background." Sara shivered and pulled her robe more closely around her body. She wished she didn't feel so uneasy sometimes with Deanna, because she was really her only ally. "Thanks for coming to my defense, though. I appreciate it."

"Your friend left a message, by the way." Deanna rummaged in the pocket of her emerald green minidress. She smoothed out a piece of notepaper. "Something about the number on his business card was being disconnected on the first of the month. He'd let you know the new number as soon as he got it." Deanna handed the piece of paper to Sara, who carefully folded it in half. "How did he know you were here?"

"All he had to do was read the papers."

"You didn't give him our number here?"

"No, I didn't. We're not unlisted, Deanna."

Deanna got up to shut off the teakettle's shrill whistle. "He must be a bit of a sleuth," she said as she poured boiling water into the two cups. "The phone is in Paul's name."

Sara took a deep breath. Her sense of isolation heightened once again. "Sam's a very resourceful man."

Deanna carried the teacups over to the table, then went to the refrigerator for lemon. "I didn't know you kept in touch with your friends from your working days. Until I came to work for you, I never stayed on a job long enough to make close friends."

There's a lot you don't know about me, Sara thought as she squeezed some lemon into her teacup. "I haven't kept in touch," she finally answered, taking the sugar bowl from Deanna. "Sam and I bumped into each other the day before yesterday at the Trump Tower."

"The day of your shopping expedition?"

Sara nodded, sipping her tea.

Deanna grinned. "No wonder you were so cheerful when you got home. Is he handsome?"

"Yes, he is, but I think you're getting the wrong idea." Sara had an acute need to keep that part of her life private. "He was a good friend, and I imagine that article concerned him."

"Did you mention you were coming out here?"

Sara had to stop and think for a moment, because his kiss had obliterated her memory of all else. "I may have in the course of conversation," she answered finally. "I hope you're not implying Sam had anything to do with the press being here."

"I'm not implying anything," Deanna said. "Paul told us to think of anyone who might have leaked the information."

"Our place out here is no secret," Sara said, trying to keep a rein on her temper. Things had been smooth with Deanna for some months now, and she didn't want to change anything. "It wouldn't take a great deal of deductive reasoning to figure out we just might come out here to observe the anniversary." She stopped for a moment. "Why, the limousine driver could have leaked the information." Her voice was cracking, and she sipped at her tea to soothe her throat.

Deanna put her teacup down. "Don't get testy, Sara. We're just trying to protect you, you know." The woman's voice was soothing, almost too soothing. It grated against Sara's nerves.

"I'm old enough to take care of myself."

"Under normal circumstances, of course; but this is a difficult time right now, Sara, for all of us. With Max's anniversary just a few days away—" Deanna stopped and looked down at her hands.

"I appreciate that, Deanna, but Sam is a good friend of mine. He would never hurt anyone."

"Things change," Deanna said. "You haven't seen him in years."

"This is ridiculous." Sara pushed her hair off her face with an impatient gesture. "I'm not planning on running away with him or anything."

"Consider the subject closed." Deanna turned to face Sara, a smile back on her face. "Part of being a friend is risking anger to keep a friend safe."

Sara suddenly remembered how Deanna had showed up in Paris the day after Max's death, as broken with grief as Sara. She managed to give time and friendship to Max's widow at the time Sara needed the understanding of a woman the most. It was something Sara couldn't forget.

"I think my fever fried my brains," she said finally. "I'm sorry if I was harsh to you."

Deanna's face lit up with her smile. "No apologies necessary. If Sam is your friend, that's all I need to know. Now, off to bed with you." She pushed Sara toward the door of the kitchen. "We can't have you getting any sicker, can we?"

Annoyance battled with affection as Sara headed down the hall toward her bedroom. Had Deanna always been so protective of her? Sara had the quick impression of being a four-year-old sent back to her room after a brief visit with the adults. It wasn't the way a twenty-seven-year-old woman should feel.

It wasn't at all the way Sam made her feel.

There was one thing to be said for insomnia: it gave Sam eight hours extra to work.

It had been two nights since Sam had been able to sleep, two nights since he'd bumped into Sara at the Trump. His body had gone into some strange kind of emotional overdrive, his adrenaline system creating havoc where none had existed before.

He'd thrown himself headlong into work, because anytime he let down his guard, he was engulfed by waves of longing so intense they terrified him. It was as if five years of game playing, five years of pretending he wished Sara Paisley Chance well in her new life, had ripped the shield from his heart and left it vulnerable and exposed.

He had wanted Sara from the day they met in front of the Obelisk. He had fallen in love with her the first time she touched his hand. He'd always thought himself a practical man, but magic, it seemed, struck when a man least expected it.

Sara was still magic.

And Sam still loved her.

4

By Sara's third morning on Long Island, most of the reporters and camera crews had disappeared. Sara suspected that Paul or Neal had spread a little Chance money around in an effort to make the local police more diligent in maintaining her privacy. Whatever the reason, she was glad.

Even her cold cooperated, and on that third morning Sara bundled up and was about to slip out the back door and down the rickety wooden steps to the beautiful, and beautifully empty, beach below when Deanna stopped her.

"You're crazy," the red-haired woman said, throwing her slender hands in the air. "You'll catch your death out there."

Sara pulled her wool scarf more tightly around her throat. "Don't worry," she answered. "I think I'd rather risk pneumonia than death by imprisonment."

"Thanks a lot!" Deanna's laugh was slightly hurt. "And here I thought I was a marvelous companion."

Sara patted the woman's arm. "Of course you are. But cabin fever's cabin fever—I've got to get out for a while, Deanna, or I'll go crazy."

"What about the press?" Deanna asked. "There's no one out there to protect you from them."

Sara glanced down at the beach. "Look," she said. "Not a soul around. I'll be fine."

Deanna looked totally unconvinced. "Be my guest," she said, opening the door, "but don't say I didn't warn you."

Sara stepped out of the warm house and into the December cold and instantly felt better than she had in days. She hadn't been lying when she mentioned cabin fever. She was used to at least having privacy in her apartment back in the city, and living so closely with Paul and his volatile personality and Deanna and her changing moods was taking its toll.

Deanna quickly pulled the storm door shut, and with a wave Sara hurried down the steep wooden stairs that led to the water's edge. A September hurricane had savaged the south shore and eroded much of the beach. The windswept dunes were now just yards from the water's edge, and Sara felt like a tightrope walker suspended between hills and sea.

Gulls swooped overhead; their screeching cries sounded mournful to Sara. She knew if she looked up toward the house she would see Deanna standing at the back door watching her, so she kept her eyes on the curving stretch of beach and quickly followed a line of seaweed and broken bottles in an attempt to get out of Deanna's line of vision.

She needed to get away from the constant reminders of a past that could never be recaptured no matter how deep the loyalty, how strong the memories. Maxwell was dead, and she was alive. It was as simple as that. She had grieved, and grieved deeply, but that time was past. Seeing Sam again, speaking with him—feeling his lips against hers, however briefly—had pushed her body and soul into the present, pushed her heart toward the future.

Sara had strolled a half mile down the beach when she realized she was out of sight of the house. Rolling dunes and scrub pines surrounded her on the left, and the dark, gray-green sea encroached upon her from the right. Unless Deanna was using a telescope, there was no way anyone could be watching, but Sara still had the uneasy feeling of eyes upon her.

A sea gull swooped down near her, split the icy water with his body, then shot skyward again, his cry sending unexpected chills up her spine.

She stopped to fix the black leg warmers that were sliding down toward her ankles when she caught a glimpse of something moving behind a dune a hundred feet away. She hadn't worn her contacts since she caught cold, and she rummaged through the pockets of her coat, hoping against hope that she'd had the presence of mind to stick her glasses in one.

Again she caught the glimpse of something bright flash briefly at the top of the dune. She squinted into the winter glare.

"Deanna!" Her voice, weak from her cold, was nearly lost in the howl of the wind. "I saw you. Come out and do your watchdogging in public."

No answer.

"Deanna, this isn't funny. Come out."

Still no answer, but someone was definitely up there; of that Sara was sure.

Beneath the layers of sweaters and shirts a thin line of sweat snaked down her back as she started toward the dune. Her sneakered feet sank into the wet sand, and her calves and thighs ached with the effort. Reaching the top suddenly felt equivalent to scaling Everest. She heard a rustling noise just on the other side of the dune. "Damn it," she breathed. "I'm a little old for hide-and-seek."

A good old-fashioned anger was bubbling up inside Sara as she scrambled for the top of the dune. It was bad enough that the press and public haunted her every move in Manhattan; the last thing she needed was to have her privacy invaded there, in the middle of nowhere.

"Listen," she began as she finally reached the top, "I'd appreciate it if you'd—"

She stopped. Two teenagers, no more than sixteen or seventeen years old, were wrapped in each other's arms. Their bodies, she noted, were thankfully wrapped in an enormous blanket. A bright red sweater lay discarded on the sand. The boy glared up at Sara, his eyes glazed with sexuality and anger.

"Hey, lady, come on," he said as the girl pressed her face against his shoulder. "Go get your kicks someplace else."

"I'm sorry," Sara stammered, unable to force her eyes away from the couple. "I thought you were somebody else."

"Well, we're not," the boy said, his voice husky with thwarted desire. "Can't we have any privacy?"

Now that was something Sara knew much about. She apologized again, then turned to hurry back down the side of the dune. Her eyes were blinded by bad vision and sudden tears, and she missed her footing and tumbled gracelessly over sharp blades of dune grass and broken shells until she finally ended up in a heap near the water's edge. Her hands were scratched through her gloves, and thin trickles of blood stained the white wool. She pulled the gloves off, then plunged her hands into the icy water, actually enjoying the sting of the salt against her flesh. It was almost enough to take away the sudden piercing desire that tore at her body and made her ache for Sam.

Those kids, those children who lay together behind the dune, held the world in their arms and probably had no idea what it meant. Sara would have willingly given up her fancy penthouse, her monied life-style, to spend one moment in Sam's arms. When she married Maxwell, she had closed off part of her heart, and now it was cracked open, and it throbbed like a wound.

This wasn't where she belonged. Running away from the publicity had seemed a good idea at the time, but she now knew it wasn't the answer. She'd run away before; she wouldn't run away from Sam again.

Sara had been curled up in a ball in the back seat of Paul Rollins's rented Lincoln for what seemed like several hours now. Her back ached, her legs were cramped, and fine fibers from the large plaid wool blanket that covered her tickled her nostrils and made her want to sneeze.

"Can I sit up yet?" Her voice was muffled by the blanket.

"Only if you want to be on the front page of every paper from here to Tibet." Paul chuckled, and she felt like throwing a shoe at him. Deanna and Neal had been totally against Sara's impetuous return to the city. Sara had argued that the press would never expect her to slip back into town so soon, and it had taken her by surprise when Paul Rollins, of all people, had agreed with her.

She groaned. "Oh, come on, Paul! I've been back here for hours—we must be halfway to California by now."

"I'm glad you're not a mathematician, Sara." She could feel him angle the car left. "Your perception of time leaves a lot to be desired."

"Your attempts at humor leave a lot to be desired." Maybe she was better off on the floor of the back seat at that. At least there she couldn't see his face. "The least you could do is tell me where we are, for heaven's sake."

She felt the car ease to a stop.

"Westhampton Beach," he said. "The stoplight near the big farm stand."

"Give me a break, Paul! We're at least out of Quogue." She started to lift her head up to take a look, but his large freckled hand firmly pushed her back down.

"I'd stay right there if I were you." His voice was annoyingly calm.

"You're a sadist. I can't breathe down here."

"Sorry to hear that." He didn't sound sorry in the least. "We're being followed by two cars filled with TV cameras and hungry reporters. Unless you feel like saying, 'Cheese' a few hundred times, I'd stay put."

The big car began moving again, and she could feel every bone-rattling rut in the road. So much for the smooth ride of a luxury car. "Why are they following us? They must be able to see it's just you in the car."

"This wouldn't be the first time someone tried to hide in the back seat, Sara." He changed lanes, and Sara's body was jostled against the left passenger door. "Just hold tight un-til we reach the expressway. I'll lose them there."

Unfortunately, they were halfway to Manhattan before the intrepid reporters finally decided Paul Rollins was not worth the chase and turned back toward Quogue. Sara, stiff, sore and very irritable, tossed the scratchy blanket aside and took her normal seat, pointedly avoiding Paul's eyes as they watched her through the rearview mirror. She maintained an aggrieved silence.

"You really should be going to Rio," Paul said as they neared the entrance to the Queens Midtown Tunnel. "It's your house, after all."

Sara shrugged and watched the dreary factories and warehouses roll by her window. "I haven't felt much like traveling."

"Might do you good," Paul continued, tossing change into the toll basket. "Not the traveling but the business. I can't make all the decisions for you, Sara."

She turned and faced him. "If you're unhappy with your position, Paul, I'm sure we can do something about it." She had to smother an urge to slap his face. "That is, if you care to make a decision on it."

"Grow up, Sara." Paul reached up and adjusted the rearview mirror so Sara's face was no longer in his line of vision.

"I'm trying to," she snapped back. "Why don't you people let me?"

Paul's face hardened, and they drove the rest of the way in silence.

All she could think about as the luxury car rolled toward Manhattan was how wonderful it would be if she were Sara Paisley again and Sam still loved her.

The telephone, disconnected and wrapped in its own cord, rested on top of a pile of cartons in the middle of what used to be Sam's living room. Okay. That was it. No more wait-ing for it to ring. Sara wasn't going to call. Even if she wanted to, now she couldn't.

It was early evening, Tuesday, December 1, and Sam had two hours before he had to be out of his apartment for good. He looked at the half-packed crates, the sawdust and glue that littered the floor, the open suitcases with sweaters and jeans spilling out, and knew the whole thing was totally impossible. The deadline had been marching toward him like an invading army, and instead of preparing to meet it, Sam had spent the past three days watching TV news and reading everything he could get his hands on about Maxwell Chance and the lovely Sara.

At least a hundred times in the past few days he had picked up the telephone and started to dial 516-28—then stopped cold, finger poised on the keypad. Each time he heard the slightly strained voice of the woman who had answered the telephone at Sara's home in Quogue a few days earlier. He had the conversation memorized.

"Deanna Rollins speaking."

Rollins, he had thought. The wife of Paul? "This is Sam Berenger. I'd like to speak with Sara, please."

Long pause. When she spoke, her voice was guarded, wary. "What number are you calling, please?"

He repeated it. "I'm a friend of Sara's."

"Many of Sara's friends have press cards. Would you be one of them?"

"No way. I knew Sara when she worked at the Obelisk." *Before she married Maxwell.*

Another long pause. "I'm afraid Mrs. Chance is asleep."

He checked his watch. "At seven-thirty?"

"She's ill. May I take a message?"

Her voice had become slightly friendlier, and conversely, he grew more wary.

"Yes. Please tell her the business number on my card will be out of service after Tuesday. I'll contact her with my new number as soon as I have it." Good, he thought. Bland, businesslike, noncommittal.

He spelled his last name for her, said good-bye and hung up.

Now, three days later, he cursed himself for not asking for the Manhattan phone number, for not calling back later, for not leaving Leonard's number, for not leaning just a bit more on this Deanna Rollins. He had already learned Sara's Manhattan number was unlisted, and try as he might, he was unable to wheedle it out of the operator.

He felt trapped between a rock and a hard place. Gut-level intuition told him his phone call to Quogue was going to be the topic of a lot of conversation out at the beach house, and he didn't want to cause Sara any trouble.

She had mentioned that these people, Paul and Neal and Deanna, guarded her with the zeal of watchdogs, and he had heard the tiniest edge to her voice when she said it. At the time he hadn't felt anything amiss, but after speaking with Deanna, he wondered if perhaps their concern was a bit overdone.

He went into the small kitchen and polished off the rest of the orange juice and the last slice of cheese in his barren refrigerator. Everyone spoke about the lack of personal privacy in a technology-oriented world, but the fact still remained that an unlisted number was an unlisted number, at least so far as New York Telephone was concerned.

He could send her a telegram at the Carberry with his new phone number. He could join the hundreds of fans who maintained their vigil in front of the building. He could hire a plane to spell out "Call me, Sara" in the Manhattan sky. If he had to, he could get a job as a window washer and write his phone number on her window.

He could go quietly crazy.

Privacy.

That oddly free feeling Sara had been experiencing during the past twenty-four hours since she returned to Manhattan was a phenomenon called privacy. Now as she stood in the middle of her bedroom, after Paul left to catch an early-morning flight to Brazil, and listened to nothing but the sound of her own breathing, she understood all she'd lost.

Going out to Quogue had proved to be a monumental mistake. Celebrity could not be escaped. Even her walk on the beach had somehow become yet another reminder of the gap between her existence and real life. She remembered the boy's face, the curve of the girl's shoulder as she leaned against him, the heat of the desire that had radiated from their bodies and warmed the cold early-winter air.

The only thing missing now was Sam. She had tried his old number as soon as Paul left for the airport that morning, and she was disappointed, but not surprised, to hear the disconnect recording. She wandered aimlessly for a while, then settled down on top of her bed with a few hundred snapshots spread out on the satin comforter, trying to sort them out for Max's biography. Maybe ridding herself of old obligations would help her see her way clear.

She sifted through a stack of photos taken when Maxwell was in high school. Maxwell's parents had believed in public education and despite their wealth had sent their only son to a highly rated South Philadelphia public school where he met Paul Rollins and Paul's sister, Deanna, children of a bus driver and a salesclerk. Sara stared at a photo of the three of them at Deanna's junior prom. It was almost impossible to connect the youthful idealism on their faces with the realities life had delivered. She was reaching over to pick up some pictures that had slid off the bed when the phone rang.

"Sara? It's—"

"Sam! How on earth did you ever—" She scrambled back onto the bed, clutching a fistful of photos. "I thought I was unlisted."

"You are, woman. I moved heaven, earth and a part of hell to get this number."

"I thought the phone company was unbribable."

He laughed. "It is. It just happens I have friends in high places."

"You sound like a dangerous man, Sam." Her voice betrayed the delight she was feeling.

"Not dangerous. Just determined."

She leaned back against the pillows, smiling. "So who are these friends in high places? Should I tell the CIA or the FBI?"

"I suppose I could make up a story about foreign operatives and a daring escape, but the truth is my sister works for one of the major credit-history bureaus, and I threatened bodily injury if she didn't get me your number from their files."

"Give your sister my thanks."

"Not necessary. I already gave her mine for both of us."

She cradled the phone closer and lowered her voice even though there was no one around to hear her. "I tried to call you."

She could hear his slight exhalation of breath. "I hoped you would."

"Didn't you know I would try?" *How can you not know how I feel?*

"I wasn't sure." His voice filled her with pleasure.

"Your phone was already disconnected."

He explained the problem with his apartment.

"Where are you staying now?" she asked.

"Leonard had me send all my equipment to his penthouse yesterday—"

"Refinishing equipment in a penthouse?"

"Hard to believe, isn't it? He said he has an empty room where I can work."

"From what I remember of Leonard, he was a terrific man." Sara had seen him a number of times when Sam was working on renovating the strip of stores that included the Obelisk. "Evidently he still is."

"Terrific," Sam answered, "but tired. Very tired."

Sara was quiet for a moment. "Are you staying with Leonard now?"

"He and Margaret want me to, but I'd rather sleep on the subway than inconvenience them any more than I already have. I'm taking over their place on the fifteenth—I think that's enough."

"So where are you now?"

"Not too far from you, actually. I'm at the Westbury." There was a long silence. "I haven't been able to stop thinking about you, Paisley."

Sara's eyes closed briefly as she savored his words. "I'm glad to hear that." She thought of his beautiful gold-rimmed eyes and how they would look lit with passion, with love.

"Are you all right?"

"You saw those pictures?"

"Every damned one of them."

She sighed. "And the articles, too, of course."

"Couldn't miss them. I didn't believe any of it, Paisley."

Her voice took on a defensive edge. "Why not? Everyone else in New York seems to."

"Because I know you. Because I know the kind of woman you are."

"I need to see you, Sam." There. The words were out before she could think twice about them.

"Great. How about right now?"

She laughed. "I'm in scruffy jeans and a sweatshirt. I need time to get presentable."

"I'll take you any way I can get you, Paisley."

"You've never seen me quite like this, Sam."

"There are many ways I haven't seen you."

Visions of Sam and a wide, welcoming bed made it hard for her to think. "Should I take that as a compliment?" Her words were light and easy as she tried to hide the sudden desire that flared.

"Definitely. Now, how about I pick you up in half an hour and we go for lunch?"

"No." The word came out quickly, harshly, and she hurried to explain. "I mean, I'd rather we meet somewhere. There are still a lot of fans downstairs and—" The fans did concern her, but her main concern was not having to explain Sam to reporters.

"Quite a cloak-and-dagger existence you have going for you, Paisley. How do you manage to get anything done?"

"It's not as bad as it sounds. It's just the lower my profile is right now, the happier I'll be. Any ideas where we could meet?"

"Let me think." A pause. "The perfect one. Hop a cab up to the Metropolitan. They have a carry-your-own-tray cafeteria where, I guarantee you, no one will bother us. If you don't mind plastic tuna and cardboard cake, it's our best bet."

She looked at her bedside clock; it read eleven-thirty. "How about one?"

"How about right now?"

"Twelve-thirty."

"Eleven forty-five."

"Twelve-fifteen's the best I can do, Sam. It'll take me at least that long to put on my mascara."

"Never let it be said I stand in the way of beauty. Twelve-fifteen at the entrance to the cafeteria. Deal?"

"Deal."

For a second after they hung up, Sara sat perfectly still, relishing the marvelous feeling of having something to do in the middle of a day, of having a destination, someone to see. And although she felt disloyal to even think it, she loved the fact she had absolutely no one to explain her plans to, no one's tacit approval to seek.

But then she realized it was eleven-forty, and she leaped from her bed, scattering pictures and notes on the carpet, forgetting them as quickly as they hit the floor. She rushed through her office toward her bathroom, knocking one of Maxwell's Grammy Awards off the shelf by her desk. She hesitated, looking at the shiny statuette nestled in the thick pile. Later. She had plenty of time later to arrange the museum pieces that had been her life these past two years.

She hurried to make herself beautiful for Sam.

Jack Farrell had spent two days poring over old newspapers when it hit him, one of those bolts of lightning that were enough to bring a sinner back to religion.

A museum. Some kind of old furniture on display. A small cocktail party with a reception for the press. Not at all the kind of thing Jack usually covered, but it was good for a few photos that the *People* page in *Time* magazine just might like.

"Aww-right!" There, tucked in the file cabinet that served to hold both his photo gear and his jockey shorts, was the article and photo he'd been looking for.

Artisan Named Chairman of Ad Hoc Committee at Metropolitan

Samuel Berenger, whose display of Early American cradles appeared at the Metropolitan Museum of Art last year, has been named chairman of an ad hoc committee whose purpose is to put together an exhibition of federal period furniture tentatively scheduled for February 1986.

Mr. Berenger, who is largely self-schooled in furniture restoration, said—

That was his man, all right. Same sandy hair, same clean jawline. Unfortunately, he remained as elusive as ever.

Jack had Sam's name, he knew his occupation, he even knew where he lived, but he'd be damned if he could locate him. Berenger's phone had been disconnected, his apartment was empty, and there wasn't a trace of a forwarding address or number to help him out.

He grabbed his camera equipment and put the clipping of Sam into his jacket pocket. Maybe he could wander around the museum and see if anyone there could give him a clue to the whereabouts of the mysterious Mr. Berenger. If nothing else, the Metropolitan was usually good for a celebrity or two.

Sam checked his watch for the sixteenth time: 12:11. "Okay," he told himself as he leaned against the entrance to the cafeteria at the Metropolitan Museum of Art, "calm down."

"Beg pardon?" A young blond woman with lovely eyes stopped directly in front of him on her way out. "Did you say something?"

His face burned with embarrassment. "Just talking to myself again," he said with a grin. "Occupational hazard."

"You must be a painter," she said, tossing her hair off her shoulder and aiming her best smile—and it was a beauty—at him. "All painters are self-absorbed."

He leaned against the wall and crossed his arms over his chest. "So I've heard." Correcting her would take too much time.

"I'm a painter." She gestured toward the sketchbook peeking out of her leather shoulder tote.

He nodded but gave her no encouragement.

"Have you seen the Temple of Dendur yet?" she asked, referring to one of the Egyptian exhibits. "I was just on my way and—"

No games, he decided. "Thanks for the invitation," he said kindly, minus flirtation or subterfuge, "but I'm waiting for a very important woman."

She tilted her head at him for a second, then shrugged her shoulders. "Such is life," she said, and walked away.

She was really a lovely creature, tall and slim and well proportioned, but Sam felt not the slightest attraction toward her. All he could think of was Sara. He checked his watch again: 12:13. Was there another cafeteria he knew nothing about? Had she changed her mind?

He turned and started heading toward the public phones near the rest rooms when a low, familiar voice beside him said, "Cold feet, Mr. Berenger?" and he turned and saw Sara, her beautiful blue eyes looking up at him. His heart pushed against his rib cage.

"I was going to call you," he said. His words sounded juvenile, silly. He had no words to convey the relief, the joy, he was feeling. "I was afraid you forgot which museum."

She arched one dark brow and grabbed his wrist, flipping it over until she could read his watch. "Twelve-fourteen. I shouldn't even be here yet." She dropped his arm and turned to leave. "Maybe I'll disappear for sixty seconds more."

Laughter broke the uneasy feeling that had swirled around him. He reached out and put his hand on her shoulder, drawing her closer. "Like hell you will." He bent over and gently touched her lips with his. Again the scent of violets and springtime surrounded him, and he felt light-headed with delight and desire. "I'm glad you're here," he said into the soft curls near her ear.

She leaned against him for a split second. "So am I."

Sam could barely feel the curve of her back through her fluffy down coat as he propelled her into the cafeteria. They teased and joked their way through the buffet line. Sara found them a little table against the wall, opposite a group of parochial schoolgirls in navy blue uniforms.

Sam held her chair out while she sat down. *"Table à deux, madame,"* he said, bowing with a theatrical flourish. "Marvelous view of the wastebasket."

Sara laughed. "It's wonderful to be away from all the kitchen noise."

He took her hand. "It's wonderful to be with you."

Shyness overtook her. She looked down at the trays laden with tuna sandwiches, pickled beets, cole slaw, rice pudding and chocolate cake. "We're going to have to stop meeting like this," she said, smiling into his oddly beautiful eyes. "Calorically, you're an occasion of sin."

"I can think of better ways to sin." He held out an Oreo cookie, and she shook her head no. "Come on, Paisley. You could use it." He appraised her. "You've lost weight since you got sick."

"Seven pounds," she admitted. Stress, rather than her cold, had made eating difficult. "All in the wrong places, as usual." She held her sweatshirt away from her body and rolled her eyes. "Voluptuous I'm not."

"Lovely, you are." He popped the cookie into her mouth.

For a few minutes they did some serious eating, punctuated only by bursts of "Where's the salt?" and "Do you want your pickles?" Although the food was barely serviceable—institution style at its most mundane—Sara found herself enjoying it as if they were at Lutece.

Choosing the cafeteria at the Metropolitan was a stroke of genius on Sam's part. In her faded jeans and New York Jets sweatshirt, Sara fit in well with the crowd of art students who habituated the museum. If anyone recognized her, they were doing a great job at keeping it secret, because she hadn't noticed so much as a sidelong glance in her direction. Was this precious feeling of anonymity possible? Could she recover the priceless pleasure of ordinary life?

Across the table from her, Sam finished his sandwich and started to tuck into a large slab of chocolate cake.

"What did people do for a place to talk before restaurants were invented?" he asked, washing down the cake with a gulp of milk. "Where did they go?"

"Good question." She sampled the rice pudding. "The movies?"

"Didn't exist."

"The library?"

"Can't talk."

She thought for a moment, then snapped her fingers. "Eureka! They stayed home."

He reached across the table and shook her hand. "Brilliant deduction, Paisley," he said with a grin. "Obviously a solution possible only in less complicated times."

She thought of her own home and the lack of privacy and nodded. "Afraid so." She tried to make her voice light but failed. "Is this going to be the way it is for us? Restaurant after coffee shop after luncheonette, trying to cram in a good talk between doughnuts and coffee?"

His eyes met hers and locked. "Are you afraid to bring me home, Sara?"

She made a gesture of disgust. "Of course not! It's my home, after all. I make the rules."

"Then what?"

She searched her mind for a logical explanation but came up empty-handed. "I don't know." Sam started to say something, but she held her hand up to stop him. "This situation has never come up before, Sam. I'm feeling my way along."

His eyes widened. "You've never brought a friend to your house?"

She shook her head.

"What about when Maxwell was alive?"

"There were many people around all the time, but they were mostly his friends, his associates first, then mine."

"Relatives?"

She shook her head again. "None living. My father died when I was sixteen, Mother died the year after I married." She took a sip of coffee. "I think I have cousins in California somewhere, but obviously we're not close."

"In-laws?"

She shook her head again. "Where do you think the name Last Chance came from?"

He thought of his own network of family back in Nebraska and felt a stab of sympathy for her. He tried to joke. "I have a couple of sisters I'd be glad to sell you."

She grinned. "I make myself sound like Little Orphan Annie, don't I? It's not bad at all— I have Deanna and Neal." She stopped.

"I think I spoke to Deanna when I called you at your beach house."

Sara nodded. "She gave me the message."

"I'm surprised," Sam said. "She didn't sound too thrilled about it."

Sara was quiet for a moment. "That's her way," she said finally. "She probably thought you were another reporter."

Sam felt there was more than that going on with Deanna Rollins, but he changed the subject. "I thought there was another member of that triumvirate—the friend whose name is in the Suffolk County phone book."

"Paul. I wouldn't exactly call Paul a friend."

Sam sat up straighter. He was feeling the same odd sensation he had experienced when he spoke to Deanna on the phone. He would have to more slowly here. "Any particular reason?"

"Bad vibes, I guess." She picked up her coffee cup, then stopped when it was halfway to her mouth. "For instance, he popped up at the door to my room the night before we left for Quogue, and I—" She shrugged. "What can I say? It's nothing concrete; he just makes me feel uncomfortable. Always has."

"Physically uncomfortable?"

She shook her head. "Emotionally. I don't think he ever really thought I was the right woman for Max."

"Were you?"

Her brow creased. "Was I what?"

"Were you the right woman for Max?"

She met his eyes and made the decision to answer his question honestly. "No, Sam, I don't think I ever really was." While she had been good for Maxwell, he had needed someone to share his extravagant life-style, not a woman like Sara who fought for privacy and shunned the limelight.

"That's not what the press had us believe."

"Don't get me wrong," she said. "We were happy enough together. It's just we never quite meshed." She brought her hands close together until her fingertips nearly touched. "We almost did, but there was always a gap." She looked down for a second. "You have to remember how we met to really understand." She thought back to how she had felt five years ago when she decided she and Sam could never have a future together and took the business opportunity in Rio. She had been filled with pain and love and a deep yearning that threatened to destroy her. But she said none of that. "Maxwell needed me," she said. "And that was what I needed at the time."

Sam stared at her so intently that he seemed not to blink. "Did you love him?"

"I cared for him."

He brushed aside her answer. "Did you love him, Paisley?"

"Yes," she answered finally, honestly. "I came to."

"Do you think your marriage would have lasted?"

She hated his questions but knew she needed to answer them if they were to get past all that had come before. "Who can say? I felt a strong responsibility to make it last, but responsibility isn't always enough." She took another sip of coffee, not even noticing it was cold. "We were having a lot of trouble right before he died. So many pressures—his work—" she hesitated "—my own insecurities. People around us twenty-four hours a day, seven days a week. Not exactly the best atmosphere." She could sense the tension flowing from Sam as he listened. "We had been in Europe for three months on tour, and we'd been arguing a great deal. Max wasn't— He didn't take care of himself, and no one seemed to care." Her voice broke for a second, and she coughed slightly to give herself a chance to recover. "I was beginning to sound like a real fishwife—'Slow down, Maxwell.' 'Let's get away for a while, Maxwell.' Finally, after I packed my clothes and threatened to leave him, he decided I was right. We would disappear to our house in Brazil, just the two of us, and try to work things out."

Sam's eyes reflected the pain in hers. She continued. "We weren't even going to tell Paul and Neal. We were just going to catch a plane as soon as Max completed the charity auto race outside Paris. You know the rest." Everyone knew the rest.

"Did he love you, Sara?" In a way, Sam hoped Max had.

She nodded. "He did. I believe he really did." She smiled sadly. "Despite all the crazy stories about him, he was a kind man. He was generous with time and money—I have an obscene number of rings and bracelets that I never wear." She took a deep breath while she remembered. "However, there was a part of himself that he always withheld, and I never really tried to reach it." She fiddled with the worn sleeve of her sweatshirt, pulling at a pale blue thread. "In that way, we were very well suited." She wanted to say that no one had ever listened to her quite the way Sam had, that no person, male or female, had ever made her want to share her childhood dreams and her adolescent fears, that nobody had ever come as near to her heart as he had; but an innate sense of loyalty to all that had been good with her marriage kept her silent.

Sam reached for her hand and held it under the table, resting her hand on his knee. "I stopped reading the papers after you left the Obelisk," he said. "I couldn't stand seeing the pictures of you with Max." How many times had he pictured Maxwell Chance, blond and bronzed and burning with genius, waiting for Sara to come to his bed? How many times had that image haunted Sam's dreams? His grin was rueful. "I used to fantasize your marriage would break up and you'd come running back to me."

Her chest hurt with the memories. "I didn't know you were there to run to. When I knew you, you were technically a married man."

"And when I wasn't one any longer?"

"Are you asking me if I would have left Max for you?"

He swallowed. "I have no damned right to ask it, but yes, that's the question."

She tightened her grip on his hand. "No, Sam, I doubt if I would."

"Okay." He had to remind himself that he valued honesty. Right then he would have wished for a beautiful lie. "The lady is blunt."

"I may have married quickly, Sam, but I didn't marry lightly. I took it very seriously."

"I didn't walk down the aisle with a divorce lawyer at my side, you know." He felt like striking back. "Believe it or not, I had daydreams about a golden wedding anniversary myself. I just picked a woman who didn't share the same dream."

She had pulled her hand away from him at his sharp words. Now she longed to stroke his hair and take away the hurt look in his eyes, but she withheld. "Some women do."

"Not all women are ready to make new commitments."

"Some women might be."

He could feel his pulse pounding at the base of his skull. "Are you, Paisley?"

"Yes." From the first second she'd seen him on the escalator five days ago, she'd understood that everything that had happened in her life had brought her to that moment for a reason. The Fates had decreed long ago that she and Sam would be lovers, and she knew, with a certainty that bordered on madness, that it would be soon.

Across the table from her, Sam began to laugh—a loud, uninhibited sound that drew amused looks from other patrons in the cafeteria.

"Sam, be quiet!"

He grabbed both of her hands and raised them near his lips. "I'd like to take out an ad in the *New York Times* and announce my intentions."

"You're getting carried away, Samuel. We haven't even had our first date yet." She shivered as his lips grazed the palms of her hands. A feeling of inevitability washed over her.

He gestured toward the empty plates on their table. "What do you call this, then? Looks like a date to me."

"It does look like that, doesn't it?"

"If you count breaking baklava at the coffee shop the other day, this is our second date."

"Second date? Better be careful, Sam. I think that means we're going steady."

"Remind me to give you my class ring." He wanted to give her his class ring, his school sweater, his thoughts, his heart, his child.

They finished eating and wandered about the museum for a while. Sara enjoyed lingering in front of the Renoirs, especially the enormous portrait of Madame Charpentier and her two golden-haired daughters.

"Only a happy man could capture joy like that," she said, marveling at the maternal beauty of the woman and the innocent faces of the two little girls.

'd like to see your paintings sometime." He touched her hair gently with his hand.

She glanced at him. "I haven't painted in years, Sam."

"Five years?"

She nodded, then turned back to Renoir. Sam, however, was not to be deterred. A strong, sensual memory had returned to him.

"You used to draw me."

She looked up at him. "What?"

"You used to draw me," he repeated. "When I was working on the renovation at the Obelisk, you used to stand in the doorway and sketch me."

He watched her face and saw surprise slide into memory.

"I tried to be discreet," she said, a small smile curving the left corner of her mouth. "I thought the door hid me."

"It didn't." He could still feel the way her eyes had traveled over his body, could still feel the way he had wanted to take her right there on the floor of the gallery. Knowing Sara was there watching him, his awareness of his body had become almost unbearable. Each powerful bunching of the muscles in his shoulders, each movement that caused his biceps to harden to steel, had been heightened. He knew she found him beautiful to watch, and his pleasure in that was great. Those times when she secretly sketched him had remained among his most powerful erotic memories.

They moved through the gallery, admiring the choppy, turbulent brush strokes of Van Gogh, the ballerinas of Degas, the hazy loveliness of Monet's water lilies at Giverny. Sara kept up a steady stream of chatter, thankful for her fine-arts background that enabled her to maintain conversation when her mind was somewhere else.

So he had known she watched him. Those times she sketched him had been so intense for her, so poignantly sensual, that she had been sure he must have been aware of her presence. Although he never once turned toward her, never so much as tilted his head in her direction, she had sensed that the need in her was too strong to go undetected. However, he had kept his back to her, and she'd had the exquisite pleasure of watching him bend over a workbench and draw a saw through a thick piece of wood in a way that made his muscles ripple dangerously beneath his tanned skin.

Sara had longed to toss away her sketch pad and plunge her hands into warm clay to try to mold for herself the swelling musculature and sheer male beauty in front of her.

She glanced up at Sam and saw him watching her intently, his eyes deep, unfathomable. She knew exactly how he would feel beneath her hands, and she shivered.

"Cold?" he asked.

She met his eyes. "The contrary," she said softly.

He drew his index finger along her left cheek and tapped her earring. "I know," he said. "I feel it, too."

Finally, at around three-thirty, they decided to leave. Every painting, every piece of sculpture they saw, only seemed to heighten the electricity between them. They were stopped at the top of the steps to the museum outside so that Sara could pull on her cap and gloves when Sam noticed a crowd on the sidewalk.

He shielded his eyes against the sunlight and squinted into the distance. "They're filming something down there," he said to Sara.

Sara adjusted her scarf and glanced toward the crowd of people and camera equipment at the foot of the staircase. "Recognize anyone?"

"I don't— Hey, wait a minute! I think that's Caroline Kennedy. What is she now? A movie star?"

Sara laughed and put her hand in Sam's. "She works at the museum, Sam. I'm surprised you didn't know that. They're probably filming something for PBS."

They started down the wide staircase, past the mimes and violinists, the aspiring singers and jugglers, who practiced their crafts on the steps, hoping for tips from passersby. Two tall young men in plaid shirts and down vests lingered at the edge of the crowd of the television crew. They were talking intently but suddenly grew quiet when they noticed Sara.

"Uh-oh," she said, ducking her chin more deeply behind her red-and-white scarf. "I think I've been recognized."

"Just keep walking," Sam said, his voice calm and controlled. "As soon as we get past this crowd, I'll flag down a cab."

Sara's knees began to wobble. "Damn it. Why do I always let this bother me?"

"Don't worry," he said. "I think they'll leave you alone. After all, they have a Kennedy to gawk at."

Before Sara could respond, they heard the rumble of footsteps and excited shouts of "Sara! Sara!" Sam put his arm around her and began to quicken his pace as he looked out at the tangle of limos and buses and cars on Fifth Avenue and watched for an empty cab. The footsteps were getting closer. Sara stopped.

"Are you crazy?" he said. "Keep walking."

"What's the use?" she asked. He could almost see the vibrations of her tautly stretched nerves beneath her pale skin. "They'll get us one way or another."

In the blink of an eye they were surrounded by people, all speaking, all demanding, all wanting the same thing—a piece of Sara. A few of the women had copies of one of Max's unauthorized biographies, and they thrust them in Sara's face along with a Bic pen and asked for her autograph. Sam found himself pushed fifteen feet away, separated from her by a solid block of humanity. Sara seemed outwardly calm, but Sam could see the fear in her large blue eyes, and he noticed the way her hand held the pen in a white-knuckled grip.

The news that Sara was there spread up and down the street like a brushfire. The PBS camera crew was approaching them, visions of free-lance sales to the *Post* and *People* magazine dancing in their heads. Even the mimes had forgotten their artistic vows of silence and called out her name. Sam started to sweat, beads of perspiration rolling down the back of his neck.

"Sara!" His voice was lost. She looked up at him, puzzled. "I'm getting a cab." She frowned at him and shook her head. Damn it. "I'm getting a cab!" he bellowed, elbowing his way roughly out of the crowd that was closing around her, sealing him out.

Sara, meanwhile, watched Sam step out into traffic, his arm raised to flag down a taxi, a bus, a horse-drawn carriage—anything that could get her out of there. Panic rose up and around her like the ocean over a drowning man. The day was no longer sunny, no longer uncomplicated. She signed two more books, then looked over at Sam again. Where were all the cabs, anyway? They usually only disappeared when it rained.

"We miss Maxwell.... You must be terribly lonely.... I went to mass on his anniversary and prayed for him.... Are you going to release those songs he recorded in France...? Write 'To Laura, Maxwell's biggest fan'...." She began to wonder if they were even speaking English. The more people crowded around her, the less she understood a word anyone was saying. For a terrifying second sound seemed to recede as she looked into a sea of faces, mouths open like hungry fish waiting to be fed. She was on the beach at Quogue again; she was at his grave site. She was nowhere at all. She felt dizzy and had to blink to bring everything back into sync again.

"No answer, Sara?"

She turned to her right toward the voice. A tall red-haired photographer stood there watching her. Why did he look so familiar?

"I—I beg your pardon?" Even her own words sounded foreign and peculiar to her.

"Is it true you're having trouble adjusting to Maxwell's death?"

She stared at him. "Death is always difficult to adjust to."

The crowd turned from the photographer to Sara and back again. They practically salivated for gossip.

Another reporter, tape recorder thrust forward, pushed to the front. "Any rebuttal to the rumour you've been unable to work on Maxwell's authorized biography?"

Her head snapped toward him. "Where did you hear that? The deadline isn't until August. The book will be ready on time." Good God. What the hell was happening? She tried to look over the heads of the crowd to catch sight of Sam but couldn't. "Excuse me, please. I have to leave."

The red-haired photographer pushed his way next to her. For some strange reason he seemed familiar. "Who is that man you're with, Sara? A new romance on the horizon?" There was something definitely familiar about his angular torso, the rhythm of his speech, but she couldn't grasp it.

The crowd began to buzz. The sound was angry, betrayed. Sara wouldn't cheat on Maxwell. Sara was Max's wife. She would always be. A vision of Hindu widows engulfed in a funeral pyre caused a shiver to run through Sara's body.

"Is he your lover?" The reporter pushed the tape recorder closer to her mouth, and she shoved it back toward him.

"I don't have to answer that."

His voice grew louder. "You won't answer that? Should I take that to be a 'yes'?"

The photographer angled in front of her. Click-click-click. Three quick shots into her soul. She could see it now: woman in panic.

"Sam!" Her voice was shrill, reed thin, barely audible over the noise from the crowd.

"Sam?" "He's her lover." "How could she do that?" "Max is dead only two years." "Did you see that article last week?" "They say she drinks." "Drinks?" "It's cocaine." "Didn't you know Max did drugs?" "She's the one who got him hooked on them." "Bitch."

They started to touch her, tugging at her coat sleeve, grabbing for her hand, her arm, anything they could get. She owed them. She owed them her autograph; she owed them her time; she owed them her life. She'd asked for this when she married Maxwell, and they'd make damned sure she paid the price. Once again she had swung from saint to sinner.

A hand clutched at her thick dark curls as she tried to make her way toward the street, and she blindly smacked at it, pushing it out of her way. Her scalp stung as strands of hair were yanked out.

"Don't touch me!" Was that shriek coming from her? "Don't touch me!"

They had ruined her husband's funeral. Not even at the most solemn of occasions were they able to control their lust for power, their urge to be close to those who did what they dared not. Before her she saw the yawning grave littered with flashbulbs and candy wrappers and flowers ripped from the massive arrangements that flanked the coffin. She heard the keening sounds of fans who ringed the area, the shouts of police to keep away, the curses of photographers being cheated out of their best shots of the grieving widow.

They had taken and taken and taken from her in the past, but she'd be damned if they'd take the rest of her life, as well.

"Sara!" Sam's voice, clear and loud and blessedly strong, reached her. "I've got a cab."

He stood at the curb, holding open the door of a big fat yellow taxi. She took a deep breath and started walking toward him, her eyes fastened on his handsome face, her mind clearly making the turn away from her past.

Another reporter ran over to her, clutching notebook and pencil to his chest. "A statement, Sara? Just one statement before you go?"

She turned to face him, her blue eyes traveling slowly over the hollow faces of the people crowded before her. The red-haired photographer poised his camera, twisting the lens to bring her into sharper focus.

"A statement?" She caught Sam's eye over her shoulder and smiled. "I'm going home, gentlemen."

That was statement enough for now.

5

Sara's words stopped the reporters cold. They stared at her as she entered the cab, and it wasn't until Sam climbed in and slammed the door shut that they once again came to life, racing en masse toward the taxi as it pushed its way into traffic. At that moment Sam would have preferred a car crash to another encounter with those ghouls.

The cabbie was shooting quizzical looks at them through his rearview mirror, and Sam could imagine the questions he'd love to ask. He leaned forward and tapped on the Plexiglas divider.

"The Carberry," he said, raising his voice so as to be heard through the partition. "An extra five if you get us there quickly."

"You got it." The man's full attention turned to the obstacle course called Fifth Avenue.

Sam leaned back on the bench seat and looked at Sara.

"Did anyone get rough with you?" He wanted to touch her but was uncertain what her boundaries were at the moment.

She shook her head, dark curls drifting across her face. "Nothing to speak of." She looked away from him and out the window.

A five-dollar bill can work wonders. Before Sam could think of something comforting—or even intelligent—to say to Sara, the taxi pulled up in front of the Carberry, and

Larry was whisking them through the gates and into the lobby.

The Carberry was a security buff's delight. There were guards near the mailboxes, there were guards near the staircase, even a guard who made visitors sign in before approaching the elevator banks. All of these transactions were recorded by tiny cameras that whirred discreetly overhead. It was enough to make the innocent feel guilty. He felt like letting out a cheer when Hector, the elderly elevator guard, ushered them inside a car and pushed P for penthouse.

"I made it!" Sam wiped his brow with the back of his hand and grinned at Sara as the elevator doors slid quietly shut. "I'm surprised they didn't fingerprint me out there."

Sara smiled for the first time since they escaped the mob at the museum. "It must be your trustworthy face." She fished her ring of house keys from the bottom of her shoulder bag. "One thing we are in the Carberry is secure."

"Secure?" He rolled his eyes. "The Pentagon's security system seems second-rate compared to this place."

"We've had one or two near misses," Sara said as the elevator began its slow, smooth ascent, "but no real trouble." She looked over at Sam and grinned. "I must say, you made a friend of Larry for life."

Sam plunged his hands into the pockets of his short gray jacket. "The man made sense. Who's to say a volcano erupting in Hawaii can't have an effect on the weather in New York?"

She laughed. "On the weather, yes, but on truck drivers? Really, Sam!" Some of the tension that had crackled between them during the taxi ride disappeared.

She'd been quiet during the drive home, and she blessed Sam for not pushing her into meaningless conversation. Too many odd feelings had been rushing through her for her to sort them out easily and find words for them. The quick transition from intense desire to intense fear had shaken her badly. Sam had simply sat next to her, holding her hand, chuckling softly at the curses in a foreign tongue that flowed from the cabbie as the taxi picked its way through rush-hour traffic. Finally, as they approached the building, she turned to Sam and said, "You'll have coffee with me, won't you?" and she thought her heart would burst at the happy expression on his face when he said yes.

The elevator reached the penthouse floor, and Sam stood to one side for Sara to exit first.

"I can't wait for you to see my rolltop desk," she said as they walked down the long hallway toward her door. "I found it up in Stockbridge a few years ago when Max was on tour, and it was love at first sight."

They both knew there was much more going on than a simple trip to see a rolltop desk, but neither was willing to admit it. Sam waited while she sifted through her keys, found the right one, then slipped it into the lock.

She frowned. "How odd." She looked up at Sam as she turned the doorknob. "It doesn't seem to be locked."

"Are you getting forgetful in your old age, Paisley?"

They went inside, and she closed and locked the door behind them. "Not that forgetful," she said, putting her shoulder bag down on the pedestal table. "I remember noticing that the key was sticking a little when I put it in the lock before I left."

"Could your housekeeper have left the door open?"

"No. We suspended services until the tenth. Nobody knows I'm back yet."

"You'd better have a look around." Sam followed her into the enormous chrome-and-glass living room. "Make sure nothing's missing."

"Who could get into the building?" she asked as they glanced around the obviously untouched room. "Maybe I am getting a bit senile, at that." She had been so excited over meeting Sam at the museum that it wasn't impossible she had forgotten to lock up behind her. Unlikely, perhaps, but not impossible.

She turned, and Sam followed her to her office.

"What about that Rollins guy?" he asked. "Maybe his flight was canceled and he came back."

A jittery, humming feeling had settled itself inside Sara's bones. She glanced back at Sam. "It's a gorgeous day outside, Sam. I doubt if that happened."

"Anything's possible, Sara. There has to be a rational explanation."

She thought about Paul and his compulsively well-ordered way of doing things and shook her head. "Even if Paul came back, he'd never leave the door open. He's the kind of man who replaces the battery in his watch every six months so he's never caught without the right time." She opened the door to her office and flicked on the recessed overhead lights. She motioned Sam inside with a sweep of her arm. "Here we are."

The explosion of color in Sara's office took Sam by surprise. After the studiedly elegant neutrals of the rest of the apartment, the riot of primary colors in textures ranging from silk to nubby wool stunned his senses.

He walked around, running his hand along the pine bookcases, letting his fingertips caress the jade silk robe flung carelessly over a rocking chair, breathing deeply of the faint smell of violets that emanated from it. He was lost in sensory euphoria.

"Sam!" Sara's voice, sharp and loud, jarred him back to the present. He walked over to where she stood before the desk.

"Something's missing." Her voice shook slightly. She pointed to the spot on the thick rug where Max's fallen award had crushed down some of the pile. The plush remained dented. The award was nowhere in sight. "I dropped Max's Grammy just before I left the house."

"You probably picked it up and put it somewhere."

She shook her head. "I didn't pick it up. I remember thinking I'd do it later." She met Sam's eyes. "Someone has been in here."

"Don't be so sure." Sam tried to sound calm despite a surge of anxiety. "You may have put it on the desk and it's hidden under two tons of unanswered letters."

"It was right there when I left." Her voice was sharper than she had meant it to be, and she saw a look of surprise, then concern, pass over Sam's face. "Someone took it."

"Maybe the cleaning service—"

She brushed his explanation aside with a wave of her hand. "I said they won't be back until the tenth."

He leaned against the desk and met her eyes. "Someone took it?"

She nodded. "Someone took it."

"But how could anyone get into this place? They practically X-rayed me downstairs before letting me up in the elevator with you."

She thought for a moment. "Deliverymen can get in. Telephone repairmen, other tenant's visitors."

"How would they know you lived—"

She laughed. "Everyone knows! You knew where I lived, didn't you, Sam?"

"I see your point."

She started to sift through the papers on her desk. Sam grabbed her wrist.

"Maybe you should leave things alone. Fingerprints and all that."

She shook her head, dark curls bouncing gently around her face. "I can't call the police." Sam moved his hold on her wrist to her hand. She could feel his solid goodness flow into her.

"You've been robbed, Sara. You should bring in the authorities."

How little he knew about the hazards of fame. "They'd laugh," she said, linking her fingers with his. "A missing Grammy? It hardly even rates as petty larceny."

"Someone broke into your apartment. That counts as something."

Anxiety tingled along her spine. "I don't want them to get involved in this."

"Is there a reason?"

"Rock stars don't have the greatest reputations."

"You're not a rock star."

"Close enough for NYPD." She removed her hand from his and paced the room, stopping near the window and looking down at the empty courtyard fifty stories below. "Paul Rollins got arrested twice for possession of marijuana."

Sam laughed. "Hardly a capital offense these days, Paisley."

"There's more, Sam."

He moved closer to her. She could feel his breath ruffle the curls at the back of her neck.

"Max had a cocaine habit when I met him. I didn't know it until after we married." She twisted her head slightly and looked into his eyes. "Every cop in New York knew about it, though."

"They'd hold it against you?" He sounded disbelieving.

She hesitated. "I don't know. I think Neal paid them off a few times—hush money, I guess you'd call it. I don't want any more bad publicity. Do you understand?" She watched as a number of expressions flickered across Sam's face.

"So Saint Maxwell had a fatal flaw?"

She chose to ignore the edge in his voice. "He was only human, Sam. He never pretended otherwise." She moved away from him and leaned against the windowsill. "He was finished with drugs long before he died."

Sam sat on the edge of a small file cabinet adjacent to her rolltop desk. "I don't understand why anyone messes with that garbage."

How could she explain to Sam that she didn't really understand herself? "It's a tougher life than you could imagine." The incredible fatigue that drains a performer night after night, the need to summon up energy from some depleted source in order to give one more show for one more audience. "He hated his weakness. When I met him, he was trying to pull away from all of that." She drew a design in the condensation on the windowpane. Both she and Maxwell had been trying to pull way from something—or someone. "But we're getting off track. The problem now is, Who got into the apartment?"

She crossed in front of him, picked up the telephone and quickly punched in the number of the house in Quogue.

"Are you calling the cops, after all?"

She covered the mouthpiece with her hand. "Deanna. She and Neal will know what to do." She turned her head slightly as she listened to the telephone ringing in the distance.

Sam folded his arms across his broad chest and watched her. Only a portion of her profile was visible to him, the slightest curve of jaw and jut of cheekbone, and in it he saw the untapped strength of a woman he hoped really existed. He had the feeling she would need all the strength she had at her disposal in the weeks to come.

She put the receiver back in the cradle and walked to the window. "No answer." She rested her forehead against the glass for a moment. "They're probably out walking the beach."

Sam reached out and touched a dark curl, which wrapped itself around his finger. The very softness of it seemed a miracle to him. "I'm glad there was no answer."

She faced him. Only inches separated them. Only years kept them apart.

"Why?" She could manage but one word.

He forced his thoughts away from her lips. "Because I think you should keep this to yourself."

"A second ago you wanted me to call the police."

"That was before I started adding up the facts."

"Facts? What facts?" She sat on the edge of the windowsill and gripped it with both hands. "Someone broke into my apartment and stole Max's award. That's the only fact I know of."

He shook his head. "Think about it, Sara—the reporters waiting for you in Quogue, the intimation you're drinking or worse." He gestured toward the desk. "Now this. There's a pattern here."

She scowled at him. "I should have paid more attention to my Nancy Drew books when I was a kid. What are you getting at, Sam?"

"Paul Rollins is the one person who's involved in every incident."

"Paul wasn't in Quogue from the beginning."

"Exactly. He wasn't in Quogue. Maybe he leaked the information to the reporters."

"He wouldn't have to stay in Manhattan to do that."

"But he is the only one who came back to Manhattan with you this time, isn't he?"

Sara stood up and straightened out the hem of her sweatshirt. "Now there's no love lost between Paul and me, but what on earth would he want with Max's Grammy?"

"You must be kidding!" Sam gestured toward the courtyard that just a few days ago had teemed with mourning fans. "Do you have any idea what it would go for out there? The ultimate souvenir."

"This is ridiculous. You're letting your imagination get carried away, Sam."

"All right, maybe I am. But you have to admit, it's a real possibility."

Quick, vivid images snapped through her brain like slides through a projector. Paul coming into her bedroom when she was hiding the dresser-drawer key. His curious lack of anger over the newspaper photo of Sara and the intimation of drug abuse. His eagerness to give her a ride back to Manhattan when it was no secret he had never particularly enjoyed her company. The things he had said to her when Max died—things she had never forgotten.

"I don't know," she said finally. "I just—"

Sam took her hands in his. "No one broke in, Sara. Whoever got into this apartment had a key."

That was one fact she couldn't deny. There had been no signs of a break-in and her lock was pick-proof.

"There are only five keys to the apartment," she said, counting them off on her fingers. "I have one, Mrs. Raines our cook, Deanna, Neal—" She hesitated.

"Paul?"

She nodded. "And Paul. But that doesn't mean he'd do anything like this."

"Let's see what we have here. Deanna and Neal are in Quogue, so it can't be them. Mrs. Raines?"

Sara shook her head. "She's on holiday in Ireland." She picked up a postcard from her desk and showed it to Sam. "Documented proof."

"Forget Raines."

"Maybe I didn't lock the door." She tried to force a smile but failed. "I'm pretty forgetful, you know."

He wasn't buying it. "We've come full circle again, Sara. We're back to Paul."

Sara's gaze darted around the room, lingering on the artwork on the walls, the statues on the tabletops, as if clues were hidden in the room like the scattered pieces of a child's puzzle. "What should we do now?" she asked. "Dust the doorknobs for fingerprints?"

"Would you know what to do if you found any?"

"No. I was hoping you would."

"Sorry, Paisley. My detective training is as skimpy as yours. The Hardy Boys didn't cover this. Besides, the prints on the doorknobs probably belong to you and me."

"It scares me to think someone was in here without my knowledge."

He put an arm around her and drew her close. "I don't think anyone is out to harm you physically."

"I hope you're right." As much as she wanted to stay close to him, she forced herself to pull away. "Sam, would you do me a favor?" He nodded. "Go downstairs and ask Larry if he saw anyone coming in or out of my elevator this afternoon."

Sam clicked his heels and saluted, an off-center grin on his face. "I think you like playing Nancy Drew."

She gave him a playful push. "Off with you!"

She walked him to the door, carefully locking it behind him, then looked around her apartment. It had once been as familiar to her as the sight of her own face in the mirror every morning. However, as she walked slowly from room to room, searching for a clue—anything that might help her figure this whole mess out—she felt as if someone had just dropped her into alien territory without a road map. Nothing seemed familiar to her: not her clothes, her books, the expensive vases and imported crystal. Except for her office, her beloved private room, Sara Paisley just might not have existed at all. Her mark was as ephemeral as a sand castle at high tide.

She went into the kitchen and poked through cupboards and cabinets searching out the coffeemaker and the filters, hunting up cups and saucers and teaspoons. Her movements as she filled the pot with water and set it on the stove were slightly clumsy. The set of muscles that governed self-sufficiency had atrophied badly.

She was about to pour the coffee when she heard a series of three sharp raps at the door.

"Good news?" she asked as Sam entered the apartment and she locked the door after him.

"No news at all," he said. He sniffed at the blossoming smell of coffee as he followed her into the kitchen. "Larry wasn't there."

"Larry's always there. Did you look outside?"

He leaned against the counter, fiddling with the arrangement of silk flowers that rested in a wicker basket while Sara poured the coffee. "Of course I looked outside. There was a young guy in his place. Said Larry went home at five—something about vacation starting."

Sara put the coffeepot down hard. "How about Hector?"

"I found him," Sam said, adding a healthy splash of milk to his coffee. "You know he's practically senile, don't you?"

Sara motioned for Sam to sit down at the butcher block that served as a kitchen table. "He's not senile," she said protectively. "He's just a little forgetful."

Sam swallowed some coffee. "Forgetful is when you leave your keys on the table. Senile is when you can't tell a man from a woman."

Sara's dark brows zoomed together in a frown. "What does that mean?"

"Hector said he saw Rollins coming out of your elevator this afternoon."

"Paul."

"That's what I thought at first, but then Hector said something about perfume, and I began to wonder about old Paul. Is he—"

Sara laughed. "Hardly. Did Hector actually say Deanna was here?"

"No. The only things he was sure about was the name Rollins." Sam scratched his head absently. "Could the old guy actually mistake a man for a woman?"

"Hector's forgetful, but I don't think he's that bad. He probably got distracted by someone coming out of one of the other private elevators."

"So we can assume he saw Rollins leaving on his way to the airport?"

"I guess so. Did he mention if the person had luggage?"

Sam groaned. "It was hard enough to pinpoint the gender, Paisley. I'd still be down there if we were checking baggage."

The nervous energy she'd been feeling dissipated suddenly, and she leaned back in her chair. "So you think Paul took the Grammy?"

Sam was watching her face carefully. "It would seem that way."

"I can't believe he hates me that much. What did I ever do to him?"

Sam shrugged. "I never met the guy, Paisley. I can't answer that."

She pushed her chair back and got up, then began pacing the wide modern kitchen. "I hate this." The vehemence in her voice alarmed Sam. "Do you know I haven't been able to go out to a movie or a baseball game or anything normal since I married Maxwell?"

She leaned across the kitchen table, her blue eyes pinned on Sam's face. "Do you know how that feels?"

"Unhealthy, I would imagine. Why did you allow it?"

"You think it's something you can choose to allow or not allow, Sam?" She gestured broadly, encompassing the world outside the apartment. "It was part of the package that came with Maxwell. I just didn't realize it at the time."

"Would it have made a difference if you had?"

Her thoughts went back to the woman she had been at that time. "Probably not," she answered. "I wouldn't have understood it even if I'd known about it." She moved back around the table and sat down opposite Sam. "You don't understand, do you?"

His grin was quick and slightly lopsided. "Guilty as charged. Frankly, I think you supply some of your own shackles, Paisley."

Anger, hot and intense, rose inside her. "Frankly, I think you should mind your own business."

He stood up and faced her. "Do you mean that?" His usually open face had closed itself to her eyes.

"Yes," she said, her ego bruised. All of her lifelines seemed to be slipping away at once. If she were forced to admit that perhaps—just perhaps—she had become a voluntary prisoner of fame, she would have to acknowledge her fears, and she just wasn't ready for that. Not now.

"Then there's really not a whole hell of a lot left to say, is there?"

She looked down at her oval nails, watching the way the overhead light reflected in the clear polish. "I guess not." She wouldn't blame Sam for getting out. What did he need with Sara Paisley Chance and her psychological hang-ups, her physical fears?

Sam turned and crossed the kitchen, passed through the metallic living room, then headed through the hallway to the apartment door, conscious all the while of Sara's soft footsteps right behind him. *Say something.* His stomach lifted up inside his body and twisted into a knot of tension. *There's a way out of this, Paisley. You can live a real life if you want to.*

He stopped by the small table and waited, hands crossed low in front of him. She stood, her back held unnaturally straight, by the closet door.

"My jacket?" he asked, gesturing toward the closet.

Her shoulders seemed to sag slightly. "You left it in my office."

He followed her, noting how she straightened her narrow shoulders and kept her head rigidly upright. Her small, slender body was nearly lost inside the oversize New York Jets sweatshirt; he was just able to make out the curve of her waist and the gentle roundness of her hips as she walked. He wanted to protect her, but she was a grown woman, after all. Protection wasn't what she needed. Love was.

The gray jacket was draped carelessly over the back of a chair. One of the sleeves was turned inside out, as if it had been discarded in a hurry. Its silver industrial zipper glittered across the lamplight from the desk. Sara hurried across the room toward it. He hesitated by the doorway; his eyes memorized each detail of the room, as if he could discover the essence of Sara hidden there.

Sara's back was still toward him as she picked his jacket up. She reached her hand inside the sleeve and slowly brought it right side out. Her long fingers smoothed out the upright collar.

"Sara." Her name escaped his lips as if his heart had a will of its own.

She lowered her head, pressing her face into the soft folds of his jacket. Her dark hair tumbled across the gray material, like curls of black smoke against a pewter sky.

His heart thundered inside his body; he could feel blood pounding against the pulse points in his throat, his wrists, his temples. Everywhere.

"Don't leave."

Had he imagined the words? In three steps he was next to her.

"Say it again." The words tore at his throat. *Please let her say it again. Let it be real.*

She looked up. Her face was streaked with tears. Her eyes seemed larger, bluer. Her nose was red, and he suppressed a grin. Even at its most human, most vulnerable, her beauty touched every part of him.

"I don't want you to leave, Sam."

He took the jacket from her hand and tossed it on the floor. It fell to the carpet with a soft whoosh. Sara stepped into the circle of his embrace as easily as if they had been lovers parted by one night, not would-be lovers parted by years of separate living.

He closed his eyes and buried his nose deep in her dark hair, nuzzling close to her neck. Violets filled his senses, and he felt disoriented, giddy almost. If someone had asked him his name, he would have had to check his driver's license.

"I'm afraid, Sam." It took every ounce of emotional strength Sara Paisley Chance had to push herself away from Sam's intoxicating nearness and form a coherent sentence. "I'm starting to believe Paul is at the bottom of all this."

"Everything points to him, doesn't it?" Sam sat on the edge of her file cabinet, then pulled her over closer, pinning her body near him with the strength of his thighs.

Sara took a deep breath, trying to clear her mind of the exhilarating feel of Sam's nearness. How easy it would be to place herself in his arms with the naive trust of an infant and allow him to take charge of her life the way she'd allowed first Max, then Deanna, Neal and Paul, to do. "It does," she answered, "but the one thing missing is a motive. I can't figure out what's in this for him."

Sam brushed a stray curl off her forehead, letting it slip slowly through his index and middle fingers. "Money, for starters."

Sara hesitated. "I doubt that. He's a shrewd man. He earns a terrific salary, not to mention a portion of the royalties on a few of Max's songs. He's too well off to take risks just for money."

Sam's laugh was mirthless. "Paisley, no one's that well-off. We all have our price. It's just a question of finding someone who'll meet it."

She moved away from him a fraction. She felt as if she were alone in a dark forest with dangers lurking just out of sight. "I never took you to be a cynic, Sam."

He stroked her wrists with his thumbs, trying to ease her tension. "Not a cynic," he answered, "a realist."

"A realist," she repeated. From her lips the word sounded cold, calculating.

"It's not a dirty word, Sara. It wouldn't hurt you to take the rose-tinted glasses off occasionally."

She yanked her arms away from him and stepped out of his warmth. "I know more about the real world than you could ever imagine, Sam," she said, thinking about the long nights with Maxwell, when he was caught in the web of cocaine and paranoia, struggling to break free.

He reddened, remembering that this woman had seen her husband die violently and had strength and dignity enough to get through a chaotic funeral with her sanity and her self-esteem both intact. "I'm sorry," he said. "That was an incredibly patronizing thing to say."

"Yes, it was." An unexpected smile flashed across her face. "But I'm relieved to know you can be as stupid as the rest of the human race."

He smiled back at her, feeling his muscles relax. "Better be careful, Paisley," he shot back. "You're beginning to sound like a cynic."

"And here I was trying to sound like a realist."

Her words were light, bantering, but he understood the full measure of her meaning. Inside the slight body, behind the candy-box pretty face, was a strong woman trying to find her way. If their relationship were to amount to anything, he would have to travel alongside her, not attempt to lead.

"Okay, realist," he said, reaching for her hand, "where do we go from here?"

She chose to ignore the other level of his meaning. "I get my old Nancy Drew books out of mothballs and do a little investigating."

"Any room for an old Hardy Boy fan?"

"Moral support?"

"I can offer you more than that, Sara."

She nodded her thanks. "I know you can, Sam. It's just that I don't even know where to begin."

"I do."

This time the kiss was not easy, neither soft nor gentle. For the first time in all the years they'd known one another, they were alone. No passing crowds, no specter of wife or husband, no eager photographer to break the dangerous spell they had willingly fallen under. Once again time encircled Sara, weaving around the two of them until the only thing she could be certain of was that this moment with Sam's lips on hers was the moment she had been moving toward all her life.

"Sara," Sam murmured, not taking his lips from hers. His breath warmed her face.

"I know," she whispered, catching at his lower lip with her teeth and gently tasting him. She could feel his response against her hipbone and she burned. Her body was pure sensation.

The sense of inevitability, of destiny, was so strong that her knees buckled beneath her and Sam swept her up into his arms and carried her to the softly cushioned couch where he lay down beside her, cradling her in his arms all the while.

His hand brushed the soft faded material of her sweatshirt, snaking under the waistband and touching the firm bare flesh of her abdomen, making her quiver with both desire and fear.

"Tell me to stop," he whispered against her lips. "Tell me to stop, Sara, and I will."

She couldn't speak. His warm, moist mouth was doing wonderful things to her throat, to her collarbone, her shoulder, while his hand slid under the sheer fabric of her bra and cupped her breast, surrounding it with his power and heat. She wanted to touch him—only she knew how much she wanted to touch him—but she was finding it impossible to make her hands do the things her mind longed for them to do. She closed her eyes and pressed her forehead against his shoulder, hating herself for the tears that suddenly started but unable to stem the flow.

Perhaps he sensed a change in the rhythm of her breathing or a tensing of her muscles, for Sam moved his head back so he could see her face. One hand remained against her stomach, while with the other he raised her face so her eyes were forced to meet his.

"Ah, sweet Sara," he said in a gentle voice. "Have I hurt you somehow?"

She shook her head and touched his cheek for a second. "Never that."

"But you want me to stop?"

His eyes were so beautiful—she had never seen eyes as strange and beautiful as his. She knew they saw straight through to her heart. If there was going to be a future for them—as she prayed there would be—it would have to be based on a foundation of truth.

"Yes, Sam, I do want you to stop." She swallowed hard. Honesty of such magnitude was more difficult than she had figured it to be. "I don't want to make any mistakes this time," she said. "Not with you. When we make love, I want it to be for all the right reasons."

"There will be no mistakes with us, Sara. I promise you that."

She ran her hand along the strong angles of his jawline. "I've never given all of me to any other person."

"Not even to Max?"

She shook her head. "There was always a part of me I could never offer him."

Sam could feel anxiety coiling inside him. "And that was?"

She smiled softly at him. "The enormous part of my heart that belonged to you."

He took her hand from his cheek and pressed a kiss into the palm, then closed her fingers over it. She felt that kiss straight through to her soul. "I want you, Sara," he said. "I don't know how long I can wait for you."

She brought his hand to her breast and placed it there so he could feel the erratic beat of her heart. "See what you've done to me, Sam, what you've always done to me?" His hand closed over her flesh, and her breath caught for a moment. "Just a little longer," she said. "I want everything to be right for us."

He was quiet for a moment before he spoke. "So where do we go from here, Paisley?"

"I wish I knew." She leaned against his hand and closed her eyes for a fraction of an instant. The moment for romance had come and gone quickly; however, the declaration, the promise, had been made, and Sara instinctively knew Sam took it as seriously as she. "I can't offer you anything until I find out what's going on around here. I don't want there to be any ghosts between us."

"Ghosts don't frighten me," he said, his wry grin returning to his face. "They can't hurt us. It's the living, breathing types we have to watch out for."

"Like Paul?"

"Like Paul."

"I'm not going to let him get away with this," Sara said, pushing her curly hair away from her face with one hand. "The only thing I own that's truly mine is my reputation, and I refuse to let him take that from me."

Sam looked at her, a puzzled frown on his face. "Your reputation is all you own?" He gestured around the massive apartment with his expressive hands. "Is this an illusion?"

She sighed. "We had a prenuptial agreement. This apartment is part of one of the foundations Maxwell set up in his estate. I'm kind of a glorified caretaker. Only the house in Rio is mine."

"What did you two have, Paisley? A marriage or a business arrangement?" He was angry, perhaps overly so.

"Look, Sam, try to understand how it was. Maxwell was an extremely wealthy man when I married him. I had absolutely nothing to do with his wealth. I didn't know him when he was just starting out; I didn't help him get his first break. He needed to protect himself.''

''Damn it.'' Sam's control broke with a force that almost frightened Sara. ''You pulled him through cocaine addiction, and he felt he had to protect himself from you?'' His expletive was pithy and exceptionally vulgar.

''I didn't want anything from him.'' *Just love,* she thought. Just someone who needed her. ''I didn't give a damn what I signed. If we had divorced, I would have walked away without a cent willingly. What difference did signing something make?''

''I believe what you say,'' Sam said. ''Why couldn't he?''

''Because he didn't know me the way you do.'' She folded her arms across her chest. ''Is that what you wanted to hear?'' Sam said nothing. ''Damn it, Sam, why are you making me feel like I'm on trial here? I'm the victim, not the accused.''

His shoulders sagged, and he leaned back against the desk, feeling the sharp edge of wood dig into his left buttock. Why in hell was he putting her through this? Was the thought of her being married to Maxwell Chance so threatening to him, after all, that he had to grill her on every decision she'd ever made?

''I'm sorry,'' he said at last. ''I have no right.''

She didn't disagree. ''You can ask me anything you want, Sam, but don't ask me to defend my marriage. I loved Max, and I'm not going to lie to you to make this easy for us. Our relationship wasn't perfect, but we were willing to work at it.''

Sam felt Maxwell's presence in the room as strongly as if the other man were standing between him and Sara, his shaggy blond head thrown back in laughter. He was wrong: ghosts were every bit as dangerous as those who lived and breathed.

He shifted awkwardly from foot to foot, suddenly feeling like a gauche high school kid. He cleared his throat. ''Listen, do you want me to stay with you tonight? I don't really like the thought of you being alone in this mausoleum."

She chuckled, and her good humor returned. "Thanks a lot—and after all we spent on decorating."

He matched her light tone. "Get your money back, Paisley. The only room with any life is this one."

She inclined her head graciously. "Why, thank you, Mr. Berenger. This happens to be the one room I decorated."

She put her arm through his and walked him out to the door. "I'll be fine," she said as she watched him pull up the zipper on his gray jacket. "I've been alone before. Besides, I think whoever stole the Grammy knew exactly what he was doing." She paused for a beat. "I also think he's headed for Rio de Janeiro right this minute."

Sam nodded, jamming his hands in his pants pockets. "What will you do after I leave?"

"Go through every item in my office, for starters, and make sure nothing else is missing."

"Good idea." He bent down and kissed her forehead. "If you need me, call, Sara. You know I'm there for you."

"I know you are." She'd always known it. She put an index finger at either side of his mouth and turned the ends up into a smile. "Don't look so grim," she said. "I think the worst is over. With a little luck I'll be yesterday's news by this time next week." She smiled up at him. "How could things get worse?"

Sam kissed Sara again but said nothing. He knew the sound of whistling in the dark when he heard it. He was afraid he was whistling the same tune himself.

6

Jack Farrell stifled a yawn and tried to ignore the fact that he was slowly freezing to death. This wasn't the life he'd pictured for himself. Where was the caviar and champagne, the good life New York City had promised him? All Jack could think about was getting back in his beat-up Volkswagen and heading for home.

He'd been standing on the southwest corner of the Carberry for two hours now, Nikon loaded and ready to shoot, and so far all he'd seen were two prominent attorneys, one aging movie star and a slightly dotty doorman heading off for his two-week Christmas vacation. Nothing worth even a Polaroid snapshot.

It wasn't for lack of trying. When Sara Chance and Berenger got into that taxi by the museum, Jack was into his Volkswagen before the other reporters had a chance to think. The six months he'd spent in L.A. trailing movie stars in their Mercedes and Rolls had put him in good stead; despite their head start, Sara and company were never more than half a block away. Unfortunately, an ill-timed red light at Seventy-first Street, coupled with the fact he couldn't afford another moving violation, slowed Jack up, and by the time he reached the Carberry, both taxi and passengers had long departed.

Damn it. He blew on his hands in an attempt to warm them, then jammed them into the pockets of his worn raincoat. His shoulders were hunched against the wind that whistled off the East River a few blocks away.

He had to be nuts, standing in front of an apartment building like some inept private eye, waiting to take a picture of a woman whose only claim to fame was that she married a famous singer who had the bad luck to get himself killed.

He moved closer to the side of the building in an attempt to shield himself from the wicked wind that whipped up the street. He should have gone into commercial photography, lining up cans of Campbell's soup in patterns designed to induce harried shoppers into taking some tomato or chicken noodle home with them. He should have gone into fashion photography, spending his days taking pictures of long-legged women with eyes that incinerated film. Wedding photography, passport pictures, family portraits. Anything but this.

But Sara Chance was news right now, and Jack Farrell was nothing if not ambitious. He'd read all the stories about her, seen the photos those lucky bastards had taken out in Quogue. She'd looked stoned out of her mind. Hardly the tragic young widow who had intrigued the public two years ago. Then the public had taken her to their hearts, turned her into someone larger than life.

He lowered his head into the upturned collar of his coat. If there was one thing the public liked better than creating a modern heroine, it was knocking that same heroine down on her rear.

It was the name of the game.

All he needed was one great picture of Sara and this guy Berenger and he could make enough money to keep himself in Johnny Walker Red and long-legged blondes for a year.

He leaned against the hood of his VW and waited.

As soon as the door to the elevator slid shut, Sam's face fell quickly into lines of worry. He hadn't wanted to leave Sara, but she seemed to want privacy. It was hard for him to tell exactly where the boundaries were drawn in their brand-new/long-standing relationship, and he'd felt awkward about pushing his thoughts onto her.

It hadn't been difficult to see that the idea someone close to her could be responsible for the odd happenings of late was abhorrent to Sara, but Sam felt there could be no other answer. He was a practical man, fully the product of his middle-class, middle-American upbringing. When all signs pointed in one direction, he was not inclined to look elsewhere.

He'd give her time to think about it all, but soon he would start to voice his opinions more strongly. If they were ever going to have a future together, they had to make sure the past was relegated to the past, where it belonged. For a moment, Maxwell Chance had stood between Sara and him as vividly as if he were still alive, and until the whole thing was straightened out, Sam and Sara didn't stand a chance.

The elevator glided to a halt at the lobby, and Sam strode through the silent hall. Hector was long off duty, and a young man with military bearing nodded to Sam as he headed for the door.

Sam was deep in thought as he came out and didn't notice the man leaning against the VW until the sharp pop of the flashbulbs stopped him in his tracks.

"I thought you didn't know Sara Chance."

Bright dots of white light were still dancing in front of Sam's eyes, but that slightly nasal voice was instantly recognizable.

"Don't you guys ever give it a rest?" Sam was curt, annoyed. This he didn't need.

The photographer chuckled. Sam could see him tilt his head in the direction of the Carberry. "Don't you?"

"I'd be careful what I say, pal."

The younger man fiddled with his camera, snapping the lens cap on and off. "You owed me a picture," he said. "What's the big deal if you and the lady Sara are making it together? A little publicity never hurt any—"

Something clicked inside Sam as abruptly as the camera had clicked just seconds ago. Before he even had a chance to think, he had the photographer backed up against the rusted fender of the Volkswagen, his hands digging into the sharp bones at the base of the younger man's throat.

"Hey, come on, man. Cool down!"

"You should have thought of this before you took that damned picture."

The photographer's eyes were wide. In the phosphorescent glow from the streetlights, Sam was able to see fear clearly visible. Fear that he had caused. Disgust displaced rage. Sam removed his hands from the man's throat.

Jack Farrell believed in quick judgments and even quicker actions. This guy was obviously serious about Sara Chance, serious enough to risk a lawsuit from a rather unscrupulous photographer. New tactics were required. Without taking his eyes from Sam, he flipped open his camera, exposing the film to the streetlight. "Satisfied?" He broke eye contact and pulled the film out, handing the tangle of black plastic to Sam.

"Keep it."

Jack shrugged and tossed the exposed film in the open window of his VW. He ran a finger around his shirt collar, stretching his neck awkwardly and grinning. "You got a pretty good grip there, Sam Berenger."

Sam's face clearly registered his shock, and Jack hid a small smile of pleasure.

"How in hell do you know my name?"

"You're pretty well known around the Metropolitan." He reached into his raincoat pocket and pulled out a small notepad with a frayed blue cover. "Exhibition of Early American cradles 1800-1818—consultant on restoration of furniture from the Empire period—chair of the ad hoc committee working on an exhibition of Federal period furniture tentatively scheduled for February 1986." He flipped the notebook closed. "Care to hear any more?"

Sam raised his hand. "No, thanks. I get the general drift."

"You may not be as well known as the lovely Lady Sara, but you've had your moments."

The kid was brash and bright, and Sam's anger battled with a crazy kind of admiration for his style. "I bow to your sleuthing skills, Mr.—" He extended his hand in a gesture of peace.

After a second's hesitation, the photographer shook it. Sam noted the slick feel of sweat on the palm. So he wasn't as cool as he seemed.

"You have my name," Sam continued. "I have no doubt I could get yours if I call the *Post*. You might as well save me the trouble."

"Jack Farrell. How did you know I work with the *Post?*"

"I'm not without my own sleuthing skills, Jack."

The balance had abruptly shifted. Sam could feel the advantage tilt in his direction.

"How is she?" Jack asked, tilting his head toward the Carberry, toward Sara. He rotated his shoulders forward in an attempt to magnify their bulk.

The action touched something in Sam. There was absolutely no point in pretending he didn't know whom Jack was talking about. "Sara's fine," he answered. "Just fine."

One of Jack's thick red eyebrows arched. "I find that pretty hard to believe."

Sam had to force himself not to launch into a long and detailed diatribe on Sara's persecution at the hands of the press. He met Jack's eyes head-on. "Sara Chance is just fine."

"Can I quote you on that?"

Sam grinned. "If you have to."

Jack started scribbling in his notebook, his head bent forward so Sam could see the childlike whorl of hair in the middle of his scalp. Jack looked back up. "Can you explain why she looked stoned in that picture?"

"Cold medicine."

Jack smirked. "Too many aspirins?"

"Too many questions. Listen." He stepped closer to the young photographer, making sure that his proximity slightly intimidated the other man. "You might find your career a hell of a lot more rewarding if you get out of sleaze journalism and into the real thing. Other people's pains are not Pulitzer Prize-winning material."

"Thanks for the lecture." Jack stuffed his notebook back in his pocket. "Reaganomics and the defense budget won't pay my rent." He hefted his camera, which hung around his neck from a battered leather strap. "This will."

"There's more to life than paying the rent," Sam said. "Money isn't the answer to everything." He only had to look at Sara to know that was true.

"The hell it isn't. Sara Chance is public property, Berenger. Don't blame me if she's suddenly camera shy."

"If you want to dig into Sara's life, maybe you should try to find out why your buddies in the press are hell-bent on slinging mud on her."

"Are you saying there's no basis in fact?"

"That's exactly what I'm saying."

"She's not into kinky sex?"

Sam grabbed the lapels of the photographer's coat.

"I take it your answer is no." Jack yanked himself away from Sam's grasp.

"Where'd you hear that?" Sam demanded.

Jack straightened out his raincoat. "Front page, this week's *National Enquirer*. It hits the stands tomorrow."

"Did you write the story?"

Jack looked aggrieved. "I have my standards, too, Berenger. They may be low, but I still have them."

Sam had to hand it to Farrell. He certainly knew how to maintain arrogance under pressure. He'd go far in the Fourth Estate.

"Come on, Berenger. Tell me your side of the story."

What was the point in saying any more? Sam simply shook his head in dismay and without another look at Jack and his ambitions walked back toward the Westbury Hotel.

He could escape people like Jack Farrell.

Sara, unfortunately, could not.

* * *

The Grammy Award. A piece of coral they'd picked up on a beach in the Mediterranean. Their wedding picture.

As soon as Sam left, Sara had made a search of her office and come up with a list of missing items. She sat at her desk, staring at the pencil-written list until nearly dawn, when she fell asleep with her head resting on the cool wood of her rolltop. She awoke somewhere around nine, showered and changed, then came right back to her desk, hoping that perhaps while she slept, all the loose ends had tied themselves together.

They hadn't. The missing items still seemed to have no common element. The Grammy was work related. The coral and the photo were personal. She'd been trying to convince herself that it had to be a stranger, a fan anxious to connect with anything that had belonged to Maxwell, but she was finding it harder and harder to fool herself.

A fan wouldn't have been so selective. A fan would never have left behind the stack of sheet music in Sara's bedroom, the work diaries, the hundreds of photos of Maxwell in the box near Sara's bed. A fan would probably have been an amateur at breaking into an apartment and would have left behind signs of forced entry. This whole operation had been entirely too slick for that. Only someone who had known Sara and Maxwell personally would have attached any value to a three-inch piece of coral tucked in a pigeon-hole compartment on a crowded rolltop desk. Only someone who had shared their day-to-day life.

Someone like Paul.

Memory rushed in on her like the tide.

The spring before Maxwell died had been an especially hectic one. He'd done a cross-country tour, only his second since his breakup with Last Chance, had produced and starred in three specials for HBO and had written several satirical short stories for *Esquire* and *Playboy* that had catapulted him to an even higher level of fame.

Fame, though, always exacted a price from him.

Sara and the others in the entourage had watched as Max grew exceedingly short-tempered, given to angry, sudden outbursts that alarmed everyone, Maxwell included. He was beginning to show signs of manic-depressive mood swings that Sara realised could easily precipitate a return to seeking relaxation in drug use.

She had approached Neal and Paul, and the three of them decided that what Maxwell needed was a vacation—a vacation preferably somewhere where Maxwell Chance was unknown.

So, two weeks later, Sara and Maxwell, plus their entourage, boarded a jumbo jet for Greece and three weeks of seclusion and serenity on a small island near Cristina Onassis's island of Skorpios. Paul's sister, Deanna, met them there. It had taken some doing, but Sara had finally grown accustomed to the beautiful redhead's penchant for popping up wherever Maxwell happened to be. Deanna had quit her third job in eight months and was at loose ends and not against spending a few weeks in Greece.

Maxwell and Sara spent hours sunning and sailing, simply allowing themselves to slow down to match the low-keyed pace of Greek life. Even though Sara would have wished for more time alone with her husband, she was overjoyed to see the way his moods evened out, the way his eyes no longer held the hint of desperation she so often saw there.

One afternoon the five of them were strolling the beach. Deanna had just remarked that it was probably the first time in years that Max's American Express card had been idle for so long. Sara remembered being surprised that Deanna knew anything about Maxwell the adult. She had assumed their friendship had fallen by the wayside during high school.

Paul picked up the teasing from his sister. "You must be going through consumer withdrawal, Chance," he said with what Sara perceived as a remarkably poor choice of words. "Are we going to have to fly to Athens so you can get a shopper's fix?"

Max, though, had taken it in his stride. "No need, Rollins. There are enough beautiful things on this island to satisfy me."

He had looked Sara squarely in the eyes when he said it, and they ignored the teasing that continued unabated from the other three. A piece of coral, smooth and peachy pink, had washed up on the beach a few feet away from them, and Maxwell bent down and scooped it up, rinsed the grains of sand from its surface, then presented it, with a flourish, to Sara.

"For you," he said. "As beautiful and real as you are."

It was one of those rare moments when Sara felt she had glimpsed the man Maxwell could be if the world would disappear for just a moment. Deanna had laughed and made a joke that Sara's diamond engagement ring was more her idea of a gift, but for Sara that one piece of coral was more valuable than diamonds or emeralds or the fleeting pleasures of fame. Even the teasing from the others hadn't dimmed the sense of joy that one simple gesture of Maxwell's had given her. That brief, exquisite moment in her marriage helped her hang on to her sanity, her wholeness, after Max died.

"We're back."

At the sound of Deanna's voice in the doorway, Sara was catapulted out of her reverie with a bang.

"Did I scare you?" Deanna, looking rested and beautiful in a loose-fitting black dress cinched at the waist with a gold mesh belt, glided into the room. "You look like you saw a ghost."

Sara quickly recovered her equilibrium and moved some unanswered correspondence on top of the list of stolen items. Sam's words, "Maybe you should keep this to yourself," suddenly seemed quite wise.

"This apartment is too darned quiet," Sara said instead. "You could march the circus through here and I'd never hear it." How could she tell Deanna she suspected her brother of a crime?

Deanna fingered the slender platinum chain that held her diamond pendant. "Maybe I should trade this in for a cowbell?" Her face was lit up with a sparkle Sara could only attribute to an extremely satisfying love life.

"If you do, let me know. I'll take the diamond."

Deanna laughed and sat down in the chair opposite Sara's desk. She crossed one long, slim leg over the other and patted the pendant at her throat. "Come on, Sara! Coveting my puny diamond with the treasure chest you have stashed away?"

"That's not exactly a puny diamond," she answered, sitting back down. "It's about the same size as my engagement ring."

Deanna was looking down, inspecting a flaw in her manicure. "I haven't seen you wear your ring in a long time, Sara."

Sara, unwilling to talk about her feelings on conspicuous wealth, hedged. "Well, the stone was a little loose, so I put it away."

"At Quieroz's in Rio?"

Sara nodded, not entirely positive but not wanting to pursue the conversation. Max had made most of his purchases at Alex Quieroz's shop, and Sara had continued to store many of her pieces in his vault just as Maxwell had. However, the engagement ring wasn't stored there; it was hidden in a tiny box in the rear of Sara's closet. Using Quieroz's had made sense back in the days when Max was alive. Now that Sara hadn't been in Rio in over a year, a trip to hide an engagement ring seemed a bit foolish. A hiding spot was a hiding spot. It hardly mattered where it was.

Sara changed the subject. "So, when did you get back? I wasn't expecting you until tomorrow."

Deanna looked up from her inspection of her nail polish and glanced over at the clock on the opposite wall. "About an hour and a half ago. Neal was getting cabin fever. And besides," she said with one of her dazzling smiles that Sara envied, "they light the Christmas tree at Rockefeller Plaza tonight. Neal wouldn't miss that for anything."

Sara sighed. How she would love to be there, too. She and Sam would bundle up—or actually she would, because he never did seem to feel the cold—and they would walk from the Carberry to Rockefeller Plaza, enjoying the music and lights and people, enjoying each other.

"Why don't you come along with us?" Deanna stood up, smoothing her dress to its above-the-knee length.

Sara shook her head. "No, no. I appreciate the offer, but there will be a lot of cameras and reporters there." She shook her head again for emphasis. "That's one thing I don't need—more publicity."

Deanna's laugh was throaty. "I see your point. Is Max's missus hooked on tinsel and carols?" She lowered her voice dramatically. "Film at eleven."

A ripple of alarm fluttered along Sara's veins. She laughed along with Deanna, but there was something about her words, the tone of her voice, that made Sara feel exposed and vulnerable. This whole unsavory business was making her suspicious of everyone. If only there were some way she could introduce Sam to everyone—especially Paul—without drawing undue attention to their relationship. Then it hit her: a party. A big, everyone-is-invited Christmas party just like they used to throw when Max was alive.

"Listen," she said, hoping her voice sounded normal, "I may not be able to go to the tree-lighting ceremony, but I've been thinking maybe it's time I threw a party."

Deanna's beautifully molded jaw dropped open. "What?"

Sara laughed. "A party. You know—lights, music, people, potato chips and onion dip. One of those pre-Christmas bashes we used to throw when Maxwell was alive."

Deanna relaxed. "Potato chips and onion dip, hmm? It has been a while since you gave a party, Sara. The last time I had chips and dip I was in tenth grade."

Sara waved her hand airily. "Okay, potato chips and caviar, then. Whatever. You know all the right people to call to get it catered."

"Fortunately. Otherwise you'd bring in Big Macs and the colonel's special." Deanna grabbed a piece of blank paper from Sara's desk and leaned over to make a few notes. "When is the big event planned?"

Sara hadn't given that a thought. She glanced at the calendar, barely visible through the piles of papers on her desk. "December twenty-second."

Deanna looked up. "A Christmas party?"

"Yes. We can decorate with poinsettias and those little twinkling white lights. Drape boughs of holly and fir along the mantelpiece—"

"Hang tinsel from the Picasso in the library."

Sara's eyes widened in surprise. "Why, Deanna, I had no idea you were such a Scrooge. Don't tell me you think Christmas is humbug?"

"Let's just say when they were giving out Christmas spirit, I must have been on another line." She finished jotting down a few more notes, then stood up again. "Don't worry though, boss. I can toast the Yuletide with the best of them."

"Why on earth are you going to see them light the tree tonight, then?"

Deanna shrugged. "Neal's idea. Actually, I'm okay until we get down to five shopping days before— Then I get irritable, depressed and ready to stuff the next sidewalk Santa I see into his own chimney."

"I'm sorry."

"What for? It's not terminal, Sara. It miraculously passes by December thirty-first." She grinned. "Somewhere around midnight." She started to leave, then turned around again. "The guest list. Shall I get out the Roladex and send to the usual?"

Sara's heart speeded up, thumping quickly against the inside of her rib cage. "Uh, yes—I mean, no. There might be a few additions."

"No problem. Give me their names and addresses and I'll see to it. I found the master party list Maxwell used to use

when I was cleaning out my file cabinet. I'll just hire a cal-
ligrapher to do the envelopes and—''

''No.'' Sara's voice was stronger this time. ''You don't
understand, Deanna. I appreciate the offer, but I'd really
like to take care of them myself. It's been so long since I've
done anything like this that I thought it might be fun.''

Deanna's feathery auburn eyebrows arched in surprise.
''Well, at least let me print out a copy of the list so you don't
miss anyone.''

Sara nodded her thanks. ''I'd appreciate it.''

''May I ask who else you're inviting?''

This was it. ''It just occurred to me the other day how out
of touch I've become with my old friends.''

''Like that Sam What's-his-name who called out at
Quogue?''

''Exactly. I think it's high time I turned that around.''

Deanna paused a moment. ''Of course you lost touch.
You had Maxwell—he opened a whole new world for you.''

''I don't have Maxwell any longer, Deanna. I have to
make a new place for myself.''

''As you wish. May I assume this Sam—'' She paused,
waiting for Sara to supply the last name.

''Berenger.''

''May I assume this Sam Berenger will be coming on the
twenty-second?''

Sara smiled. Deanna couldn't help her loyalties being with
Maxwell, but Sara knew she would come around. ''He sure
will.''

Deanna picked a ballpoint pen from the top of Sara's
cluttered desk and made some more notes on the piece of
paper she held in her hand. ''How many others?''

Sara had absolutely no idea how many other people
would be willing or available to come to her impromptu
party. For all she knew, they might have to hire actors and
actresses to people the place. ''Ten? Maybe twenty?''

Deanna nodded. ''We'll plan on thirty-five. If they're
anything like Max's friends, they'll descend on this place
like vultures and eat everything in sight.''

Sara pushed her chair back and stood up. "I hope you know I want you and Neal and Paul to come, too."

Deanna's cool hazel eyes met Sara's and didn't waver. "No, I didn't know."

Sara walked around to the other side of the desk and put an arm around the taller woman. "It wouldn't be the same without you guys. You know that." This was not turning out exactly as planned.

"Well, you seem to be changing everything. I didn't expect this to be any different."

"Deanna, I..." Sara's voice trailed away. She was at a total loss for words. Deanna—cool, able, friendly Deanna—had been replaced by a woman whose emotions seemed terribly close to the surface.

Then, as quickly as Deanna had become hurt and moody, her face lit up with a smile, and the discomfort between the two women disappeared. "Did you listen to me? I think I really am turning into Scrooge. Shall I blame my age?"

"Why not?" Sara was able to cover her confusion easily. "You didn't have much of a birthday celebration last week, I'm afraid."

"Didn't need one," Deanna said, patting the large patch pocket on her short black dress. "That gorgeous cigarette lighter you gave me is something to celebrate all by itself."

They were chatting pleasantly about the Trump Tower and all the beautiful things to be found therein when the telephone on Sara's desk rang. Sara hesitated a moment before answering, and Deanna, apparently sensitive to Sara's need for privacy, flashed her a smile and left the office.

"It took you a while, Paisley."

"You're getting impatient, Berenger." Sara picked up the cordless phone and carried it to the window, feeling as warm as if she were perched in front of a crackling fire. "It only rang three times."

"Three and a half," he answered. "Not that I'm counting, you understand."

"Of course." She balanced on the edge of the parsons table that fronted the large window and looked down at the courtyard below. "I missed you last night."

There was a short silence. "I'm glad to hear that. I didn't sleep so well myself."

She grinned and held the phone closer. "Worried about me?"

"Actually, I stayed up all night worrying about the falling interest rates."

"Liar."

"Want me to tell you what I really thought about?" His voice was low, an intimate sound that nestled close to her ear.

"Yes," she said, almost surprised she could find her voice at all.

"You, Paisley." He paused for a beat, and she found herself holding her breath for his next words. "I thought about how it will be when I finally make love to you."

"Sam." Her voice was husky and soft, his name an endearment on her lips.

"Do you know how many times I've thought about what it will be like to hold you in my arms, to—"

"Sam!" His words had become so intimate, so compelling, that she feared she would lose touch with the reality of her present situation. She forced a small laugh. "You never know who might be listening in to our conversation."

"Don't tell me you have a party line?"

"No party line," she answered, "but some things are better said in person."

They laughed for a moment. When Sam spoke again, his voice was all business. "Did you find anything else missing?"

"Afraid so." She hurried back to her desk and fished the list out from under the letters she'd covered it with when Deanna came into the room earlier. "Max's Grammy." She hesitated a moment. "A few pages from Max's journal had obviously been read." She explained about the cigarette burn at the edge of the pages.

"Were they important pages?"

"Actually, no. They were just a few random selections. Not of any value from what I could see." She took a breath and continued. "Our wedding photograph and a piece of coral we'd found on a vacation in Greece."

"A piece of coral? What the hell—"

"I know. I can't figure it, either."

"What was special about it? Was it set in gold or studded with diamonds?"

She shook her head. "No. Just a plain, ordinary piece of coral. The only people on earth it meant anything to were Maxwell and me."

"Did anyone else know about the coral?"

"Know about it? Of course." She explained about the Mediterranean vacation. "We're right back where we started from, Sam."

"Paul Rollins."

"Exactly. And I don't know what to do about it."

"Is he still in Brazil?"

"He won't be back until Thursday."

"We could search his apartment."

She laughed. "Forget it. Someone's always around. We could never get away with—" She stopped abruptly.

"Paisley?"

Excitement sizzled through her body like a jolt of pure electricity. "We could do it tonight. Deanna and Neal are going to the tree lighting."

"Tonight?" Suddenly, Sam didn't sound so sure. "I was only kidding, Paisley."

"It's our only chance, Sam." Sara's laugh held a tinge of recklessness. "If you'll pardon the pun."

"What if he's in there?"

"He's not. I'm sure he's in Brazil."

"What in hell are we looking for?"

"You tell me. You're the one who wanted to search his apartment in the first place."

"Yeah, and I'm beginning to wonder about my sanity. What we're thinking of is illegal, Paisley."

"So is burglary." Adrenaline gave her confidence she hadn't known she possessed. "If I'm living with someone who hates me this much, Sam, I have to know about it. I have to know if it's Paul."

They made plans to meet at four-thirty in front of a leather-goods store down the block from the Carberry. After they said good-bye, Sara found herself feeling half-crazed with anticipation and anxiety. If you had a key to the apartment, it wasn't considered breaking in, she rationalized. Arriving uninvited, perhaps, but breaking in? Hardly.

Jack Farrell yawned and dragged his hand through his thick springy red hair, which was still wet from his shower. He'd thought the cold water pounding down on his head and shoulders would help him return to the land of the living, but he still felt exhausted. The night before he'd stayed in front of the Carberry until 2:00 a.m. on the off chance that Berenger would return or Sara would emerge. By the time he tossed his camera into his beat-up Volkswagen, his body was so stiff with cold that he could barely fold his frame around the steering wheel and drive off.

He stumbled into the office at around seven. He occasionally did stories as well as photos, and he typed two very pedestrian efforts into the system—one about Caroline Kennedy's new job and the other about drug dealing on the Upper West Side—handed some film to the photo department, then beat it home for some sack time.

Maybe if he wasn't so obsessed with Sara Chance, he could get out there and do some serious work—nail the kingpin of a major drug ring, find Jimmy Hoffa, discover that Mayor Koch really lives in New Jersey. Something. Anything would be better than this ridiculous feeling he had that there was a story behind the story the public had been reading about Max's widow.

He pulled some clean underwear out of his file cabinet and eased his narrow body into a T-shirt and shorts.

He was getting soft; that's what it was. He'd actually felt some compassion for her yesterday in front of the Metropolitan when the reporters had surrounded her, twitching at the scent of fresh blood. His better instincts, instincts he tried very hard to ignore, kept telling him Sara was being set up.

Spending another night pounding the pavement in front of the Carberry made as much sense as swimming in an empty pool. Any idiot with an Instamatic could get a picture of Sara coming in and out of the apartment building. That was nothing special.

But waiting inside the Carberry? That was something else entirely. If he could just get inside that fortress, he'd bet his telephoto he could get a story that would make *Time* and *Newsweek* sit up and beg. He'd have enough Johnny Walker Red and long-legged blondes to last him until next Easter if he could pull that off.

He'd make Charlie Perez sit up and take notice, and at that moment the picture of Perez staring at Jack's story with undisguised envy sounded even better than a blonde with legs that went on until tomorrow.

7

Manhattan streets grow dark early in December. By three o'clock in the afternoon, the pale winter sun begins its descent, and all across the city apartment lights are switched on, illuminating the windows for passersby.

Sara watched the building across the street as the third-floor window filled with light. She watched the fifth-floor window where a woman with long blond hair held a baby in her arms and pointed toward the street below and to the many apartments where lighted menorahs and Christmas trees twinkled a holiday message of love and good cheer.

And then there was Sara, who stood alone on the crowded street, waiting for Sam to come along so they could break into someone else's apartment.

Peace on earth. Goodwill to men.

This was insane. She had to be totally, completely out of her mind to even consider doing something as ridiculous as breaking into Paul Rollins's apartment. What on earth had gotten into her this afternoon that such a crazy idea would even occur to her? Sara Paisley Chance, who never so much as tossed a gum wrapper in the street, was actually going to search someone else's home, rummage through his belongings, invade his privacy in the same way she hated to have hers invaded.

But then she thought of that lurid issue of the *National Enquirer* that Neal had brought to her attention at lunchtime, and she knew she had to do it. She hadn't been able to bring herself to read the story, but the headline was permanently burned into her memory: "I Made Love to Max While Sara Watched—Seventeen-Year-Old Fan Tells of Kinky Sex and Wild Drugs."

Bile, hot and acrid, rose in her throat, and she swallowed hard to calm herself. If Paul were to blame for the terrible stories and strange things that had been happening to her, she had to know. She had to deal with it—and him—head-on before she could ever think of starting a life with Sam.

"You're early." Sam's voice, low and warm, tickled against her ear, and a tiny swell of holiday cheer bloomed inside her chest.

"You're late." She slipped her arm into his. "The clock in the luggage store says four thirty-three."

He pulled his thick navy sweater up over his forearm and showed her his watch. "The clock on my wrist says four twenty-nine."

Out of nowhere, she grew annoyed. "Perhaps you should have it checked."

He tilted his head and looked down at her, a puzzled expression on his handsome face. "Paisley? What's wrong?"

"You have to excuse me," she said, "but I always get testy when I'm about to break into someone's apartment."

They turned down the block that led to the Carberry's front entrance.

"Having second thoughts?"

She nodded. "And third and fourth and fifth. What if someone catches us?"

"No one's around to catch us, Sara. Paul is in Brazil, and the other two are out for the night. We're home free." He squeezed her hand. "Besides, we have a key, right?"

She nodded.

"See? No problem. We'll get in and out in nothing flat."

"A simple little once-around-the-apartment?"

He grinned. "Exactly. Before you know it, we'll be back in your place, drinking wine and eating dinner."

"Eating dinner?" She couldn't help but laugh. "Only if you know how to cook."

"You've got it. We'll pick up some steaks at D'Agostino's, and I'll show you how to broil the best T-bones this side of Omaha."

"Make that a Big Mac and an order of fries and you've got a deal."

Sam could feel some of the tension slip from her body as they approached the front gates to the Carberry Towers. He, however, felt coiled like an overwound mainspring ready to snap. They waited while Larry's replacement unlocked the gates, then walked ahead to open the front door with a flourish. Sara smiled her thanks, ignoring the small group of fans lingering beyond the iron fence, some of whom mumbled vague obscenities in her direction. Even though Sara had called him at Leonard's and warned him about the *Enquirer* article, the swiftness with which trash spread still amazed Sam.

Once inside, they strolled past the guards, past the video camera that hung suspended from the ceiling near the elevator bank, and they waited while Hector fumbled around with his uniform jacket, then held the elevator door open for them to enter.

Sara pushed the penthouse button, and the doors slid shut. The elevator car rose as if it were cushioned on pillows of air. Sam would never get used to the subtle differences between the rich and the rest of the world.

"Do you have the key?" he asked.

Sara nodded. "I always keep my keys handy."

He started to remind her he wasn't talking about her house key when she motioned very subtly for him to keep silent.

"They have a surveillance unit in the elevators," she explained as they left the elevator and walked down the hallway toward her apartment. "The security team monitors all of them with a video unit and a backup sound system."

Sam exhaled loudly. "Good thing you stopped me when you did. We could have ended up with Mr. T and the A-Team waiting for us at the door."

Sara chuckled and unlocked her front door, ushering Sam inside.

"Hardly that," she said as she closed it after them. "More likely a very discreet, terribly polite SWAT team with pleasant smiles and .357 Magnums."

Sam's laugh was a shade nervous. She probably wasn't kidding. "Life-styles of the rich and famous?"

"Exactly." She tossed her key chain down on the round table in the foyer, then motioned Sam through the apartment and into her office. He followed her, enjoying the sway of her hips beneath the baggy sweatshirt. She turned and faced him, hands resting lightly on the polished surface on her rolltop desk. Her fingers seemed to be trembling. "Well, I guess this is it."

"I guess so." Sam tried to sound as if it were a casual conversation. "Shall we get the show on the road?"

"Just like that?"

"You were planning on sending out engraved invitations?"

She grimaced at him. Humor, evidently, had been put aside. "I think I should call first."

He looked at her, puzzled.

"In case someone's there," she explained. "Better to find out on the phone than in person."

"Did you get this from your old Nancy Drews?" He leaned against the modular sofa and watched as she picked up her cordless phone.

"No," she answered. "Remington Steele."

Sam started to say something when she placed her finger over her lips and shushed him. "It's ringing," she whispered.

He folded his arms across his chest. His heart was thumping so hard, in both anxiety and anticipation, that he could feel it pounding against his forearm. Sara put the phone back down on top of the desk; it nearly disappeared in a pile of papers.

"Coast is clear." Her light blue eyes seemed larger than usual. "This is it."

"You're sure, Paisley?"

She nodded, her face obscured for a moment by a cloud of dark curls. "I have to know if Paul is responsible for all of this."

"Okay, then. Lead on."

She lifted the edge of her faded gray sweatshirt and removed the key that had been safety pinned in place. "There's no entrance from my apartment," she said as she led Sam back out into the hallway outside her door. "We have to go in the front."

Sam looked up at the high ceiling, searching for remote cameras. "Is this area under surveillance also?"

Sara, who was about to fit the key into the lock, hesitated a moment. "I don't know." Then she straightened her shoulders and opened the door. "It's too late to worry about it now." She flashed a smile at Sam, who took his cue from her and smiled back. "Just act as if we belong."

How ironic, Sara thought. Acting as if she belonged was exactly what she'd been trying to do all her life.

She opened the door and stepped into the dark apartment. Behind her, she heard Sam fumbling along the wall, then the click as he flicked the switch and soft, recessed lighting bathed the entrance hall with a muted amber glow. Sara moved into the living room and gasped. Nothing in Paul's personality had prepared her for the beauty of the artwork he collected.

"Look at this," she said, gently drawing one finger across the shoulders of a marble god that rested on the mantelpiece. "This is magnificent."

Sam came over and inspected the piece. "The guy knows his artwork," he said, emitting a long, low whistle. "This is a Sanzeri. In twenty years it will be priceless."

"I had no idea Paul was a connoisseur." She stepped farther into the living room, running her fingers lightly over exquisitely carved marble icons on a plain oak parsons table.

Sam peered closely at a framed lithograph on the far wall. "A signed Lichtenstein," he said with an appreciative whistle. "Just how much does this guy make a year, anyway?"

Sara looked around the room at the museum-quality pieces and shook her head. "Not this much."

"How do you think he can afford these things?"

"Beats me. But if E. F. Hutton is talking, I'm ready to listen."

Sam laughed, but they both knew the implications. Was it possible Paul had been making a very lucrative profit peddling information, true or false, about Sara and Max? Sara couldn't bear to think about it now.

"I'm getting the creeps in here," she said finally, rubbing down the goose bumps that had popped up along her arms and legs. "Let's get this over with."

Sam went off to check the kitchen and bath, while Sara headed through the hallway to Paul's bedroom. She had expected to have the distasteful task of sifting through piles of embarrassingly personal items and was pleased to discover his room almost monastic in its simplicity.

A queen-size mattress rested on top of a platform bed made of pale, bleached pine. A fitted cover of some kind of soft-looking navy material covered the mattress, leaving the platform itself exposed. Sara bent down and noticed that a large drawer was built into the platform on the other side. She slid the drawer open. Underwear was stacked neatly on the left side of the drawer, and Sara felt guilty as hell as she sifted through the shorts and T-shirts. A few crewneck cashmere sweaters occupied the center space. Their soft silkiness slid through her fingers. Nothing concealed there except exceptionally good taste in wearing apparel. Finally, she removed the pile of starched and impeccably ironed dress shirts that rested in the right side of the drawer. Again nothing.

The closet likewise yielded no clues. A large stereo system filled the wall opposite the bed. She poked around the components but found nothing amiss.

So much for sleuthing.

She left the room and headed through the living room to the large, amber-tiled bathroom where Sam stood inspecting the medicine cabinet.

"Anything?" he asked.

She shook her head. "Nothing. The man is obscenely tidy, I must say." She peeked around the corner of the medicine cabinet and looked inside. "Anything here?"

Sam chuckled. "Not a thing. The only thing I've discovered is Rollins has a thing for Colgate toothpaste and Lagerfeld cologne."

"Can't base a case on that, can we?"

"Not in this state, anyway." Sam closed the medicine cabinet, then clicked off the bathroom light.

They went back into the living room. Sara moved toward the door. "Let's go," she said. "I don't want to press my luck."

Sam looked around the living room. "Did you check his desk?"

"What desk? I didn't see one."

Sam pointed toward another parsons table to the right of the living-room window. "There. That piece of furniture over there with a typewriter on it."

Sara squinted in the general direction of his hand. "I never saw it."

He chuckled. "Try wearing your glasses, Paisley. It might help."

Sam began sifting through the pile of papers that were arranged in neatly organized stacks in low metal baskets. Sara was reaching for a notebook that rested at a perfect right angle to the typewriter when she noticed that Sam's face had suddenly drained of color.

"What is it?" Her voice was no more than a whisper.

Sam threw the folded piece of paper down on the desk as if it were on fire. "The bastard," he said, slamming his fist down hard against the tabletop. "The lousy, stinking bastard."

"Sam?" She reached for the paper he'd tossed down. He grabbed her wrist with his hand. "Let me see it. I have to know."

He loosed his hold on her and watched as she picked up the paper, looked at it and, to his horror, began to laugh.

"You have one strange sense of humor, lady." He couldn't keep the outrage from his voice. "That's one of the most disgusting personal attacks I've ever seen. If someone I trusted was thinking of sending that to me, I'd—"

"Calm down, Sam. I've already seen the letter."

He was growing more confused by the second. "What is this, a carbon copy?" He reached for the phone. "I'm going to call the cops. They can be waiting for him Thursday when he gets off the plane from Rio."

"Don't bother," Sara said, her brief amusement at the situation fading away. "Paul didn't write this."

Sam put the receiver back down. "How do you know?"

"Because I gave him this letter."

Sam leaned against the desk and stared at her. "Have I gone crazy, or have you?"

"Neither." She rummaged through the stack of papers and pulled out six more letters, all in the same small neat typeface, all filled with the most stomach-turning accusations Sam had ever seen in print. "I've been getting one a week since the end of October. I gave them to Paul to hang on to in case things ever got out of hand."

"And you're sure he's not responsible for these?"

She nodded. "Positive. He even brought in a detective, but there was no way to trace them. They were sent out of the general post office near Penn Station, and there were no identifiable fingerprints on them."

Sam said nothing as they quickly returned Paul's desk top to its original condition. They were both quiet as they took a last look around the apartment to make sure everything was in order, then went to leave.

"Wait!" Sam grabbed Sara's arm. "I hear the elevator."

Quickly, Sara closed the apartment door again, then leaned her forehead against it. "Oh, no," she whispered. "What if it's Neal and Deanna?"

"What if it's Paul?" Sam countered.

Sara's senses heightened until she felt painfully in touch with every sight and sound and smell in the hallway. The elevator had indeed stopped at the penthouse floor, but she hadn't been able to tell if anyone exited. They stood quietly for four minutes by Sam's watch, waiting for the inevitable sound of the key scratching in the lock.

It never came. Finally, Sara breathed normally again. "False alarm," she said, matching her words with a false smile.

"False alarm? You either want the penthouse or you don't, Paisley. It's hard to make a mistake on that."

"No, it's not," she said, easing the door open a crack and peering into the dimly lit, empty hallway. "There are three penthouses at the Carberry, and they all have their own elevator." She opened the door wide and stepped outside. Sam followed her. "People have made that mistake before."

"What about the elevator man downstairs? Doesn't he watch out for that?"

She laughed as she closed the door behind Sam. "You've met Hector—he has enough trouble sometimes remembering what day it is." She glanced down at Sam's watch as she went to unlock the door to her own apartment. "Besides, he's off duty by now. I don't know how sharp the night man is."

Once inside Sara's apartment, they moved quickly to her office. Neither one seemed terribly comfortable in the living room, and the kitchen was only as good as it was functional, and for Sara that meant not at all. She offered him a glass of brandy, and when she brought it back in to him, he was sitting on the sofa, tracing a finger along the red silk bargello pillow she had designed what seemed like a hundred lifetimes ago.

"Sit down," he said, accepting the drink with one hand and patting the spot next to him with the other. "You look like you're ready to explode."

She couldn't sit. She paced. She felt flushed with a nervous, pointless energy. "That was a total waste of time," she said, stopping for a minute by the window. "We still don't know a blasted thing."

Sam sipped his brandy. "We know Rollins has great taste in art."

Sara glared at him. "Don't be flip."

"Sorry." One eyebrow was arched in surprise. "Let me rephrase that. We know Rollins can afford some pretty damn fine artwork."

Sara shrugged. "So?"

"That means he has money, Paisley, and plenty of it. He has to be getting it from somewhere."

She dismissed his statement with a brusque wave of her hand. "There was still no evidence to prove he's responsible for what's been happening to me."

"What did you expect to find, Paisley? A signed confession?"

Her feathery dark brows slide together in a scowl. "Well, this was your bright idea in the first place," she snapped. "I still find it hard to believe Paul could—"

"Damn it to hell!" Sam stood up, spilling a few drops of brandy on his corduroy slacks. "Are you going to stick your head in the sand again? I thought you were more of a fighter, Paisley."

His words hit home. She felt the sting of tears behind her eyelids. "It helps when you can identify the enemy, Sam."

Something in her voice defused his anger quickly and completely. Could she have had any doubts about him?

"I'm not the enemy, Sara." He eliminated the space between them and put his hands on the fragile bones of her shoulders. She looked so forlorn in that ridiculous New York Jets sweatshirt of hers that he felt an almost-overwhelming surge of love for her.

Her heavily lashed blue eyes met his, sweeping him inside her soul. "I never thought you were," she answered. He lowered his head toward her until their lips made a brief, painfully sweet contact.

Desire pulsed in the air between them. Sam slipped his long fingers through the soft curls that wreathed her face, gently caressing her scalp. She felt as if she were all sensation, a combination of fire and sweet, sweet rain.

"Get your coat," Sam said, releasing her from his magical touch, releasing himself from her power.

Sara was still in sensual thrall to him, and it took her a moment to return to reality. "Why?" she finally managed.

"We're going out for dinner."

She hesitated. "I can't," she said. "What if someone—"

"No one will recognize you," he broke in. "Get your coat." He followed her to the living room where they had left their coats on the couch. "Okay," he said, grabbing her handbag from the floor. "Now brush your hair off your face."

"Have you gone crazy?" She didn't know whether to laugh or be annoyed.

"Don't ask questions, Paisley. Just do it."

She took her brush from her pocketbook, and moving to the mirror over the table in the hallway, she smoothed her dark hair off her face, then anchored it back with two tortoiseshell combs she'd kept in her makeup case. "Ugh," she said, turning toward Sam. "I look horrible."

He grinned at her. "Not horrible, just different."

She looked back at her reflection. "I'm beginning to see your point."

Sara took over from there. In a few moments she had applied a dark red lipstick she'd bought ages ago but never worn, popped out her contacts and put on her oversized glasses, then tied a wool challis scarf over her head.

"*Voilà!*" She turned to Sam with a grin.

He started to laugh.

"Don't say it," she warned, waving her index finger at him in mock-warning.

"I wouldn't dare," he said. "But you do look just like a—"

"Bag lady," she finished for him. "I could stop a clock."

"Not too glamorous," he agreed, "but I'll make a bet no one recognizes you tonight."

"I'll say a prayer no one recognizes me tonight," she said, glancing at her altered appearance in the mirror one last time. "You'd better be right, Sam. This could do more to hurt my reputation than anything they've done to me so far."

They left the apartment. Sara made sure to double lock the door behind them. Sam pushed the button for the elevator, and they were so engrossed in debate over where they would go to eat that neither one noticed the tiny squeak as the door to the fire stairs opened a crack, then swiftly closed.

Jack Farrell's close call left him sweating despite the draft that swirled up the stairwell. He had been just about to come out of hiding when both Sara and that Berenger guy came out of the apartment on the right. He dived for the fire exit as if a three-alarm blaze were on his tail and prayed neither of them heard the door squeak shut behind him.

He needn't have worried. From the bits of conversation and laughter that made it through the heavy steel door, their thoughts were on things other than nosy photographers and libelous stories.

For a second, as he crouched in the shadows, his narrow body shivering with the cold, Jack wondered if Berenger and Sara were lovers. He wondered what it would feel like to hold her in his arms, to bury his face in the soft, fragrant mass of curls that framed her face.

He wondered if he was going crazy.

He heard the elevator doors slide open and the whirr of machinery as it eased its passengers back down to the ground floor.

It was time to get to work.

* * *

Sara hadn't really needed all the Soave she and Sam had polished off in order to feel euphoric. The simple fact of anonymity had been enough to send her emotions skittering skyward. A fine line runs between anxiety and elation, and the unexpected gift of normalcy coming right on the heels of their escapade in Paul's apartment sent her teetering over the edge.

"I don't know why I never thought of changing my appearance." She gestured with a breadstick toward her slicked-back hair and eyeglasses. "I can't believe this is all it took."

Sam broke off a warm piece of Italian bread from the loaf that rested in the wicker basket in the center of their table. "It's more than the glasses and red lipstick, Paisley," he said. "It's attitude."

"I don't follow you."

"Would you believe Marilyn Monroe was able to get around unnoticed?"

Sara took a sip of wine. "I find it hard to believe Monroe could take a deep breath without it making headlines."

"That's where you're wrong. The story goes that she and a reporter were walking through Central Park one sunny Sunday afternoon and he was amazed that no one recognized her. 'Is it that you're not wearing makeup or sequins?' he asked.

"Monroe laughed and shook her head. 'Not at all,' she said. 'I'm just not being Marilyn Monroe right now.'"

Across the table Sara frowned. "What is that supposed to mean?"

Sam chuckled. "Let me finish. Monroe went on to say that her star personality could be switched on and off like electricity. It had nothing to do with makeup or the lack of it."

Sara laughed. "I don't believe it."

"Neither did the reporter, but Monroe insisted it was true. They made a bet that without fixing her hair or slipping into something low-cut and sexy, she could make a mental transformation and instantly attract the same fans who were strolling by her right then, unaware of her existence.''

''And who won?'' Sara asked. ''The reporter, right?''

''Wrong. Monroe's posture changed, her skin suddenly glowed with energy and excitement, and right in front of this man's eyes she became a movie star. Fans mobbed them, and they had to run for their lives.''

''Sounds like one for 'Ripley's Believe It or Not,' if you ask me.'' Sara poured herself some more wine, then topped off Sam's glass, as well. ''I still don't understand how this relates to me.''

Sam shrugged. ''I'm not sure how it does, either. But maybe if you become less conscious of who you are, others will follow suit.'' He gestured toward her altered appearance. ''It's not just the sleight of hand we played. Anyone with a sharp eye would know who you are. It's just now you don't feel like you should be noticed and therefore you're not giving off that little electrical charge you usually do.''

''Highly improbable theory, Mr. Berenger.'' She grinned at him, and they both were silent as the waiter brought their food.

''Maybe it is,'' Sam said as the waiter moved away from them. ''But the point is, you can have a life, Sara. It *is* possible.''

Sara looked down at her food and speared a piece of chicken with her fork. ''In New York City? I doubt it.''

Sam reached across the table and took her free hand in his. ''Not in New York,'' he said. ''With me.''

''But you live in New York.''

He took a deep breath. How in hell had he forgotten to tell her? ''January first I'm supposed to move up to Maine.''

''You're what?'' Sara dropped her fork, and it clattered against her plate. Chicken and spicy sauce splashed onto the white tablecloth.

He explained about Karl Bergmann and the opportunity presented to him.

"But your business," she said, not really caring about his business at all. "How will it get along without you?" *How will I?*

"It's worth a year away from my business," he said, still holding Sara's hand in his. "You can't put a price tag on what Bergmann is offering me." He told her a little about Bergmann's methods and how craftsmanship of that caliber was going the way of dinosaurs and clean water.

Sara watched his eyes light up as he spoke about his work—his art—and in that instant she understood what made Sam different from anyone she knew. He cared. He truly cared about what he did, and that caring went beyond the size of his paycheck and the extent of his bank balance.

"I'll miss you," she said, her words tearing at her throat from inside.

"You don't have to miss me at all, Paisley."

She met his eyes. "I would never ask you to stay here."

"I can't stay here," he said, "but you can come with me."

"To Maine?"

"You make it sound like I was heading for the Australian Outback."

"It might as well be," she answered. All of her high spirits had vanished. "It's cold up there, Sam."

He thought of his life without her. "No colder than it's been here," he said quietly.

She looked down at her hands, at the wide gold band on her left ring finger. She had been so intent on figuring her way out of the maze her life had become that the very real decisions ahead of her had gone ignored. There wasn't just her future to consider; there was Sam's as well.

"What ties you to New York, Sara?"

Her answer took a moment to formulate. "It's my home," she said finally, for lack of a better answer. "It's where I've always lived."

"That's your past. What about your future?" he asked softly.

She looked away, then back again into Sam's beautiful eyes. "I can't answer that."

"Can't or won't?"

"Both. I can't give you a quick answer, and I'm not certain I'm ready to hunt for a serious one."

"You're an honest woman, Paisley."

"I'm trying to be."

Sam released her hand, and they continued eating. He could see her face change as her buoyant mood gave way to something quieter, darker. He'd been so close; he could almost feel how close he'd been to making her understand that the prison she lived in was partly of her own design. Yet she had slipped away from him and was hiding once more behind vague responsibilities and broken promises.

He hadn't meant it to sound that way, but in mentioning his January first target date for being in Maine, he had placed a tacit deadline on their relationship. They were old enough and had been through enough in their separate lives to understand that what they could have together would not last forever untended. If she'd had career or family or some tangible commitment tying her to New York, he would have searched heaven and earth to find a way to satisfy both of their needs.

But she hadn't.

What she had was fear and loneliness and a dependency on the old life she'd known, and he couldn't allow that to determine their relationship. They'd come too far for that.

It had all gone too easily. Maybe that was why Jack's stomach was doing backflips.

From the second he'd walked up to the gate at the Carberry and the guard mistook him for Paul Rollins, he'd been home free. Whereas he'd been expecting to be booted out on his butt, instead he'd been ushered in like one of the chosen few. Whereas he'd expected to be sneaking up the service stairs like a hood, he'd glided up the private elevator to the penthouse floor like visiting royalty.

The one hitch had been when Berenger and Sara nearly caught him approaching the doors at the end of the corridor, but a handy fire exit had saved him. Chance had even had the decency to forget to lock the door to Rollins's apartment, giving Jack free snooping access. He didn't even have to pick a lock.

Too smooth, he thought as he looked through the stacks of papers Rollins had neatly piled in a wooden file box beneath the table he used as a desk. Too easy.

He sat down on the floor and began to read Paul's notes on his life with *Last Chance.*

Too good to put down.

It was only seven o'clock when Sam and Sara finished dinner and left the restaurant. Although the sky was dark, Fifth Avenue was crowded with Christmas shoppers hurrying up to Bendel's or down toward Lord & Taylor. Sidewalk vendors roasted chestnuts, and the smoky, pungent aroma made Sara even more melancholy than she already was.

They had been fairly quiet since Sam dropped his bombshell about moving up to Maine for a year, concentrating instead on food and drink instead of life and its problems. She was at an impasse, and she knew it—effectively blocked between her past and her future, her present tied up in lurid headlines and shady motives. She could talk all she wanted about her responsibilities toward Max's charitable foundations, but she knew it was all a sham, a cover for the real reason.

She could never consider a life with Sam until she had a life she could call her own.

Sam had asked her if she wanted to take a walk over to Rockefeller Plaza for a quick glimpse of the Christmas tree, but her holiday spirit had disappeared, and she declined, saying she thought she'd better get back to the Carberry "in case."

"In case of what?" Sam asked as he stepped out into the street and whistled for a cab.

"In case Deanna and Neal get back earlier than I thought," she mumbled as she slid across the ripped leather seat of the taxi and Sam got in and gave the driver instructions to stop at the corner of the Carberry and keep the meter running.

"Damn it, Paisley. When are you going to stop acting like a frightened child around those two?" he said as the cab pushed its way into traffic.

"I resent that."

"You should," he answered. "That's a hell of a way for an adult to feel in her own house." He took her gloved hand in his. "Why don't I just go upstairs with you and you can introduce all of us and have it over with."

"Not now!"

"Tomorrow." He was relentless.

"Sam, for goodness' sake—"

"Damn it, Paisley. We don't have time for this." He forced her to meet his eyes. "We never had time for this."

"Humor me, Sam. Please."

She smiled, but he didn't return it. She had disappointed him; she could feel it in every cell in her body. "How about December twenty-second?" she asked, forcing the smile to remain on her lips. "Are you free to come to a party?" No answer from Sam. She leaned over and put her face in his line of vision. "Very exclusive guest list." She told him about her plan.

"Will your unholy trinity be there?"

She nodded. "Among others. I even want to ask the old crowd from the Obelisk."

He ignored that, returning instead to Paul and Neal and Deanna. "They'll know how we feel about one another?"

She hesitated. "They'll know whatever they need to know."

"Do they need to know we're serious?"

She looked into his eyes and knew she held the key to their future. The wrong answer and he'd disappear up to Maine, and she wasn't fool enough to think any one woman would be given three chances for happiness with the same man. "Yes," she said. "They need to know."

In the darkness, Sam reached for her hand and lifted it to his mouth, pressing his lips against the pulse in her wrist, and she shivered with longing.

The cab stopped at the corner of the Carberry. The streetlight had burned out, and the cab was shrouded in a darkness that was intimate, intense. The driver was slumped in his seat, battered cap pulled low over his eyes, grabbing some rest while the meter clicked away Sam's dollars and cents.

It was as close to privacy as they could manage.

Sam slid closer to her and pulled Sara into his arms. He seemed so sure they could have a future, but she had long ago forgotten how to hope for one. Sara closed her eyes and pressed her cheek against his, enjoying the slight scrape of his five-o'clock shadow against her skin. He felt warm and alive, and it had been a very long time. She felt herself melting like a quick-burning candle. *This is enough*, she thought, the scent of him filling her mind and heart. *If this is all I ever have of him, this is enough.*

Sam could feel her heart thundering like a skittish colt; its vibration could be felt even through the thickness of her down coat. Anger for the years they had lost came out in the way he kissed her. The springtime scent and womanly feel of her only managed to remind him of all they'd lost, of all he wanted to find. *This isn't enough*, he thought. *I can never have enough of her.*

However, taxicabs—even with a driver willing to feign deafness and blindness—are not the place to declare oneself. As the passion rose swiftly between them, both Sam and Sara realized they must say good-night.

"Call me when you wake up," he said, kissing her once more as the cab pulled up directly in front of the Carberry. "I want to be the first voice you hear in the morning."

"Call me tonight," she answered quickly as the doorman hurried toward the taxi. "I want to be the last voice you hear before you sleep."

Then, suddenly, just before the door swung open and she was ushered back into reality, Sara leaned toward Sam and kissed him once more, committing his scent and touch to memory.

"Soon," she said, touching his mouth with one finger.

"Very soon," he answered.

Time was running out.

8

Sam's scent lingered with Sara after she left him in the taxi. It was ridiculous, considering the state her life was in, but the mere fact of his existence was enough to cause a very foolish grin to wreathe her face, and she didn't care if the security men monitoring the penthouse elevator thought her mad. She had never felt more sane, more whole, in her life.

Not even during the best of times with Maxwell had she experienced such a feeling of well-being, of completeness, as she had just moments ago with Sam. With Max, things had been frenetic, exciting, lived always on the edge of despair or elation. She had never had the opportunity to savor him as she was savoring her stolen moments with Sam, to know the thrill of the inevitable.

She had just exited the elevator and was heading toward her own apartment when she noticed a pool of light seeping out from under Paul Rollins's door.

How odd. She could have sworn she turned out the light. Was it possible Deanna or Neal was in there? She had no desire to bump into either one of them, she was filled with the sight and sound of her hours with Sam and didn't want reality to intrude again.

Lord knew, Paul could afford the electric bill, if his art collection were any indication. She hesitated, then flipped to Paul's key on her key ring. She'd go in, take a quick look around, douse the lights and forget all about Paul Rollins's apartment. She'd had more than enough of it for one night.

The first inkling that all was not quite right came when the key didn't unlock the door. It didn't have to; the door was already unlocked. Sweat broke out on her forehead and around the bridge of her nose. She took her glasses off and jammed them in her coat pocket, then drew her hand across her brow with a jerky, nervous gesture.

"Damn it!" she whispered. How could she have been so clumsy, so stupid, as to leave the door unlocked. Paul seemed to hate her as it was; if her stupidity had cost him his art collection, she wouldn't be at all surprised if he contemplated murder.

She stepped into the large hallway that divided the living room from the rest of the apartment. Everything seemed fine. She continued to the bathroom, then to his bedroom. The rooms still had the vaguely monastic stamp she'd noticed when she was in there earlier. Her breathing slowed down closer to normal as she went back down the hall and headed for the living room.

Red hair, burning in the lamplight of the brass fixture that hung over the desk, caught and held her gaze. A wave of nausea crashed over her, and she grabbed onto the back of an angular chrome chair for support. Paul, his back mercifully toward her, was sitting on the Oriental carpet near the window, paging through a stock of manuscript pages that apparently had been stored in a wooden file box both she and Sam had overlooked earlier.

How long had the man been back from Brazil? He was supposed to be away for another four days. How close had he come to discovering her and Sam while they were searching his apartment?

She started to move closer to Paul, praying she'd know what to say when he turned around and cut her with those sharp eyes of his.

How the hell was she going to get out of this?

* * *

Jack, on the other hand, was totally oblivious of Sara's presence not twenty feet away from him. Paul's words had transported him away from this upwardly mobile Manhattan apartment and back to Philadelphia some twenty years earlier when Max's poor-little-rich-boy routine ran smack into Rollins's lower-middle-class reality. It would make compelling fiction.

As fact it was overwhelming. So overwhelming, in fact, that it wasn't until he felt a hand tap him on the shoulder that he had any idea there was another soul in the room with him.

"Paul?" The voice was soft, clear and slightly shaky.

Jack hesitated before turning around. "What?" he asked, trying to buy a few seconds' time before the inevitable.

"When did you get back? I thought you'd be gone until Friday."

Jack took a deep breath, swallowed hard, then turned around to face Sara Chance.

"Oh!" She took a step backward, stumbling over the chair by the tabletop desk. "Who are you?"

The look in her wide blue eyes was one of such fear that Jack stood up, knocking manuscript pages to the floor, and instinctively reached to steady her.

"Don't look so frightened," he said. "I'm not going to hurt you."

She was edging toward the telephone in the hall. "One step closer to me and I'll scream." She put her hands in front of her in a defensive gesture. "This building is crawling with security guards. One loud noise and they'll be up here in a flash."

He stopped in his tracks and raised his own hands in a gesture of defeat. "Believe me, Mrs. Chance, I'm not here to hurt anybody." He went to grab his press ID from his inside coat pocket, but her low gasp made him stop. "No guns," he said, smiling what he hoped was his best smile at her, "no weapons. I just want to give you some ID."

She nodded and picked up a large chrome objet d'art that rested on the floor near the entrance to the living room.

"Don't come any closer," she said, raising it overhead. "Just toss your ID on the floor near me."

He did. She reached into the pocket of her blue down coat, extracted an enormous pair of eyeglasses, slipped them on and picked up his press pass.

Her hand was shaking. As she bent her head to read the fine print on the press pass, he could see she took a long breath to steady herself. He watched her eyes skim line by line over the information.

John Peter Farrell
548 East 82nd Street

6'1" 156 pounds.   Rd hair   Brn eyes

Birth date: 4/15/59

"I have O-negative blood," he said suddenly from across the room.

She looked up. "That's not on the card."

"I know," he said. "I was volunteering the information."

"I don't think I'll be needing it."

"Maybe you won't," he said, gesturing toward the angular sculpture she still held aloft, "but if you bean me with that thing, I'll be a prime candidate for a transfusion."

"I'll keep that in mind." She took another look at the press card, then tossed it back at him. He caught it before it hit the ground. Suddenly, her expression changed. "I know you! You were one of the photographers at the Metropolitan the other day."

Jack nodded. "Guilty," he said, shooting a nervous glance at Sara's upraised hand. "I'm also the one your pal Berenger knocked over the day you two were—"

"You guys don't give up, do you?" Anger suddenly supplanted fear. He could actually see her jawline harden as she put the metal sculpture down. "Do you get some strange kind of charge out of harassing people?"

"Not people," Jack corrected, "stars."

"I'm not a star."

He twisted his neck and ran a finger along the inside of his collar. "Close enough. You were married to one."

"Maxwell is dead," she said, stepping closer to him, her slender hands gesturing angrily. "Can't you let him be?"

Jack shrugged. "I don't make the rules," he said. "I just play the game."

Sara's blue eyes were on fire. "Well, the game stinks." She backed away from him, heading once again for the telephone. "I'm going to call the police."

"Hey, come on!" Jack's voice went up half an octave. "I was just trying to earn a living."

Sara's eyebrows arched. "Really? Doing what you did usually earns someone five to twenty at Ossining."

He grinned. "Whaddya know? Sara Chance has a sense of humor."

She reached for the phone, which rested on a low table. "Give me one good reason why I shouldn't call the cops."

Jack took a deep breath. He might as well go for broke. "Because if you do, I'll tell Rollins you and Berenger broke in before I did."

She shook her head and picked up the phone. "Who'll believe you?" she asked, waving an enormous ring of keys at him. "I have keys; you don't."

She was really going to call the cops. Sweat broke out around Jack's hairline and across the bridge of his nose. He took five steps forward and grabbed her hand before she could finish dialing the number. "Why did you and Berenger break in here earlier, then?"

Her wide blue eyes grew even wider, and he saw a trace of fear, of despair. He felt a surge of pity for her but pushed it down.

"We didn't break in," she stammered, the phone dropping lifelessly from her right hand.

"I know Rollins is away," Jack pressed, "and I saw you and Berenger come out of here."

"I was bringing in the mail," she said, putting the phone back in its cradle. "Mr. Rollins is in Rio."

"You can do better than that, Mrs. Chance."

She turned on him, her blue eyes flashing with anger. "So can you, Mr. Farrell." Her voice held the sting of a whip. "At least I live in the Carberry. I'd say you were a long way from East Eighty-second Street right now."

Damned right, I am. "Just looking for a story," he said calmly.

"In another man's apartment?"

"It's all part of the job. I'm looking for answers."

"To what?" She crossed her arms across her chest. "My drug problem or my kinky sex life?"

"Whichever. I'm not fussy."

She glared at him. "Why don't you try finding out who's been spreading all these lies about me?"

His brain snapped into overdrive. Now they were getting someplace. "Any ideas?"

He could see part of her close down. "Oh, no," she said with a low, mirthless laugh. "I'm not going to help you ruin my life."

She didn't need to. The very fact she and Berenger had searched Rollins's apartment told him everything. He wished he'd had time to read all of the papers stacked beneath the desk; maybe they held some answers. So far all he knew about was Paul's loyalty to Max, his misgivings about Sara and the foundations Max's estate was bankrolling.

"It seems to me we're in something of a Mexican stand-off here," he said slowly, forcing his body language to remain casual, unthreatening. "We both have something to hide, and we don't trust each other." He grinned. "It could be a long night."

"I have plenty of time," she said calmly; however, he could see the strain in the tightness around her mouth. "Now let me ask you a few questions. Why did you pick Paul's apartment to search? I would've imagined you'd search mine."

"Looking for cocaine and nubile young men?" he asked, alluding to the offensive newspaper articles that had been appearing the past few days.

"Something like that." She watched him closely.

He ran a finger around the collar of his shirt. "The truth is I didn't know which door was yours, and since this one was unlocked, I decided to start here. Just the luck of the draw."

Those blue eyes of hers were fastened on him like magnets. "What would you have done if they were all locked?"

He shrugged. "Choose one, then unlock it."

"Picking locks is another of your talents?"

"Probably my major one."

"That seems an odd skill for a newsman."

"Relax," he said, grinning at the look on her face. "I came upon it honestly, if that's possible. I did the photos for a story on burglary prevention for *Family Circle* a few years ago, and one of the ex-cons we interviewed gave me a few pointers."

"I'm sure it's come in handy."

"Listen, Sara, you might not believe this, but I don't want to hurt you."

"Excuse me for being cynical, but you Fourth Estate types are not my favorite people at the moment."

She hesitated, then made a move toward the telephone once again. He saw his career crumbling around him like most of his dreams had. It was a tough world out there, and it was time she knew just how tough.

"Don't," he said in a low, measured voice. "You'll regret it." She looked frightened, but she held on to the phone. She had more guts than he figured. "Put down the phone, Sara, unless you want your picture and Berenger's on the front page of the *Post* tomorrow morning."

"You're lying." She lowered the phone a fraction. "You don't have any pictures of us."

"But I do." He could see that picture of Sara looking up into Berenger's eyes as clearly as if it were in front of him.

"I don't believe you."

"Do you want to take the chance?" he asked. "How would you like your boyfriend's name plastered across the *Enquirer* with yours?"

Bingo—the magic words. She put the phone down for the last time.

She looked close to tears. A part of him felt sorry for her, but another, larger part of him looked around the penthouse and figured she'd known the rules when she started playing the game.

"Get out," she said, her voice strangled with fear and anger. "Get out before I change my mind."

Jack picked up his coat from the floor and slid a few of the scattered pages from Paul's manuscript into a sleeve.

"Watch the morning paper," he said as he headed toward the apartment door. "There'll be a little message for you."

He just got the door closed behind him when he heard something slam against it, then shatter into a million pieces.

"Sorry," he said out loud as he waited for the elevator. He had the right to a bit of fame, too.

Sam kicked at one of the many satin covers on the bed in one of Leonard Klein's many guest rooms and held the phone closer to his ear. It must be his hearing. Sara couldn't have said what he thought she said.

"Okay, I'm taking a deep breath and counting to ten." He pulled the cord free of the nightstand and paced the room. "Give it to me again, will you?"

Again she raced through her speech like a high school kid in a public-speaking class, and again she said the same unbelievable thing. "Jack Farrell broke into Paul's apartment tonight."

"And you didn't call the cops?"

"And I didn't call the cops."

"No doubt about it," he said, sitting on the edge of the bed and forcing himself not to hurl the telephone out the window. "You're certifiable. Absolutely insane. Was it something in the Soave tonight?"

Her voice was subdued. "Don't you think you're over-stating the case a bit, Sam?"

"Overstating?" He stood up and resumed his pacing. "Lady, when I get around to overstating the case, you'll know about it. I'm still dealing with plain facts."

He could hear her take in a long gulp of air before she spoke. He knew he was being hard on her, but damn it! She was making one of the major mistakes of her life, and he wasn't about to watch her bring the sky down on her shoulders without registering his objections.

"I wish you'd cool off for a second, Sam, and think about the way it was," she went on. "I was caught red-handed in Paul's apartment—both of us were."

"Both of us?"

"Jack saw us leaving Paul's." She paused, allowing her words to take their full effect on him. "What could I do but play ball with him?"

Sam leaned against the windowsill and looked out at the illuminated darkness of Fifth Avenue far below. "Correct me if I'm wrong, but didn't you catch Farrell curled up with a book? If that's not getting caught red-handed, then I'm a one-eyed—"

"Sam." Her voice cut off one of his earthier expressions. "You're missing the point entirely. Jack and I were both caught—we both have something to lose."

Sam sank back down on the satin-covered edge of the bed. "One of you sure as hell has something to gain."

"Damn it!" Her voice was higher pitched, louder. "I hate the telephone. If I were with you right now, face-to-face, I know I could make you understand the way it was."

She repeated the same litany of how the police would never take her seriously as she had spouted before.

"I'd like to sit down and have a long talk with this Far-rell," Sam said when she paused for breath. "I've got a damned good right hook. I'd straighten him out."

"Don't say things like that, Sam. It scares me."

"You should be scared," he countered. "You're in way over your head, Paisley. This guy's out for glory."

"Can't you understand? He said he'd smear you on every front page. I couldn't let you get involved in this. I couldn't do that to you."

Sam's temper was moments away from erupting. If they were in the same room, he might have strangled her. "Now let me get this straight. He broke into Paul's apartment, and you're helping him to get away with it. Right?" She said nothing. "Is that it?" Still nothing. "Damn it, Paisley, answer me."

"Why should I bother? It seems you've got it all figured out already."

He slammed his fist down onto the soft surface of the bed. The mattress absorbed the blow and took away any satisfaction. "I thought we were in this together," he said, trying to keep his voice from being heard three boroughs away. "I thought this was our problem."

"You don't understand how awful it is to be hounded, Sam. If the press finds out about you, your reputation will be shot. Farrell will make sure of it."

"Screw my reputation," Sam exploded. "I don't give a damn about my reputation. You were just intimidated by that guy. That's all."

"He has pictures—"

"Bull. Did you ask to see them? Did you ask for negatives? Do you have any proof they even exist?"

"Well, no, but—"

"You could have stalled for time. Damn it, Paisley, you should have made him squirm."

"We're running out of time, Sam. You said so yourself."

There was a long and uncomfortable silence before Sam spoke again. "I thought the party was going to be our chance to observe Paul at work. I thought that was where I'd get my opportunity to do a little sleuthing."

"We'll still have the party, Sam."

"I suppose our filter-and-lens friend will be invited?"

"Don't be ridiculous."

"How do you know he won't crash it?" He could tell by her hesitation that she hadn't thought of that. He grinned. "Got you with that one, didn't I, Paisley?"

"What can I tell you, Sam? I don't have all the answers. I just know I can't stand this much longer." Her low sigh curled itself around his ear. "I want my own life back again."

"You should have thought of that before you married Maxwell."

"You should have thought of the consequences before you said that." Click.

"Sara?"

Nothing but the dial tone spoke back to him.

"Damn it!" He slammed the receiver back down on the cradle and stormed around the room, dragging his hand through his thick brown hair and wishing he had never given up smoking. He needed something as hot and angry and destructive as his mood to keep him from calling her back. The second his words were formed and already on their way to Sara, he'd known he'd gone too far, but he was too stubborn to pull them back, to soften their sting. In the deepest part of his soul, the part where he resented every year, every day, every hour of Sara's marriage to Maxwell Chance, he had meant to hurt her. He had meant to let her feel the hidden sting of his pain and hers, of all the moments they had lost.

"Son of a bitch." He wanted to break something, hear the satisfying crunch of splintering wood or the icy shatter of breaking glass. The only thing that kept him from giving in to his rage was that he was staying in another man's home, as another man's guest, and there was still enough of the gentleman left in him to keep him on this side of civilized behavior.

He headed for the temporary workroom in another part of the Kleins' apartment. He would call her. She was far too important—she'd always been important—for him to let pride or jealousy keep them apart. But first he had some very uncivilized aggressions to rid himself of before he made the call.

Sara had never hung up on a living soul in her life. Her working-class parents had instilled such rigid guidelines of social etiquette in her that she even listened all the way through recorded sales messages before hanging up. Rudeness just wasn't part of her vocabulary.

However, as she slammed the receiver down and listened to the satisfying noise it made, she had to admit that there just might be something to giving head to one's anger. Sam's attitude about her decision not to call the cops on Jack Farrell had so enraged her that if she'd had a better working vocabulary of vulgarities, she might have chosen to fry his ears with some choice language rather than abruptly terminate the conversation.

"It's my life, damn it," she said out loud as she stared at the phone and willed it to ring.

She was sick to death of taking orders, of checking her every move with a higher authority, a guardian, a jailer. She was sure Sam's reasons for doubting Jack's reliability were probably valid, but this was her life and her problem and if she screwed it up, then so be it. At least she'd made her own mistakes.

Great speech, Paisley, she thought, rubbing a hand across her eyes in a weary gesture. *Why didn't you make it to the man who counts?*

Sam had just stepped out of the shower the next morning and was trying to revive himself from a sleepless night when the front door chimes to Leonard's apartment, his current home, sounded. He hurried through the large apartment, wrapped the large white towel tightly around his middle and flung the door open.

"I wouldn't blame you if you slammed the door in my face, but I really hope you have better self-control than I." Sara, bundled to her eyebrows in coat, scarf and cap, stood on his doorstep. Only her large blue eyes gave any clue at all to her identity. "Say something, Sam. If I'm going to get turned out on my ear, please do it now, before I feel any more ridiculous than I already do."

Sam hiked the towel more firmly around his body as he looked at her. Right then he felt he had the market cornered in feeling ridiculous. He stepped aside and motioned her in with the hand that wasn't occupied with the towel. "Come in. I'm not exactly dressed for entertaining, but—"

Sara's eyes suddenly darted along his body, lighting for a moment on feet, legs, discreetly sliding over the towel and returning to his eyes. A slight flush stained her cheeks, and he grinned despite the anger he still felt. "Am I what you expected?"

She tugged off her cap and scarf and stuffed them into the pocket of her big blue coat. "I'm afraid my expectations about you never went this far, Sam."

If they hadn't been on such shaky emotional ground to begin with, he might have followed up on that remark with a few provocative comments about his own expectations of her, but it definitely was not the right time. Instead, he led her into the living room where she deposited her coat on the arm of a delicate brocade chair, then perched on the edge of the sofa opposite it.

"Have you had breakfast?" he asked, the polite host in his formal towel. "I was just about to—"

Her first smile teetered at the edge of her mouth. "I can see what you were just about to." She waved one slender hand in the general direction of the rest of the penthouse. "Finish your shower, Sam. I've always found it hard to talk to someone who has better legs than I have."

He managed a comic frown. "I'm not sure if that's a compliment or a put-down."

"Neither am I." She picked up a copy of *American Artist* from the glass coffee table and began to leaf through it. "Do what you have to, Sam. I'll wait."

By the time he finished changing into a pair of brown cords and a taupe sweater with sleeves pushed up to the elbows, Sara was in the kitchen fiddling around with the Silex coffee maker.

"I didn't think you were domestically inclined," he said as he took the glass bubble from her and fit it snugly into the bottom part of the coffeepot.

"You're wrong," she said, pulling out a shiny red bar stool from beneath the work counter and sitting on it. "I'm fascinated with cooking and all the other things that go along with running a home." She pushed her heavy dark hair off her face with her left hand. "I've just never had an opportunity to try my hand at any of them."

He adjusted the flame beneath the coffeepot, then leaned against the counter, arms folded across his chest, and watched Sara watch him.

"Well, Paisley?"

Sara had rehearsed her speech all night. She had repeated it over and over during the taxi ride from the Carberry to the Trump until the sounds became as meaningless as a mantra. Why was it so hard now for her to say what was on her mind and in her heart?

"I shouldn't have hung up on you," she began, fastening her gaze on his beautiful eyes and trying to push the vivid image of his muscular body draped in the bath towel from her mind. "That was a stupid, childish thing to do."

"You won't get an argument from me."

"What?"

Sam grinned. "It *was* a stupid, childish thing to do."

"You deserved it."

"So did you," he answered, "but I managed to restrain myself."

"I bow to your superior self-control." This wasn't going along quite as expected. "The least you could do is try to make this easier for me, Sam."

"Apologies are meant to be difficult. If they were easy, what would stop you from hanging up on me again?"

"If we were on the phone right now, I would hang up on you again." She glared at him. "Since when do you come on like a Sunday school preacher, anyway?"

"Must be my midwestern background rearing its head again."

"You don't have to look like you're enjoying this quite so much."

He bowed to her and turned away until only his back was visible. "Is this better?" he asked.

"Damn it, Sam. Turn around and listen to me, please. I've been rehearsing this speech for twelve hours now. Let me say it once and get out of here." She held her breath and waited, only relaxing when he turned around and resumed his spot, leaning against the counter.

He wasn't laughing anymore. Those beautiful eyes of his were as serious as she'd ever seen them. "I'm listening, Sara."

"We're not married, Sam. There's no commitment between us yet—" He started to say something, but she raised her hand to stop him. "An unspoken one, yes, but nothing tangible." *Nothing for me to base my decisions on.* "These newspaper articles, the break-in—everything that's happening is happening to me, to Sara Chance."

"Sara Paisley Chance," he interrupted.

"No, Sam, to Sara Chance. To Max's widow, not to the woman you want to know. It's my life I'm trying to recover, and ultimately these have to be my decisions. I may have made a mistake with Farrell, but I did it, and there's no backing out now." Once again she described the situation in Paul's apartment where the two would-be "burglars" found one another red-handed. "He's looking for his first big break," she said, thinking of his address in a not-too-great part of Manhattan. "He doesn't dare risk my calling in the cops."

"So you're saying his only interest is money?"

She frowned. "Of course. What else could it be?"

Sam dragged a hand through his still-damp hair. "You," he answered, watching her so closely she felt as if she couldn't breathe. "Sara. Just Sara."

She shook her head. "No," she answered. "And besides, I'm not his for the taking," she said. "I'm not anyone's." *Not anymore.*

He moved closer to her, pulling the air out of her lungs as he approached, making the December chill seep out of her bones as he neared.

"But what if a man asks, Sara Paisley?" His knees were pressed against hers, his body leaning down close to her as she tried to sway from him without tipping over on her perch. "What if a man were to ask?"

She put her hand up and rested it against his chest, trying to keep a distance between them, trying to regain her sense of balance. "I come with ghosts right now, Sam. I come with a whole baggage of ugliness and lies that I wouldn't wish on another human being." *Especially not on someone I love.*

"My shoulders are broad," he said, allowing her to regain the space that had been between them but keeping his fingers entwined in her hair. "I can support the weight."

She shook her head. "For a while, maybe. But it would take its toll—believe me, I know. I want to clear Sara Chance's name before I can remember how to be Sara Paisley." He said nothing. "Am I making any sense at all?"

"I want you, Sara," he said bluntly as the pressure of his fingers against her scalp increased pleasurably. "I want you in my bed and in my life. But I want all of you, and if the only way I can have all of you is to wait a little longer, so be it." He tugged at her hair, and her face tilted up toward his.

"Ah, you're a patient man, Sam Berenger," she said softly.

His mouth came closer to hers. She could smell the sharpness of peppermint on his breath, the clean warmth of his body. "For a little while longer," he said, then touched her lips briefly, fleetingly, with his own. "But even my patience has its limits. I can't wait to catch you between husbands, Paisley."

"That's not an original line," she managed. The touch of his lips had almost made her dizzy. "I think Rhett said that to Scarlett." She followed the curve of his jaw with her finger. "Besides, it was you who was attached years ago, Sam. Not I."

He kissed her again. This time it did make her dizzy. "That's true, Paisley. But the fact remains that life, unfortunately, has no intention of waiting for us to make up our minds."

"I know that," she said, thinking of Maxwell, of endings and beginnings. "I've made up my mind."

He moved away and looked so deeply into her eyes she felt as if she were being devoured. "And?"

How could he sound so unsure of himself? Hadn't she made her feelings obvious every time she whispered his name?

"Don't you know how I feel, Sam?" She took his hand and pressed it against her heart. "Can't you tell?"

His hand closed gently around her breast. She felt both powerful and dominated simultaneously.

"We need to be alone," he said.

"We are alone."

"Without time limits, without worrying about a knock at the door." The feel of his hand against her was making her dizzy. "Come away with me, Sara. Give us one night away from all of this."

"I can't." She covered the hand on her breast with her own. Thoughts of front pages and ugly gossip taunted her. "This is all I can give for now."

"All you can or all you will?"

"All I can. I told you before I would never come to you surrounded by ghosts and shadows, and I meant it."

"Will there be a time when you'll be able to?"

His unspoken question "Will I still be there?" hung in the air between them.

"The time will come," she said finally. "I won't ask you to wait forever, but—"

He cut off her words with a kiss that tore more deeply inside her heart than any knife ever could have. She belonged to him—she always had; she always would—in the same way that he belonged to her.

The shadows around her grew just a little bit fainter.

9

Sam had a lunch meeting up at the Metropolitan, so Sara walked home alone from his apartment. Sam wanted her to share his cab as far as the Carberry, but she had felt the need for fresh air and had refused. She stood on the corner of Fifth Avenue and Fifty-seventh Street for a few moments until Sam's taxi disappeared into the noon crowd, then she began strolling slowly up Fifth Avenue.

"Hey! Why doncha watch where you're goin'?" A woman pulling a metal shopping cart piled high with D'Agostino bags bumped against Sara and scowled as she passed by.

Lucky Sam, she thought. In little more than two weeks he'd be on his way from Fun City, headed toward the bucolic pleasures of New England. In another two weeks he'd be gone.

She tugged at her collar and pulled it up closer around her face against a gust of December wind and turned the corner to the Carberry. Now that the anniversary of Max's death was past, the fans didn't gather until midafternoon, so the street was quiet. However, Sara did notice Laurie, a friend of the girl who'd given the *Enquirer* that hideous story about making love to Max while Sara watched. Sara walked over to her.

"Laurie?" She bent down next to he skinny pale blonde who sat with her back against the metal gate, nose buried in the morning papers. "How are you?"

Laurie looked up. Sara had expected a flustered smile, the usual "I can't believe you're talking to me" response. Laurie, however, met her eyes head-on and said, "What do you want?"

Sara's nerves went on alert. "Is Joanne around?"

Laurie shook her head.

"Where is she?"

The girl shrugged. "She's gone away for a few days. How come?"

Sara's smile faded. "I have a few questions for her."

Laurie looked away for a moment toward the newspaper on her lap, then back at Sara. "What about?"

Sara adjusted the ring finger on her left glove. "What do you think, Laurie? That awful story she gave the *Enquirer.* That lie."

Laurie's face darkened. "That was no lie."

"You know better than that. Joanne didn't begin coming to the Carberry until after Max died. She never even met him once." She touched the girl's thin forearm, but Laurie pulled away. "Why did she do it?" She could see Laurie hesitate. "Was it for money?" Sara pressed. "Did she need money for drugs?" No response. "You can tell me." She reached out again and touched Laurie's arm.

This time Laurie leaped to her feet, waving the newspaper in Sara's face. "What do you care?" she yelled, bringing the doorman around to see what the commotion was about. "You've got all Max's money. You live in a penthouse—" She pushed the *Post* toward Sara. "You've even got another man already."

Sara took the paper, but she already knew what she'd find. There, on page 1, was a photo of her looking up at a man whose back was to the camera. Her face seemed lit from within, incandescent with love. It had been taken the day she met Sam at the Trump Tower. It had been taken by Jack Farrell.

Laurie grabbed the paper back from her and savagely ripped it with her bony hands. "'Max's Missus and Her Mystery Man,'" she mocked, reciting the headline. "'How Long Has This Been Going On?'"

"Laurie, I—"

Laurie spit on the ground near Sara's feet. "Don't tell me anything. I thought you were special. I thought Joanne never should have taken that money for telling the *Enquirer* those stories. I told her they were up to no good."

Sara's scalp tingled. "Who was up to no good? Who gave Joanne the money?"

"Forget it. Now I'm glad she did it." The pieces of shredded newspaper swirled around them in a gust of cold wind, and Laurie slapped them away with sharp, stabbing motions.

"Was it a reporter?" Sara asked.

The substitute doorman was approaching them. Laurie looked over at him.

"Laurie, you have to tell me," Sara urged, pulling the girl's attention back.

"Trouble, ma'am?"

Sara looked up at the uniformed giant. "I'm just trying to get some information from this young lady."

He looked down at Laurie and sneered. "Why don't you haul yourself out of here before I call the cops on you? I've had enough of you vermin hanging around out here." He motioned toward Sara. "Decent people live here. They don't need your kind loitering around."

"Let her be, Allen," she said to the doorman. "She's no trouble."

"You're being kind, ma'am." He turned toward Laurie and kicked the ratty blanket she'd spread out on the sidewalk. "Get out," he said. "I don't want to see your kind around here on my shift."

"Laurie—" Sara began.

Laurie picked up her blanket and her radio and looked back at Sara. "Too bad," she said with a smile that chilled Sara. "And I was just about to give you their names, too."

An obvious attempt to turn the screws and a successful one, at that.

The doorman waited until Laurie wandered away, then took the enormous brass key from his pocket and unlocked the gate for Sara.

"Don't let her kind bother you, Mrs. Chance," he said as he opened the gate for her and ushered her into the vestibule. "Not everybody believes that sh—pardon me, garbage they print in the *Post*."

Sara thanked him for his kind words, but at that moment all she could think of was that Jack Farrell hadn't been joking at all. That photo in the *Post* was only a message. This time he'd withheld Sam's name. Next time they wouldn't be so lucky. She knew how awful it felt to see baseless lies about yourself in the press; she would do anything to keep Sam safe from that.

She let herself into her apartment. She could smell something spicy and vaguely Italian drifting out from the kitchen. Sara tossed her coat over the living-room sofa and was about to head into the kitchen when Deanna's voice, coming from Sara's office, stopped her in her tracks.

"Sara! Would you come in here, please?"

Sara turned and walked toward her office. "Why so formal, Deanna?" she asked as she approached the door. "You sound like— "

"Sara, this is Detective Lenihan." Deanna, her face looking strained and tense, stood near the desk next to a short, husky man with thinning black hair. "He's from the police department."

Wings of fear began to flutter inside Sara's belly. Deanna kept tugging at the diamond at the base of her throat until Sara was sure the fine platinum chain would break. The detective, a look of studied nonchalance on his face, inclined his head in Sara's direction.

"Mrs. Chance."

Sara drew a deep breath and straightened her shoulders. "Detective." She glanced at Deanna but could read nothing but anxiety in the other woman's face. "What can I do for you?"

"We have something of yours." He dug into the pocket of his dark blue suit and pulled out the top portion of Max's Grammy Award.

She extended her hand for it, but Lenihan held tight. "Where did you find it?" she asked.

Lenihan looked over at Deanna, who was braced with her back against the rolltop desk, nervously toying with her diamond pendant. "Why don't you tell her?" he asked, shoving the award back in his pocket. "I have to call headquarters."

Sara snapped back to attention. "You can use the phone in the foyer," she said. The two women waited until Lenihan's heavy tread retreated down the hallway.

"What's going on here?" she demanded of Deanna. "Why all this cloak-and-dagger nonsense?"

"I've been going crazy all morning waiting for you to get here. Paul's out of town, and Neal's run out to Quogue for the day, and when that Lenihan showed up, I—"

"For heaven's sake, Deanna, will you tell me what in hell is going on?" Sara wanted to take the taller woman by the shoulders and shake her until she got an answer.

"They found the Grammy Award."

Sara gripped her hands together behind her back in an effort to control her rising anger. "That's the one thing I do know, Deanna."

Deanna hesitated, her eyes darting around the room. She looked like a convict on death row awaiting the call from the governor.

"Deanna?" Sara forced her voice lower, softer. "Please tell me before the detective comes back in."

"They found it during a drug raid in Harlem."

"What?"

"They had a drug raid late last night in East Harlem— remember that shooting gallery David Kennedy was found in a few years before he died?" Sara nodded. "They raided it and—"

"Found Max's Grammy," Sara finished for her. "Someone must have tried to sell it for drugs."

She heard a husky cough in the doorway and looked over to see Lenihan lumbering back into the room. "Is that your story?"

Sara narrowed her eyes. "It's not my story," she said calmly. "It's my guess."

He watched her so carefully she felt like a bacterium under a microscope. *Don't let him see he's making you a nervous wreck.*

"Pretty good guess," he said, settling down on the arm of the sofa and lighting a cigarette. "Ladies?" He held out the pack of Camels toward Deanna and Sara, who both shook their heads. "Are you always that good at guesswork, Sara?"

"Are you always this rude, detective?" It was probably the kiss of death, but Sara couldn't help herself. His attitude was driving her up the wall. "It hardly requires a Sherlock Holmes to figure, does it?"

He chuckled and took a long drag on his cigarette, his small gray eyes watching her through a cloud of smoke. "No, it doesn't," he acknowledged, casting a glance at Deanna, then back at Sara. "The clues add up pretty nicely, don't they?"

Sara nodded. "That they do. Someone stole Max's Grammy to support a drug habit. Where else would it turn up but in a shooting gallery?"

"Sara." Deanna's hand touched Sara lightly on the forearm. "Maybe you should wait until Neal gets back tonight before you say any more."

"I've already said all I need to," she answered, turning back to Lenihan. "The detective came to tell me the Grammy has been found. Right?"

Deanna said nothing, just went back to fiddling with the diamond around her neck in this new, and very uncharacteristic, gesture of hers.

Lenihan eased his bulk off the arm of the sofa and stubbed his cigarette out in one of the large marble ashtrays.

"Afraid it's not quite that simple, Mrs. Chance."

"You have to hold the Grammy for evidence?" She gestured toward his pocket. "You have to find the other half?"

Lenihan motioned for Deanna to explain.

"It—uh—it seems the girl who brought it in—"

"Joanne?" Sara broke in.

Deanna nodded. "It seems Joanne was looking for cocaine."

"I'm not surprised," Sara said. "That wasn't exactly Bloomingdale's she was in."

"Sara—" Deanna stopped and cleared her throat. "Sara, she said she was getting the coke for you."

The blood drained from Sara's head, and her legs grew wobbly. Deanna helped her to the chair behind the rolltop desk, then left the room to get water.

"I'll never get used to this," Sara murmured.

"To what?" Lenihan asked, leaning against the edge of the desk, watching her.

"To the lies. No matter how many times this happens, I never quite expect it."

"Things like this have happened before?" He flipped open a small notebook and began jotting things down.

Sara looked up at him. "Don't you read the papers?"

He nodded. "Sure. You get a lot of ink in them, Mrs. Chance. A lot of ink."

"I know. And you've probably believed every single thing, haven't you?"

"I don't believe nothing until I've got proof," he answered. "I've found it doesn't pay."

She accepted water from Deanna, who was back in the office. "You think this girl's story is true, don't you?"

Lenihan shrugged. "Beats me."

Deanna finally found her voice. "Why would Sara Chance have to lower herself like that?" She gestured toward the penthouse apartment. "Is this the home of a woman who needs to barter mementos?"

"Drugs do strange things to people," Lenihan replied laconically. "I could tell you stories—"

"Spare us," Deanna snapped. "If Sara wanted drugs, she wouldn't have to send some little groupie. She would just—"

"Deanna!" Sara didn't like the turn the conversation was taking.

"Something wrong, Mrs. Chance?"

Sara glared at him. "I just resent the implication that I could remotely be interested in drugs."

Lenihan scribbled a few words, then looked up at her. "Given your past associations..." His voice tailed off.

"If you're talking about my husband, he managed to get away from the stuff permanently."

"Lucky man." Lenihan didn't sound as if he were buying any of it. Suddenly, Sara felt guilty, and for no reason at all.

"I don't use drugs."

"Good for you." Lenihan's smile was as unpleasant as his manner. "I don't recall asking."

"It needed to be said," she answered. "I wanted it on record."

The intercom beeped twice, a sign that Mrs. Raines had lunch ready. Sara asked Deanna to go to the kitchen and explain what was delaying them. Deanna left reluctantly, casting a few glances over her shoulder as she went out the door of the office.

"She looks nervous," Lenihan remarked as Deanna disappeared down the hallway.

"We're not used to entertaining the police around here," she said. *No matter what you think.* Lenihan was perched on the edge of the sofa like an overweight parakeet. She decided to exercise one of the perks associated with being "lady of the manor" and sat up straight behind the desk as if this interlude were nothing more than business as usual.

"Don't you think this whole thing is just a bit absurd?" she asked, forcing herself not to fiddle with the letter opener on the desk. She made her hands rest calmly, innocently, on the blotter before her. "Take a look around you, Detective Lenihan. This is not the home of a woman who needs to hock trinkets for money."

Lenihan eased himself up from his spot on the sofa and made a leisurely tour of her office. He ran a ragged fingernail across the deep veneer of her desk, shot an assessing eye over the sculptures and paintings, the Persian rug hanging on the far wall.

"It must take—what? A few hundred grand a year to run this place?"

Sara shrugged airily. "I would have no idea, detective. My people take care of those details." She hated the snobbish way she sounded, but she knew it was what it would take to impress Lenihan that she was indeed comfortable with wealth.

"You have a house—where?" He waited for her to supply the town, but she stubbornly maintained her silence. "Amagansett? The Hamptons?" He took another drag on his cigarette. "Quogue?"

"Quogue."

"It's a funny thing," he said, flipping again through his notebook, "but the town hall doesn't list you as the owner."

She repositioned herself on the chair.

"Town hall lists the StopHunger Foundation, Inc. as owner, as overseen by Paul Rollins." He flipped the notebook closed. "Did you know that?"

She brushed his words aside. "I never did understand the way things were done in business," she said with a chuckle. "Tax shelters, estate problems—you know how it is."

"No, Mrs. Chance, I don't know how it is. I live in a two-room apartment in Sunnyside." He stubbed out his cigarette. "I damned well don't know how it is."

Anxiety hammered at her from behind her eyes. Sweat popped out on the back of her neck. The title on the house was news to her. She had no idea what game Lenihan was playing with her and no desire to find out the rules.

He sat on the edge of the desk, close to Sara. She wanted to move away but knew that in his eyes it would be a tacit admission of guilt. She took a deep breath and stayed put.

"I did a little investigating before I came over here," he said, watching her closely. "It seems you don't own a damned thing."

She laughed. "I'm afraid you have your facts wrong, detective. I'm quite a wealthy woman."

"Correction, Mrs. Chance. Maxwell left the bulk of his estate to two foundations: the antihunger one and another to save the wild mongoose or something."

"FAWN," she said automatically. "Foundation for Animal Welfare, North America."

He slowly looked around the room as if assessing its worth, then back to Sara. "It seems to me that without your American Express card, you wouldn't have a plug nickel of your own."

"This is ridiculous." She got to her feet and smoothed her blouse back into the waistband of her skirt. "Anyone with eyes would see that I hardly want for a thing." She started pointedly toward the door. "If there's nothing else, detective . . ."

He grinned and got up. "There's nothing else right now," he said, following her out into the hall. "But if I were you, I'd be a little more discreet when I go looking for my kicks. Fence the object first, then get the—"

"I advise you to stop right there."

Both Sara and Lenihan started at the sound of Neal's voice coming from the living room. Neal seemed totally in control, something Sara hadn't seen since Deanna moved in with him nearly two years ago.

"I'm Neal Travis," he said, approaching Lenihan, but not offering to shake his outstretched hand.

"Lenihan, NYPD. Are you her legal counsel?"

Neal shook his head. "I'm Mrs. Chance's personal adviser and coordinator of FAWN, and I highly recommend

that you stop before you say something that just might find
you in court.''

Lenihan was not easily intimidated. He plunged his hands
into the pockets of his suit and looked at Neal and Sara,
who stood before him.

"You think you run a pretty tight operation, don't you?''
He was barely able to conceal his disgust with them and
everything they represented. He directed his next words to
Sara. "I'd take a look into those foundations if I were you.
A hell of a lot of money is going in, but not too much is
coming out."

Sara's head swiveled immediately in Neal's direction. Neal
didn't react to Lenihan's words; he merely showed the detective to the door.

"Call before you come next time, officer, or your supe-
riors will hear about it.''

Lenihan gave a mock-bow toward Sara. "By the way,
Mrs. Chance, you take one helluva picture."

Neal slammed the door shut on Lenihan's amused face.
Sara's bones rattled from it.

"Are you all right?" Neal hurried over to Sara and put his
arm around her.

A few months ago she would have collapsed gratefully
against him and allowed herself to be ministered to, taken
care of; now, however, she didn't feel the need.

"Where did you come from?" she asked, removing herself from his embrace. "Deanna said you were out at Quogue.''

"I got as far as Jamaica," he said, smiling at Deanna,
who had just entered the room from the kitchen, "when I
realized I'd left some of my papers at home."

"Lucky, wasn't it?" Deanna asked, giving Neal a quick
kiss. "Was that disgusting man rough on you, Sara?''

Sara shrugged. "Not rough, exactly," she said, thinking
of some of the detective's remarks. "Unpleasant might be
a better word.''

She noticed a quick look shoot between Neal and Deanna.

"You would have been proud of her, Deanna. She was really putting him in his place when I stepped in."

Sara pushed a lock of hair off her cheek. "Do I get a gold star for it?" She sounded hard and cynical. Not herself at all.

Neal and Deanna stared at her.

"Oh, please," she mumbled. "Forget I said that. I guess I'm just feeling a little rattled right now." The truth was Lenihan had hit home with a number of his remarks about just how disenfranchised she really was, and the truth hurt. Perhaps her prenuptial agreement was more all encompassing than she had believed.

"He was an obnoxious ass," Deanna said, drawing Sara's arm through her own and leading her toward the kitchen. "The man obviously had some kind of ax to grind, and he chose you for the whetstone." She patted Sara's hand. "By the way, what picture was he talking about?"

Sara took a deep breath. "I'm on the front page of the *Post*. Again."

Neal muttered a curse. "What now? Group sex or wild drugs?"

"Neither," Sara said. "Just a photo of me."

"Alone?" Deanna asked.

"I was with a friend." What was the matter? She felt more uncomfortable with their questions than with Lenihan's.

"Anyone we know?" Neal asked.

"Your friend from the old days?" Deanna offered.

Sara had to fight to keep her nerves under control. "No one you know," she answered as they sat around the dining-room table, "and yes, my friend from the old days. Now could we please drop the subject? I'm getting indigestion, and I haven't eaten yet."

Neal and Deanna kept up a cheerful conversation during lunch, but Sara was quiet. She couldn't stop thinking about the Grammy and the shooting gallery in Harlem and the fact that, viewed through Lenihan's eyes, it didn't seem all that unlikely that she would resort to such a thing. He knew so much about her—in some instances, more than she knew herself—and he probably knew she came from a background much like his own, a background where there had never been enough money.

Neal and Deanna's conversation rose up and around her but never really penetrated. Time was passing too quickly. Farrell's "message"—the photo of her with Sam—had undermined her faltering sense of security. She had thought him a liar, a man who would say anything to get ahead; however, his producing the picture had given him credibility. He was hungry for success, and obviously he saw Sara Chance as his meal ticket. Her party—the party on which so much of her future rested—was in less than a week, and a few days after that Sam would be leaving for Maine.

Now, more than ever, she doubted she would ever be free enough to join him.

After lunch Sara excused herself and went to her bedroom to lie down, ostensibly to recover from Detective Lenihan's unexpected visit. Instead, she locked herself in her room and immediately picked up the telephone and tried to place a call to Sam, but with no luck. Lenihan's visit had done anything but fatigue her; instead, she was filled with a sickening kind of nervous energy.

As much as the detective's veiled accusations had angered her, a lot of what he had to say hit home with a particularly hard punch. When you got down to the bare-bones fact of the matter, she was living penniless in the midst of splendor. Hadn't she and Sam had a discussion a while back that touched on the same thing? That time she had been able to dismiss it as not terribly important. This time, however, she was beginning to see exactly how alone, how vulnerable, her position was. She'd stepped from her mother's protection to her husband's without the necessary step in between. When she was twenty-two, she was more than willing to hand responsibility over to another. She was no longer twenty-two. She had to be responsible for herself, and that meant understanding her financial situation.

Finally, because there was no way to avoid it and—even more important—because the time had come to deal with it, she pulled out a pad and pen and began the process of listing her assets. The list began with her jewelry and ended with the house in Brazil. She looked at her scribbled note and chuckled softly.

4BR, EIK, formal dr. 2 1/2 baths, fpl, pool, great view of beach. Must sell quickly: owner moving to New England.

She knew she still had the jewelry. But with Paul in Rio de Janeiro so often lately doing who knew what, she had to pray that she still owned the house.

"Not bad." Charlie Perez tossed the morning edition of the *Post* down on the desk. "Where'd you take it?"

Jack grinned at the older man whose envy was turning his brown eyes green. "Professional secret," he said, winding a spool of microfilm tape and slipping it back into its box.

"Ever hear about professional courtesies?" Charlie grinned. "I wouldn't mind sharing some of my secrets."

"Like hell." Jack laughed and pushed the microfilm boxes back into their slots in the cabinet next to him. All over town people were buzzing about Sara and her mystery man, and the credit line Photograph/Jack Farrell had been zipped across AP, UPI and Reuter's News Service wires. If this was fame, he could take more of it. A hell of a lot more.

Charlie lit up a cigar. "At least tell me who the guy was. You know I'll find out sooner or later."

"Forget it." Jack shoved his notebook in his back pocket. "Did you help me out on the Prince-Charles-at-the-UN story? I still think you're the one who punctured my tires so I'd miss the press conference."

"Me?" Charlie took a drag on his cigar. "What can I say, Farrell? I'm deeply wounded." He stubbed the barely smoked cigar out in an overflowing ashtray and stood up.

"Are you going to the reception at the Plaza for the Olympic athletes?"

"I didn't know anything about it."

Charlie tapped his knuckles on the desk and headed for the door. "Now you do," he said over his shoulder. "Three o'clock in the Terrace. Catch you later."

Jack stared at the door for a full ten seconds. Amazing. Just a few days ago he was the struggling kid, to be patronized and placated. Now, thanks to one hot picture, he was in with the biggies. It would take some getting used to.

However, right now he had no time to waste on Olympic has-beens. He'd spent the whole morning reading everything in the file about Maxwell Chance and the charitable foundations set up after his death. The Foundation for Animal Welfare, North America, nominally directed by Neal Travis, was based in Vancouver, Washington State. Stop-Hunger, directed by Paul Rollins, was in South Philadelphia. Neither one showed any activity. That struck him as odd. What better way to counteract the rotten coverage Sara had been getting than with a nice flow of press releases on the do-gooder work her charities were doing?

But there was one thing that was stranger still. Sara had mentioned that Paul Rollins was in Rio de Janeiro. Thanks to a long-standing relationship with an airlines reservationist he'd met at Maxwell's Plum, Jack had been able to find out that Paul Rollins hadn't gone to Rio at all. Patty had checked flights in and out of Rio from the metro area for the past two weeks, and Rollins's name was nowhere to be found. It was, however, found on another manifest.

Paul Rollins was in Vancouver.

All along Jack had felt there was a story, a big story, beneath the obvious one. Young widow on hard times was great for the *Post* and the *Enquirer.* Young widow fronting a phony charity? That's the stuff careers were made of.

Sara spent the better part of the afternoon trying to reach Sam. Finally, her restlessness escalated to such a pitch that she had to get up, had to get out of that room and away from her thoughts about Lenihan's visit, the house in Rio and her lack of money before it drove her completely crazy. She changed into jeans and a sweater and went into her office to try to do some work on the notes for Max's biography.

Deanna was sitting at the desk.

"Oh, hi," the red-haired woman said, looking up from a stack of papers on her lap. "I thought you were dead to the world in there."

Sara shook her head and poured herself a cup of black coffee from the carafe on top of the file cabinet. "I tried," she said, "but every time I closed my eyes, I saw Lenihan and that awful face of his." She shivered "There was something so menacing about that man…" Her voice trailed off, and she took a sip of hot coffee.

Deanna nodded in agreement and got up from the chair so Sara could sit down. She took the rocking chair to the right of the rolltop desk. "Neal is looking into the whole mess right now," Deanna said, looking calmer than Sara had seen her since Lenihan's appearance. "He says there's no way you can be implicated just because the Grammy showed up during the drug raid."

"I hope not," Sara said, "but he made it seem pretty serious."

"Of course," Deanna continued, looking away from Sara for a moment, "Lenihan did want to know why you never reported the Grammy as being stolen."

"What did you tell him?"

"Now that I think about it, I probably shouldn't have, but I told him you didn't feel the police department would take you seriously."

Deanna looked both upset and apologetic, but it didn't make Sara feel any better. As if the bad press she'd been getting weren't enough, Deanna had to make it sound like Sara was a holdover from the sixties with an antiauthority complex. No wonder Lenihan had been on the defensive with her.

"I wouldn't blame you if you kicked me out of here."

Sara sighed. "No point in worrying about it, is there, Deanna?" She took another sip of coffee. "I have a feeling Lenihan had a few preconceived notions of his own. He probably wouldn't have liked me if I'd turned out to be St. Joan of Arc."

"Just be happy he didn't show up with a book of matches." Sara laughed at Deanna's remark, and Deanna seemed to relax slightly. At least she had stopped fiddling with that diamond pendant of hers.

"So what's up?" Sara asked. She didn't want to be rude, but she did want to get the idea across to Deanna that it was her office and she felt like being alone in it.

Deanna waved a sheaf of papers in front of her. "Party plans. We've started getting the RSVPs back."

"And?"

"And we're getting a lot of 'sorry, buts.'"

Sara's shoulders sagged a little. "From my old crowd or from Max's?"

Deanna hesitated. "Both, actually. They claim family plans and previous engagements, but—"

"But I'm bad news right now, and they don't want to find themselves in the *Enquirer,* right?"

"Afraid so."

Deanna looked genuinely sorry, but that didn't make Sara feel one bit better. The fewer people who showed up at the party, the more Sam would stand out. She bent her head and rubbed her temples, trying to ease the dull throb that had just begun.

Deanna stood up and collected her papers. "Need an Excedrin?" she asked.

Sara shook her head and looked up at the tall redhead. "Thanks for the offer," she said, "but I think even Excedrin couldn't cure this headache."

"I have something stronger in my room. Let me get it." Deanna stood up.

"No, thanks, I'll be all right," Sara replied.

"The party will be fine," Deanna said as she headed for the door. "Christmas parties always manage to bring their own surprises." She flashed one of her glamorous smiles at Sara. "Don't worry."

Sara watched as the woman closed the door behind her. Don't worry? Easy for her to say.

It was almost midnight by the time Sara finally got through to Sam on the phone.

She began speaking the second she heard him say hello. "Oh, thank goodness! I was afraid you'd been mugged or kidnapped or—"

His warm laugh filled her mind. "Don't I even rate a hello before you start?"

She chuckled and leaned back against the pillows. "Hello," she said softly. "I've missed you."

His voice grew more intimate. "Good," he said. "That's the way it should be. Now what's all this talk about muggings and kidnappings?"

"Just an overactive imagination at work," she said, closing her eyes and summoning up his face, strong and handsome, before her. "Pay no attention. Did everything go all right at your meeting?"

He groaned. "The meeting went fine," he said, "but the rest of the day was shot to hell." He explained about a foul-up with the house in Maine. "I'll have to fly up there and straighten it out."

"Sam, no!" Her voice slid up an octave. "The party— you have to be here."

"No problem," he said. "But I have to take a flight out tomorrow morning for Bangor."

"You'll be back in time?" There was no way she could get through it without him.

"I promise, Paisley." He paused. "Anything new on your side?"

She told him about the run-in with Lenihan.

"How do you feel?"

"Well," she said slowly, "I've been doing a lot of thinking since he left."

"I can imagine."

She took a deep breath. "You know, much of what he said was true. I really own only the clothes on my back and the house in Rio. That's a frightening thing for a twenty-seven-year-old woman with no job skills and no family."

"That's nothing new, Paisley." Sam's calm voice helped to quiet her nerves. "You told me that that day at the Metropolitan."

"I know, I know." She pushed her hair off her face with her left hand. Her wedding ring caught a strand and pulled it from her scalp. "But somehow it never seemed quite so frightening as it did this afternoon. When Lenihan said it, it made me realize just how precarious my position really is."

"And?"

"I'm going to sell the house in Rio." She wished he were there beside her so she could see his face "Sam? Did you hear me?"

"I heard you." He sounded careful, cautious. "What does it mean exactly?"

She hadn't thought that far ahead. "It will give me independence from Max's estate, for starters."

"Eliminate one of the shadows?" His voice caressed hers.

"Yes," she managed, finding herself torn between reality and the sensuous thrill his voice had given her.

"I'm going to hold you to that," he said. "Our time is coming, Paisley. We've waited long enough."

Sara and Deanna were sitting in Sara's office working on some of the party details for the caterer the next evening when Paul, rumpled and tired and decidedly not tan, came in.

Deanna rushed up to kiss her brother. "So the traveler is home from his travels!" She wiped a smear of bright lipstick from his pale cheek. "When did you get in?"

Sara watched while Paul, usually affectionate toward his sister, didn't return the embrace. His eyes, instead, were fastened on Sara. "A few hours ago." His voice sounded gravelly with fatigue.

Sara forced herself to smile at him. "What took so long?" she asked, twirling her pen between her fingers. "Customs delay?"

One of his eyebrows arched for a second, then slid back to its normal position. "You know how it is with South American flights these days," he answered smoothly. "They're always watching for contraband."

Deanna gave him another hug, then stepped away to inspect his appearance. "You look tired." She planted her hands on her slender hips. "Where's the tan, Rollins? No one goes to Rio and comes back paler than when he left."

"You don't get tan in an office building, Deanna."

How odd, Sara thought. She had never seen him so uncomfortable before, especially not with his sister. Deanna offered to get him a cup of coffee, and Sara could almost swear that he breathed a sigh of relief after his sister's tall, shapely figure disappeared from the room.

He folded his lanky frame into the armchair near Sara's desk. "I saw Neal a few minutes ago," he said, linking his fingers loosely in front of his face. "He told me what happened with that detective. I'm sorry."

She must be hallucinating. He actually did look as if he were sorry. "Don't be," she said, attempting a jovial tone. "You didn't call the cops on me, did you?"

He shook his head. "No, Sara, I didn't." A series of expressions flickered across his long and narrow face, and for a second she was reminded of Jack Farrell and how the young photographer might look in another ten years. "Has this detective contacted you again?"

She tapped the desk blotter with the end of her pen. "He called this morning to ask me again why I didn't report the robbery."

"What did you tell him?"

"The truth. That I didn't think the NYPD was terribly interested in petty larceny."

Paul lowered his hands and leaned forward, his elbows digging into his bony knees. "Sara, I—"

Deanna came hurrying into the office like a red-haired whirlwind. "Here's your coffee, Paul," she said, putting a small tray down on top of the low file cabinet. She turned to Sara. "I also took some chicken out of the fridge—I hope you don't mind—and a few pieces of rye bread."

Paul nodded his thanks and began gnawing on a chicken leg. Deanna perched on the edge of the sofa to his left. "Are you back to stay?" she asked. "Will you be here for the party on Monday night?"

He wiped his mouth with the paper napkin Deanna had provided. He looked from his sister to Sara. "Party? What party?"

"I'm having a Christmas open house." Sara hesitated, waiting for some reaction. "I'm inviting all the people who used to come back when Maxwell was alive." She forced another smile in Paul's direction. "You're officially invited."

He nodded. "Thanks, but are you sure this is such a hot idea? You haven't been exactly getting the greatest press these days, Sara."

"If I wait until I start getting good press again, Paul, I'll be ten years dead. I think it's high time I got started with my life again. I've got to move forward."

Maybe she needed to have her glasses changed, because for a second there she thought she saw understanding in Paul's eyes and something very close to anger in Deanna's.

Ridiculous. Wasn't it the other way around?

10

"Please, not a blizzard." From her living-room window, Sara peered down at the street far below and groaned. "Blizzards are supposed to wait until after Christmas, not before."

Deanna, busy making a checklist of the silver and crystal before the caterers arrived to set up, walked over to Sara and looked over her shoulder at the swirling snow. "Don't worry," she said, giving Sara a pat on her shoulder. "It's already after five, and we don't have any accumulation to speak of."

"But the party starts at nine. We could be snowed in by then."

Deanna laughed and went back to her inventory work. "Sara, for heaven's sake! They only forecast flurries."

Sara tore herself away from the window. "One man's flurries are another man's blizzard." So many of the invitees had "regretfully declined" that she was almost afraid the guest list would consist of Neal, Deanna, Paul, Sam and herself. That thought alone was enough to make her stomach tilt sideways.

"This is New York City, Sara. If New Yorkers can function during a transit strike, they can make it to a penthouse Christmas party during a snowstorm. Trust me."

Sara muttered something about trust being a highly overrated emotion, and Deanna laughed. Sara went back to the window and continued to stare morosely at the falling snow. All she'd been able to think of was Sam up there in the wilds of Maine. What if he got snowed in? What if he developed plane trouble? What if the airports were closed due to weather? The "what ifs" were endless and pointless. She'd set this whole party into motion, and it was too late now to stop the process.

The doorbell rang, and Deanna admitted the entourage from the catering service: chefs and maids and butlers and a myriad of boxes and carts and bags of food that suddenly littered every available surface in the apartment. There seemed to be no room at all for Sara, so she disappeared into her bedroom, locked the door behind her and set about trying to conjure up a holiday mood.

The caterers, bless them, had had no trouble at all creating holiday splendor where none had existed before. Sara, dressed, coiffed and fully made up an hour before necessary, drifted through the quiet apartment, relishing the Christmas magic. Deanna had disappeared around six-thirty to set about doing all the things a woman does before a gala party. A little after seven both Neal and Paul had taken their leave to do, Sara supposed, whatever men do before a special occasion.

She could hear the catering staff milling about in the kitchen and the servants' quarters adjacent to it. Occasionally one, not yet in uniform, would hurry through the apartment with a repolished piece of silver or a freshly washed crystal goblet, positioning the item just so on one of the huge buffet tables.

Sam had called around six o'clock to tell her his plane had landed safely at La Guardia and he'd get to her apartment by eight-thirty. Despite her belief that a great deal rested on the outcome of the party, Sara felt at peace, able to enjoy the Christmas beauty around her.

Boughs of fresh holly, the leaves shiny green and the berries an impossible shade of red, were draped around the large windows in the living room. Armfuls of deliciously scented pine covered the mantelpiece. Sara herself had arranged tiny white lights around the edge of the mantel, and they twinkled like captured stars. She'd even picked out a small Christmas tree from a vendor over on Third Avenue that now graced the entrance hall, decorated the old-fashioned way with tinsel and garland and scores of colored ornaments.

She checked the clock in the hallway. Sam would be there in ten minutes. If it weren't for the fact that another vile story about her supposed involvement with drugs—thanks, no doubt, to Detective Lenihan—had hit the papers that morning, she would have actually been happy.

She went back into her room to check on her hair and makeup. There would be time enough later to be happy. Lord willing, there would be a whole lifetime to be happy with Sam. Right now the most important thing was to bring an end to this madness.

"Ah, Sara," Sam said fifteen minutes later, "I've never seen you more beautiful."

Sara smiled at him, her delicate beauty glowing like the lights on the Christmas tree. He found it hard to tear his eyes from her. She was wearing something soft and shimmery, the color of moonlight and stars, and she seemed so lovely as to be almost unreal.

"Stop looking at me like that," she said as she handed him a glass of champagne. "I do know how to dress like an adult when I have to."

"Evidently." They clicked glasses. "This is a far cry from sweatshirt and jeans, Paisley."

"It is a marvelous dress, isn't it?" she asked, sipping her champagne and spinning gracefully around so he could admire her outfit. "I found it the other day at a little boutique at the Trump, and I couldn't resist." She took another sip of champagne and smiled wryly. "Have to enjoy that American Express card while I still can."

Before Sam could respond, they heard the sound of bells jingling in the hallway and then a high-pitched woman's voice calling out, "Merry Christmas, everyone. The Three Wise Persons have arrived!"

He looked toward Sara "What the—"

"This is it," she said softly. "Here they come."

Sam could feel the hairs on the back of his neck rise in anticipation. He hadn't felt as tense since his tour of duty in Vietnam. A rather nondescript man with a genial face and a full head of dark blond curls entered the room first, followed by two very tall, very slim red-haired people. One of them looked enough like Jack Farrell to be his older brother; the other didn't look like anyone's brother. She was a knockout.

The woman was wearing something dark green and silky, and she used her hands when she spoke the way other women use their eyes. She hugged Sara and whispered something to her and laughed, but all the while her hazel eyes were fastened on Sam. His anxiety level went up another notch.

Sara walked over to him and took his hand, leading him over to where the two men and the woman stood. "Sam, I'd like you to meet my friends." Sara pointed first to the shorter man: "Neal Travis." The Farrell look-alike: "Paul Rollins." The woman: "Deanna Rollins, Paul's sister." She looked up at Sam, and gave him a comforting smile. "This is Sam Berenger."

Neal Travis was just starting to say something—the usual great-to-meet-you kind of party talk—and Sam had extended his right hand when Deanna walked up to him, smelling of Joy perfume and champagne, and embraced him. Her slender body was damned deceiving, because she hugged him tightly enough for him to know she had full breasts beneath her silky dress.

"So you're the man from the past our Sara has been hiding from us." Deanna offered her cheek for the obligatory social kiss. She glanced over at Sara, who stood between Neal and Paul, looking as uncomfortable as Sam felt. "I must say, he's been worth the wait, Sara."

Sam half expected Travis, Deanna's lover, to show a hint of jealousy, but he only stood there, sipping champagne and looking amused. It was Paul Rollins who seemed annoyed.

"Why don't you let the man take a deep breath, Deanna?" He looked at Sam, a slight smile on his face. "My sister's always been the shy type."

"Oh, don't listen to him." Deanna moved away from Sam. "He's the repressed one in the family." She tossed her head, and Sam's eye was drawn to a large and lovely diamond nestled on a fine chain at the base of her throat. "Not me," she said with a lazy grin. "I don't believe in repression or worry."

Neal finally staked his claim. "The woman lies," he said, turning a charming smile on Sara and Sam. "You should see her when her Bloomingdale's bill comes in. She does plenty of worrying." He put his arm around her shoulder.

His easy words dispelled the awkwardness that had been building, and they fell into a more normal pattern of conversation. It wasn't until Sara and her friends/employees began greeting arriving guests that Sam had a chance to step back and observe. He was a man who trusted his instincts. Again he thought of that long-ago time in Vietnam; there, trusting his instincts had saved his life. Maybe age and civilization had taken its toll, because he found it hard to believe his instincts could possibly be right this time.

He sipped his second glass of champagne and looked across the yawning expanse of living room at Deanna Rollins, whose hair wreathed her head like fire. Her eyes met his, and she raised her glass. He couldn't help it, but he had the distinct impression he was looking at the face of the enemy.

The elderly actor was explaining something about SAG or AFTRA or some other incomprehensible acronym, and Sara could only pray she was inserting her "Oh, reallys" in the right spots. Her full attention was focused across the room where Deanna seemed to be engaging Sam in a little long-distance flirting that made the champagne Sara was drinking taste like vinegar.

"Sara?" Paul Rollins, a glass of Perrier in his hand, was at her side. "May I see you a minute?"

She nodded, then looked back at the elderly actor. "Would you excuse me, Morris?"

Morris smiled and redirected his monologue toward a middle-aged cellist on his left.

She followed Paul into the hallway. "What's up? Have we run out of champagne already?"

"I have to leave."

"What?" She had to force her voice level down. "What do you mean, you have to leave? You just came back!"

"Something came up."

"Where are you going?" The shadows thickened around her, and she felt as if she were suffocating in them.

"Just a little business trip," he said. "Nothing to worry about."

"Rio again?" *Please, not Rio,* she thought. *Not when I'm so close.* He shook his head, and she sighed in relief.

"Sara, listen to me. I want you to be extremely careful while I'm gone. Stick close to home. And if anyone asks, say I've slipped down to the Bahamas for the holidays with a new woman."

The man was a snake. "What about Deanna? She's going to wonder where her brother's disappeared to."

The look he gave her made her shiver. "Deanna knows all about sexual urgency. She won't ask any questions."

"I don't know." If he left, her chances for a quick resolution to her problem would leave with him. "Doesn't it seem a little tacky—leaving home and hearth for the holidays?"

He laughed. "Ah, little Mrs. Sara. Ever the optimist. Not all of us have eggnog in our veins."

She remembered Deanna's feelings about the holidays. "It must run in your family. Your sister doesn't have a great deal of Yuletide spirit, either."

Again that strange, unfathomable look.

"Just remember what I said, Sara. Stay put."

"Paul, I really need more of an explanation than this—"

The discussion was over. Paul was gone before she had time to finish her sentence.

She hurried back into the living room to speak to Sam, but she kept getting waylaid by guests who still saw Sara as a key to the glamour they had once been privy to. She tried to be polite, but her eyes kept straying around the large room. She saw Sam standing with his back against the bar, effectively blocked from making eye contact with Sara by Deanna Rollins. Neal was slumped on one of the chrome-edged sofas.

Sam's face was only partially visible, and she wasn't sure whether or not he was looking for rescue. Actually, it didn't matter. She was going to rescue him whether he liked it or not.

Finally, an hour after Paul's departure, Sara made her way over to where Sam, Deanna and three of Deanna's friends from who knew where were chatting.

"Well," Sara said, casually linking her arm through Sam's and taking a sip of his champagne, "can I get into this top-secret discussion or is it off limits?"

Deanna's eyes glittered like the diamond that rested at the base of her throat. "What do you say, Sammy? Should we let Sara in on our secrets?"

Sam looked incredibly uncomfortable, but Sara was not feeling particularly charitable at the moment. "Yes, Sammy, should you let Sara in on your secrets?"

Sam squirmed visibly, as if his shirt had suddenly grown too tight. "I haven't been called Sammy since I was in first grade."

One of Deanna's friends, a small blonde, laughed. "He's certainly evasive, isn't he? Are you sure you weren't in the diplomatic corps, Sam?"

"Positive." His eyes sought Sara's. He smiled, but she could see the apology behind it. "We've been talking about my career," he explained. "Deanna was very interested in how I got started."

"Restoring furniture is an unusual way to make a living in this day and age," Deanna said, her hazel eyes resting on Sara. "Especially for someone as—" her eyes swept over Sam, then back to Sara "—athletic as Sammy obviously is."

Sara felt a powerful urge to cram that enormous diamond up Deanna's nose. "Deanna, would you do me a favor and check the kitchen? I'd like the omelets to be served by eleven-thirty. Most of these people have to be in their offices tomorrow morning, and we don't want to keep them out too late."

It was obvious from Deanna's suddenly closed expression that she understood full well Sara's attempt at wielding her power. Excusing herself, she moved away. Her three friends, feeling awkward without her, headed toward the hors d'oeuvres on the other side of the room.

"Alone at last," Sam muttered, rolling his eyes toward the ceiling. "You didn't get here a minute too soon."

He went to take her hand, but she pulled away. "You didn't look like you were suffering terribly, *Sammy*."

"Am I wrong, or are those big beautiful blue eyes of yours turning a shade of green?"

"Don't be ridiculous." She stopped. Hell, why lie about it? "You're wrong, Sam. My whole body is turning a shade of green. You didn't have to look like you were enjoying their company so damned much, you know."

He took a fresh glass of champagne from a passing waiter and offered Sara a sip. "If I looked like I was enjoying myself, it's just a compliment to my social skills. The woman is a barracuda, Paisley."

"What?"

He took a sip of the sparkling wine. "A barracuda. You know, a man-eater."

There was something about his words and the way he said them that made Sara feel as if she were at the edge of an important memory. She shook her head to clear away the cobwebs. No matter. She had more important things to discuss with him.

"Something's happened," she said quietly, smiling so Neal, who was watching them from the couch, wouldn't suspect anything was amiss.

Sam was instantly on the alert. "What? Did you get something on Rollins?"

"In a way." She drew closer. "Come with me."

The waiters were setting up the chafing dishes, so many of the guests were congregating near the tables. Sara and Sam were able to quickly maneuver through the crowded room, down the hallway and into her office where she closed the door behind them.

"What happened, Paisley?" Sam asked the second they were alone.

"The worst. Paul's gone."

"He's what?" Sam leaned against the edge of the couch, obviously stunned.

"He's gone. He pulled me aside right after the party began and told me he was going away again. On business."

Sam stared at her. "Where do you think he's headed?"

"I wish I knew."

"What do we do now?" Sam asked. "He was the whole reason for this party."

Sara looked up at him. "I think we're on our way to Rio."

"Care to run that by me again, Paisley?"

Suddenly, it made perfect sense to her. "I'm going to sell the house."

"You're crazy. The week before Christmas?"

"Okay, maybe I won't sell it right away, but I'll put it on the market."

"Paisley," Sam said, shaking his head, "I think your timing is off."

"I don't have time to worry about that." She grabbed Sam's arm. "Don't you see? He could be pulling the house out from under me—it could already be gone, for all I know. Time's running out, Sam. I have to know what's mine."

Sam said nothing. She moved away from him. "I'm going, Sam, whether you come with me or not."

He stepped toward her, then hesitated. "What if the house is gone, Sara? What then?"

"I also intend to see Alex Quieroz about selling my jewelry and permanently retire Sara Chance's American Express card." She grinned at him, and he couldn't help grinning back. "Make sense?"

"Lopsided sense, but I see your point." He pulled her over to him and ran his hands slowly up her spine, making it hard for her to think straight. "What about us?" he asked. "Will there still be ghosts?"

Rio was a dream. It had always belonged more to Sara than to Maxwell, had always been her oasis from his fame. "Not there," she said. "This trip will be for us."

He released her and handed her the phone.

"Make reservations for two," he said.

It was a little after 3:00 a.m. Sara stood by her bedroom window, looking down on the snow-covered street. There had been no blizzard, after all; the city had only received enough to cover the grime, to soften the hard edges of its reality. From where Sara stood, it was hard to believe that ugliness existed anywhere. But she knew all about illusion.

The party was long over. Sam was back in his apartment packing for their late-morning flight to South America. The caterers had magically spirited away all evidence of the party, leaving nothing but pristine emptiness behind. Neal had taken Deanna back to their apartment, mumbling that the word "champagne" should be stricken from her vocabulary.

Sara had checked for her passport, made their reservations and tossed a few things in a small suitcase. Different images from the party kept flickering through her mind, small disjointed scenes that disturbed her but made absolutely no sense at all. Most of them featured Deanna.

She leaned her head against the cold windowpane. Was she really that jealous of Deanna's apparent infatuation with Sam, or was there another deeper reason for the surge of anger and unease she had felt watching the red-haired woman flirt with him? Again she had the feeling that she was on the edge of memory.

It hardly mattered. The thing to do now was to collect the few pieces of jewelry she still had hidden deep in her closet and pack them up to take down to Rio tomorrow. Max had only purchased the finest gems. He used to tease her by saying if she left him she could live for a year on the proceeds from her engagement ring alone. And yet she had never cared much for the ring. They had married quickly and had had no formal engagement period. On their first anniversary Max surprised her with the incredible diamond, but it had never held the wealth of memories an engagement ring did for most women. She glanced at her wedding ring, a heavy and ornate antique. It was expensive but wasn't worth near what the diamond was. The memories attached to it, though, were priceless. No matter how broke she might turn out to be, she would never part with it.

She opened the closet, which was the size of her late parents' living room. She rummaged around behind some boxes of old shoes and found the velvet pouch where she unceremoniously stored the few items that weren't locked up in the safe in Rio.

"I'm sorry, Max," she said out loud, then plunged her hand inside and removed the antique gold bracelet from Rome, the platinum and ruby earrings from Cairo, the pearls from Tokyo. Her fingers felt around the soft recesses of the bag. How odd. Her engagement ring was missing. It was too big to remain unnoticed in the pouch. It was easily as big as the rock Deanna was sporting. She shrugged and brought the jewelry back into the bedroom and tossed the pieces into her suitcase. Obviously her memory was faulty and she had indeed stored her engagement ring at the vault at Quieroz's shop in Rio.

She'd know soon enough. In another fifteen hours or so, she would be in Brazil and that much closer to putting an end to all of this.

Now it was simply a matter of time.

* * *

"If we have to be stuck someplace, Paisley, this is definitely the place to be stuck." Sam stood at the edge of her balcony, which looked down over Ipanema Beach. The warm tropical sun splashed golden highlights atop his shiny brown hair.

Sara, still in the wool dress she'd traveled down in, was perched on the railing, her face lifted up so the breezes could cool her skin. "I'm afraid I'm still too tense to appreciate it, Sam," she said. "I never expected Alex's shop to be closed." They had taken a cab directly from the Galeao Airport to the jewelry shop, only to find it closed for the afternoon.

Sam moved closer to her, letting her dark curls slip through his fingers. "We should have taken Christmas into consideration, Paisley. We should—"

"Whoever thought a jewelry store would close for an office party two days before Christmas?" she said. "Where's their business sense?"

"You know the Cariocas better than I," he said with the grin of a man who could learn to like that kind of life. "You tell me."

She sighed. "Anything's possible, I guess. It's a country with its own rules." Rules that very probably contributed to their enormous national debt. "I guess we'll just have to wait it out."

Sam looked at the panorama of surf and sand and the mountains before him, then turned back to take in the splendor of her incredible glass house and shook his head. "The real question is how did you ever manage to tear yourself away from here?"

"Don't think I didn't contemplate it," she said, standing up and lifting her heavy hair off the back of her neck so the cooling breezes could reach her skin. "Max wasn't very well known here; I could have managed a private life. I even tried it for a month after he died. But when all was said and done, I'm an American, and I simply couldn't bring myself to live in another country. I wanted to come home."

"Despite the price you had to pay?"

She met his eyes. "At the time I didn't know how high it would be."

He reached for her, but she sidestepped him, feeling suddenly nervous and a bit shy. "There's so much I want you to see. Why don't we shower and change into something a bit more tropical, and I'll show you some of the sights."

Sam plunged his hands into the pockets of his khaki trousers. "A forced march, Paisley?"

Her expression softened. "I just need a little longer to relax, Sam."

He nodded. "Just a little longer," he said.

In a way Sara regretted her idea to take in some of the sights of Rio de Janeiro. She had forgotten exactly how splendid many of them were. Although they were just eight hours from New York City snow, it was summer in Brazil. Sara was wearing shorts and a halter top, and Sam wore jeans and no top at all, and they were overdressed. The Cariocas of Rio, body conscious and proud of it, were strolling the beach at Ipanema as if it were Fifth Avenue during the Easter parade. Only no one ever dressed quite like that—or in quite so little—back home.

"I should have put blinders on you," Sara said as a splendid dark woman in a minuscule monokini strolled past them. "I think I like it better back home where everyone's all bundled up in parkas and ski pants."

Sam laughed, stopped and pulled her into his arms. "You're just going to have to get used to something, Paisley, if we're going to keep on seeing each other like this."

The feel of his bare chest against her exposed midriff was intoxicating. "Get used to what?" she asked, expecting the worst.

"There's no one more beautiful, more sexy or more important to me than you." He bent low and kissed her to the applause of a group of teenagers playing soccer near the water's edge. "Can you get that through your thick skull?"

"I don't know," she said. "But feel free to try to convince me."

His hand cupped the back of her neck, then slid across her shoulder and down over her sun-warmed skin to the edge of her thin halter. "Let's go back," he said softly. "It's time."

She nodded. "It's more than time."

After the fiery sun and dense humidity outside, the house was dark and sweet and cool. The sudden change made Sara feel woozy for a moment, and she stopped in the kitchen to pour a glass of the bottled water they had picked up on their walk.

Sam stood in the doorway, his muscular arms folded across his chest, his beautiful eyes watching her. She found it hard to swallow.

"Sam?" She offered him her glass.

He said nothing, just dropped his arms to his side and approached her. His fingers brushed hers as he took the glass from her, then put it down on the countertop. He reached for her hand. She had invested a great deal of her fantasy time imagining just how the moment would be when it finally arrived. She'd imagined wine and candlelight; she'd imagined music and dancing; she'd imagined a seduction that ended with her being carried to the bed. But she had never imagined anything as wonderful as this reality.

The sun was setting over the ocean outside their window, and great streaks of red and orange filled the bedroom. The salty breeze, sweetened with the scent of the strange and beautiful flowers that grew beneath the window, lifted Sara's hair and blew the curls gently across her face. Sam, a look of intense concentration, intense yearning, on his face, laid his rough hand against her cheek, and in that second she knew that all the pain, all the unhappiness, of the past few years were worth it if it meant that such a moment could exist.

She reached up and cradled his face in her hands, drawing his lips down until they met hers, setting in motion what had been their destiny from the day they first met.

"You know what this means, don't you?" he asked, not really moving his lips from hers. "This will be our pledge, our promise."

She closed her eyes in assent. "Yes," she whispered against his lips. "Nothing will come between us again." *Please,* she thought. *Make it true.*

He reached behind her and deftly untied the bow that held her halter top in place, then slowly removed the garment from her body. She trembled slightly as his hands cupped her breasts, making her feel as if shooting stars were going off inside her head. Swiftly, she slid out of her shorts and panties, then, never taking her eyes from his, unzipped his jeans and let him lean against her while he stepped out of them.

"Oh, Sam," she whispered, letting her fingers trace a delicate pattern on his hips, "you're so beautiful."

He slid his hands up her back, pulling her close, so close that she didn't know where she ended and he began. "You're so much more than I dreamed," he said, his face buried in her hair, lips exploring a sensitive spot behind her ear. "I love you, Paisley." He moved his body in a way that made her gasp with need. "I always have."

She pulled back so she could look into his eyes, those eyes that had haunted her during the lost years. "Let me love you," she said, drawing him closer to the bed and the fulfillment of a very old promise. "Let me love you the way I should have a long time ago."

She pulled him down onto the bed and drew him with her into a world of fantasy and delight that she had only guessed existed. A world that, unfortunately, could last but one night.

"This night is special," she said between kisses.

"I know," he murmured, moving his body beneath hers with the strength she'd always known he possessed.

She couldn't speak any longer, couldn't explain that their night together beneath the star fire of Rio was a gift from an Orixa, a Brazilian deity with a fond eye for lovers. She would tell him in the morning when the sun splashed across the bed.

Morning would also bring with it a return to a very troubled reality, but thankfully it was still a long way off.

By 8:00 a.m. they were in front of Quieroz's jewelry shop, waiting for the doors to be unlocked. By eight-fifteen they were sitting patiently while Alex checked his computerized list for Sara's vault number. By nine Sara had disposed of everything save her wedding ring and her engagement ring. One she wouldn't part with; the other she couldn't find.

"Alex, are you sure I didn't put it in a separate vault?" she asked for at least the fourth time. "I was certain it was here."

"I'm sorry," he said in his delightfully accented English, "but there is no record of it."

"It must be back in New York," Sam said, squeezing her hand. "You probably found such a good place to hide it that even you can't find it."

"I doubt it," she said. "What I'm afraid of is it was stolen the day of the break-in. I never thought to check—I was so concerned about Max's papers and that damned piece of coral that I never thought to see if any jewelry was missing."

"Well, if it's gone, that's it, then." Sam's solid midwestern logic cut right through to the heart of it. "Once they pull a stone out of its setting, it can never be identified."

Alex laughed. "Oh, no, *senhor,* not true. Not true. Sara's diamond carried with it its own set of 'fingerprints.'" He looked at their confused faces and laughed again. "I could identify it in just a few minutes."

"How?" Sara asked, straightening in her chair. It didn't change the fact that her diamond ring was gone, but it was a fascinating bit of trivia. Like Sam, she had believed that precious stones, once taken from their settings, were virtually indistinguishable from one another.

"We brand them."

"Impossible," Sara said. "You'd ruin their beauty."

"Not if they are branded from within."

"You've got my curiosity," Sam said. "How is it done?"

Alex slipped his diamond pinky ring off his finger. "I'll show you." From around his neck he removed his white silk scarf, rubbed the diamond briskly, then dusted the stone with powder from a small vial that rested on the table near the telephone.

"Look."

To their utter astonishment, Sara and Sam clearly saw a heart-shaped brand on the face of the diamond. It wiped away with a touch of the cloth.

"Incredible," Sara said.

"How did you do it?" Sam asked. "Is it some kind of fancy parlor trick?"

"My son would be highly insulted," Alex said with a chuckle. "This method is his pride and joy." He went on to explain that his son was a researcher for General Electric in the United States. They had discovered that an ion implanter, commonly used in the manufacture of integrated circuits to recreate regions of different electrical conductivity in the silicon, can be used to "brand" diamonds. "It is difficult to describe in English," he said, "but what is done is he shoots a beam of charged atoms through, in my case, a heart-shaped opening in a foil mask to form this different area. It is invisible until dusted with this special powder."

"Not too popular with jewel thieves," Sam said.

"Not at all," Alex answered. He turned to Sara. "Would you like to see your brand?"

"I'd love to," she answered, forgetting the missing diamond in her fascination with this unusual process.

He buzzed his assistant in the next room, who brought in one of the rubies Sara had sold back to his store. "Watch." He rubbed the face of the stone with his scarf and dusted it with powder. Instantly, a star, sharp pointed and clear, appeared.

"That's beautiful!" Sara couldn't help smiling. "In fact, I think it looks even lovelier with the star visible."

Alex talked a bit about the research being done to make the jewel thieves' work harder, then walked them out to the door. "Will you be in Rio for Christmas celebrations tomorrow?" he asked.

Sam looked to Sara for an answer. "I doubt it," she said. "I guess we'll fly back home tonight."

"Do not worry, Sara," Quieroz said, kissing her first on one cheek, then the other. "I will check my records to make sure you had no other account with us."

Sara thanked him, and she and Sam left. She had the address of her real estate attorney in her pocketbook and managed to find a cabdriver who understood her Portuguese well enough to get them to their destination.

The house was hers, and all the paperwork was in order. The real estate attorney, young and eager, said there would be no difficulty in selling her property and assured her he would handle all details in tandem with her attorney in the States. "One month," he guaranteed. "One month and it is all done."

"You should look a lot happier," Sam said an hour later when they were stretched out on her bed, sipping cold glasses of mineral water with lime. "You've taken care of the jewelry, you've put your house on the market and in six hours we'll be on our way back to the States." He cupped her chin with his hand and tilted her head so he could see her face. "What's the matter, Paisley?"

She seemed distant, as if her mind were somewhere far away. "I don't know," she said. "I just feel a bit odd."

"Thanks a lot," Sam said with a wry chuckle. "That's a great thing to know after I've done wild and crazy things to your body."

She smiled and curled in closer to him, the memory of their most recent lovemaking casting away the demons for a moment. "I can't think at all when we make love, Sam. I'm pure emotion."

He sat up a bit and kissed her behind the ear. "Very flattering, Paisley, but I know you too well. What is it?"

She sat up in the bed, draped in a light percale sheet. "I don't know," she said, rubbing the back of her neck absently. "There's been something right at the edge of my memory for days now, and I can't seem to bring it into focus."

Sam put the glass of water down on the bamboo end table and sat up, also. "Something about Paul?" She shook her head. "Travis?" She shook her head again. "Your engagement ring?"

She started to shake her head, then stopped abruptly. "I don't know. Maybe—" She closed her eyes to focus her concentration inward. "I think it has something to do with Deanna, but I'm not—"

Sam groaned. "Oh, you mean the barracuda."

Her head snapped in his direction. "The what?"

"The barracuda." He looked at her strangely. "You know, you had the same reaction when I called her that the other night. What's going on, Paisley? Did you see *Jaws* too many times and you're afraid to go near the water? Are the sharks—"

"Shark. That's it." She closed her eyes to concentrate. "Maxwell used to call her a shark."

It had been in Greece, just a few days after the incident with the coral piece Maxwell presented to Sara. Paul was resting in the villa. Neal was showing Sara the fine points of backgammon on the patio, and Maxwell and Deanna had gone snorkeling off some reefs not too far away.

When Max came back, he was agitated and had a large angry scratch along his left cheek.

"Did you have a close encounter with a reef?" Sara asked as she brought him a washcloth to bathe his face.

"No," he said cryptically, "more like a close encounter with a shark."

Fear had nipped at Sara. "A shark in these waters? You can't go out snorkeling anymore, Max. It's—"

He grabbed her wildly gesturing hands and kissed each palm. "My beautiful Sara," he said, "you wouldn't know a real shark if you met her."

Suddenly, three years and five thousand miles later, it all made sense. The coral. The Grammy. The diamond that sparkled cruelly around her neck like captured fire.

"Deanna," Sara said. "It's been Deanna all along."

11

Jack Farrell's trip to Vancouver proved two things: Rollins had indeed been up there recently, and FAWN existed only on paper. Sure it had an office, a staff, fancy equipment—everything a real charitable foundation would be expected to have. But with the help of the gift of gab and a hundred-dollar bill placed in the right palm, Jack was able to take a look at its financial disclosure, and that look confirmed his biggest suspicion: not one cent allocated to help various zoos and wildlife preserves had reached said institutions. It was all somehow filtered back into FAWN, where it was mysteriously absorbed.

Mysteriously? Jack snickered. He was pretty damned sure that money was lining Paul Rollins's pockets with green.

The constant barrage of Christmas carols everywhere he went reminded him it was Christmas Eve. He'd been on the run constantly in Vancouver and had lost track of the days. What in hell was he doing sitting in a bar at a third-rate motel in Vancouver, Washington? He went up to his room to pack.

He'd been tossing his shirts into his suitcase when he remembered the manuscript pages he'd read in Rollins's apartment. The pages from his memoirs about growing up with Maxwell Chance. The passages about Philadelphia, about the quantum leap Rollins had taken from the slums of South Philly to hanging out with the only son of a main-line family, were indelibly burned into Jack's brain. Paul's words had painted vividly the picture of a man who now dined on caviar and prime ribs but tasted only the bitter flavor of poverty. It was a taste Jack knew intimately.

Now he leaned back in the narrow seat of the airplane and gazed out at the flat plains of the Dakota Badlands below. In another two hours or so he'd be in Philadelphia, where Rollins and Maxwell Chance both grew up, the nominal headquarters for the equally suspicious StopHunger Foundation.

He'd bet his Nikon he'd find the same setup. And if he did, he would take tremendous pleasure in blowing the whistle on Rollins.

Sara and Sam had no trouble getting a seat on the midnight flight from Rio to New York. Other people, people with homes and families, were already at their destinations, snug by a crackling fire, warmed by the Christmas Eve spirit.

As the jumbo jet took off from Galeao Airport, Sara caught a glimpse of the enormous statue of Christ on top of Corcovado peak. Although not terribly religious, Sara was usually moved by the sight of the massive figure of trust and love. Tonight, though, the sight of the statue, spectacularly lit and veiled in a thin shroud of clouds, made her shiver. She couldn't help but think of Deanna and wonder if trust and love could survive in a very difficult world.

The trip was smooth and fast until they neared New York. A large snowstorm was providing much of the northeast with the white Christmas so fervently hoped for. JFK was blanketed not only with snow but a severe visibility problem that diverted their flight down to Washington, D.C. They spent six dismal hours in Dulles Airport waiting for service to JFK to be resumed. It was well after five o'clock before they were back in New York, through customs and finally in a cab.

They spent the entire cab ride back to Manhattan talking about the best way to approach the problem of proving

Deanna's guilt. Sara was all in favor of pulling over and calling Detective Lenihan and having him go straight to the Carberry to arrest Deanna, but Sam's good sense prevailed.

"We don't have any proof, Paisley," he said, trying to ignore the way the cabbie ran a red light at the outskirts of the airport.

"That diamond is proof. I know it's from my ring, Sam. I'm sure of it."

He shook his head. "Great," he answered. "I think you're right, too, but that's not good enough to get a warrant from the cops."

"Well, what am I supposed to do, then? Go up to her and say, 'Give me your diamond, Deanna. I want to see if you stole it from me'?" The taxi went into a gentle skid as it took a curve, and Sara's breath hissed.

"We're both jet lagged to within an inch of our lives, Paisley." Sam pulled her close to him and gently stroked her hair, which was still damp with snow. "Let's take it one step at a time. Deanna's up in Connecticut with Travis until late tonight. We don't have to leap into anything before we know exactly what we're doing."

Sara pulled away from his comforting caress. "I can't wait any longer," she said. "I'm tired of waiting. We're so close, Sam, so close to everything we've always wanted."

His hold on her tightened. "That's right—we are close. So don't blow it, Paisley. If she gets suspicious, she might do anything—she could flush that damned necklace down the john."

The vision of the elegant Deanna flushing a five-carat diamond down the commode made Sara laugh. "I don't know if she'd go that far. Deanna's more likely to stash it in a Swiss bank, but you're right. I guess we should sleep on it." At Sam's expression, she added, "Alone, unfortunately."

"Not for much longer, Paisley," he said as she leaned over and kissed him quickly on the mouth.

* * *

Jack Farrell had no idea what to do. He was standing on a nasty, snowy street corner somewhere in the heart of South Philly in front of a bustling building that had the hand-painted sign StopHunger—Stop In hanging over the door. Men, women and children, who were among the many Americans who had fallen "between the cracks" of the huge social service system, were lined up outside the door for Christmas dinner. A Christmas dinner that StopHunger was obviously providing.

Jack had been there for over an hour, watching the steady stream of people cheerfully work their way inside for a hot meal and a helping of friendship. He'd spoken with them, digested their words.

"It's been here over a year now, man, and it's saved me." "My husband lost his job two months ago, and this is the only thing that keeps food in my kids' stomachs." "My social security isn't enough to pay my rent—this place gives me a hot meal every evening." "It keeps me going on . . ."

Over and over again he'd heard the same thing: praise, unqualified praise, for StopHunger. The foundation not only existed; it flourished. It destroyed all of his current conclusions about Paul Rollins.

A violent gust of wind blew around the corner. Jack pulled his coat tighter around his narrow body and huddled down lower. The snow stung his face, blowing into his eyes so that he had to cover them with his gloved hand to protect them. He didn't hear the man approach until he spoke.

"You look like you could use a square meal yourself, pal."

Jack squinted into the snow, trying to get a clear look at the man who belonged to the voice. "Who are you?" Not one of his more incisive questions but appropriate.

"I think the question is, who are *you?*"

The man had an unquestionable air of authority; he wasn't someone you could fast-talk your way past. Jack reached into his inside pocket and pulled out his press pass.

"Jack Farrell," he said, handing the card to the man. "I'm with the *Post,* among others."

"Jack Farrell." The man looked at the card, tapped it against his cheek, then handed it back to Jack. "The man who's been doing a little work in Vancouver."

Jack's stomach did a complete somersault. "I don't know what the hell you're talking about."

The tall man laughed and draped his arm around the younger man's shoulders. "Oh, come on now, Farrell," he said, pulling him toward the door to StopHunger. "I'm not going to believe that." He stopped beneath the streetlight, and Jack looked up at a face that could well be his own in ten years. "I'm the man you were checking up on." He pushed Jack through the door. "I'm Paul Rollins."

"Deanna!" Sara, only home an hour herself, couldn't hide the surprise in her voice. "When did you get in?"

Deanna stepped into the apartment and glanced down at the small suitcase resting near the foyer table. "Just a few minutes after you, apparently," she said, looking back at Sara. "Welcome home."

Sara had to fight down the feeling of anxiety that was snaking its way through her body. "Same to you," she said easily. "Where's Neal?"

"He decided to spend the weekend skiing," Deanna said, heading toward the living-room bar. She shook her head. "Although I surely don't know why anyone would want to slide down a mountain on a pair of wooden sticks."

Sara followed her into the living room and helped herself to a glass of club soda while Deanna poured two generous fingers of Scotch. "Why didn't you stay with him?" she asked, praying her words sounded as casual as they were meant to.

Deanna carried her Scotch over to the window and perched on the sill. She took a sip of the liquor, then shrugged. "I got bored with all the good cheer, frankly." She took another sip. "Besides, I hate snow."

Sara sat on the chair opposite her. "In case you haven't noticed, Deanna, it's snowing here, too."

Deanna chuckled. "I've noticed," she said, putting her drink down on the glass end table and unbuttoning the heavy black sweater she was wearing. "It just doesn't seem quite so oppressive here."

Sara watched absently as Deanna shrugged out of the sweater and draped it over the arm of the sofa. As usual, Deanna's taste in clothing was faultless. Even now, after a few hours' drive in a snowstorm, Deanna was impeccably dressed in a deep green silk blouse that scooped down low, stopping just short of exposing cleavage. Deanna leaned forward to retrieve her glass of Scotch, and that was when Sara noticed.

"Deanna, it's gone!"

Deanna looked up at her, confused.

Sara fought to control the roller coaster that was her emotions. "Your diamond necklace is gone."

What on earth was wrong with Deanna? She didn't look concerned in the slightest.

"Deanna, for heaven's sake, didn't you hear me?"

"Relax, Sara." Deanna laughed. "You sound like an insurance agent." She took a sip of Scotch. "The chain broke, and I had to take it off. Imagine if the diamond had dropped into the snow?"

Relief made Sara glad she was already sitting. She knew her legs would not support her weight at that moment. "See why I don't wear my jewelry?" she asked, trying to cover her real feelings. "I can't take the tension."

"Well, relax, Sara. I'm taking it back to Cartier's next week to have them fix the clasp."

"Maybe you should have a padlock attached."

Deanna laughed. "I'll mention it to them."

They chatted for a while about the weather, the holiday, the insanity of skiing. Deanna asked about Sara's trip to Brazil, and all Sara said was she had found the papers she had supposedly gone down there to retrieve. They pointedly avoided mention of Sam, and Sara was surprised at how easy it was to talk to Deanna and how very difficult to remember that the red-haired woman had been the cause of her pain.

It was 10:00 p.m. when Deanna returned next door to the apartment she shared with Neal. Five minutes later Sara was on the telephone with Sam.

"Paisley, will you calm down?" His voice was the only thing holding her together at the moment. "Run it by me again."

Sara took a deep breath and repeated her message. "Unless we hit her over the head and grab it, we'll never have a chance like this again. Deanna's not wearing her necklace. This is our opportunity to get hold of that diamond and test it."

"Are you planning on another trip down to Rio?"

She hadn't thought that far. "I don't know. I'll call Alex tomorrow—he could send up a vial of that dusting powder through a special courier."

"I have a better idea. Maybe he knows someone in New York who could handle it for you."

Sara congratulated him on his brilliance.

"I appreciate the kind words, Paisley, but the fact remains we still have to get our hands on that diamond. Any plans?"

She hesitated. "You're not going to like it. At least I hope you're not going to like it."

"Shoot."

"Do you remember the way Deanna acted with you at my party?"

He groaned. "The barracuda."

"Exactly. I'll bet that the only thing better than wearing my diamond around her neck would be having my lover in her bed."

Sam's expletive was graphic. "Forget it, Paisley. No way."

"Calm down, Sam. I'm not suggesting you sleep with her."

"Damned good thing—"

"But I am suggesting you give her the impression you intend to." He was quiet for a while. Sara began to wonder if he'd hung up. "Sam? Are you still there?"

"Unfortunately," he answered. "I'm beginning to see what you're driving at. I lure her out with the idea of a roll in the hay."

"Exactly." Excitement was building in Sara's blood. "And while you're wining and dining her, I'll let myself into her apartment and steal back my diamond."

"Which we'll have dusted with that powder—"

"And the star brand will show up—"

"And we'll live happily ever after."

"If we're lucky." Sara gave him Deanna's phone number. "Set it up for 6:00 p.m. tomorrow night."

"What about Travis?"

"He won't be back until Sunday."

"Where should I take her?"

Sara chuckled. "I can't plan your date for you, Mr. Berenger. I have my own worries."

They talked over some of the possibilities, then decided that the best place would be Leonard's apartment, where Sam was staying. It was private, and that would help make Deanna feel that Sam had a romantic encounter of his own in mind. He'd have dinner and drinks and soft music awaiting her; then a well-timed phone call from Sara around nine o'clock would stop the fun before it started.

"I miss you," Sara said, cupping her hand around the mouthpiece and letting her voice grow softer, more intimate.

"Glad to hear it." Sam sounded pleased. "I was beginning to wonder if our night together really happened or whether it was just some crazy dream."

"It really happened," she said. "It was the most beautiful night of my life."

"I love you, Paisley." Just the sound of his voice was enough to send delicious tremors through her body, shooting out straight from the center of her heart.

"Oh, how I love you, Sam."

He chuckled. "Words are cheap. Show me how much."

"Over the phone? I'm not that inventive."

"Not that inventive, huh? Seems to me I remember a few very—"

Suddenly she was very, very serious. "We're almost home free, Sam. I promise you that when this is over, I'll show you beyond your wildest dreams."

"I'm going to hold you to that, Paisley."

She couldn't think of anything she would love more than a life sentence in his arms.

If their guess about Deanna proved right, in twenty-four hours the nightmare would be over. She would be free to go to Sam unaccompanied by ghosts and shadows.

She hung up so that Sam could call Deanna. As she put the cordless phone back down on the desk top in her office, the lamplight caught and held the fire of her diamond wedding ring. Her breath caught. Then, without pause, she slid the antique ring from her finger and let its substantial weight rest in the palm of her right hand. "I did love you, Maxwell," she said aloud as if one of the ghosts still lingered in the room.

Part of moving ahead was knowing when looking backward was no longer wise. It had taken two years, but now, on Christmas night, she was ready to say good-bye to Max.

She was ready to say hello to Sara Paisley.

Sara had no idea how she managed to get through the next day with her sanity intact. The snowstorm kept her inside, and Deanna, apparently stricken with a case of cabin fever, was restless until she finally settled down in Sara's office to do some paperwork.

Fortunately, Sara had been able to get through to Alex Quieroz early that morning, and he gave her the phone number of his son, who lived in nearby White Plains and would be happy to help identify the diamond. Now, as she pretended to be engrossed in her work on Maxwell's journal notes, she found her eyes straying to Deanna, admiring the beauty of the woman and wondering how such ugliness could be hidden inside.

Deanna did do a wonderful job of it, though. As she wove her little story about meeting her friends for some "girl talk" and an old movie festival at the Thalia, Sara almost found herself wavering in her conviction. After Deanna left, Sara had to keep reminding herself that this woman she had called friend had already done her best to destroy Sara and now she was setting out to cold-bloodedly steal the man Sara loved.

She paced the apartment, one eye glued to the clock. Deanna was due at Sam's at seven, and Sara had decided it wise to wait until eight o'clock before going next door to retrieve the diamond. She had wanted to make sure Deanna didn't suddenly pop back for a forgotten purse or last-minute phone call.

The clock chimed the hour, and Sara jumped as if struck.

Okay, Paisley, she thought, picking up her huge key ring and letting herself out of her own apartment, *let's see if all those Nancy Drew books help you out of this one.*

She didn't dare contemplate what she would do if she couldn't find the diamond.

Something wasn't quite right.

Sam had orchestrated his pseudoseduction beautifully: the fire crackled in the hearth, the champagne was chilled to just the right temperature, and the catering service he'd called had brought over the finest caviar. In the kitchen, a beautiful dinner of Veal Oscar waited to be served. Deanna had arrived on time, bearing a bottle of Taittinger's and wearing another one of those silky, clingy numbers that seemed to be her trademark. Her eyes glittered with something he assumed was lust—for his body or her revenge, he wasn't sure. Either way, he had been positive she had bed as her top priority.

He'd been sitting next to Deanna on the sofa, giving an Academy Award performance, when he realized she wasn't buying it. Not the candles, not the wine, not the fire. Noth-

ing. Sure she was sitting close to him, her long slender thigh
pressed against his, her graceful fingers playing with the hair
that grew over his collar in the back. There was a slightly
strange quality about her that night that seemed to keep her
just one beat behind him, keeping him just a fraction of a
second off-balance.

He took a casual glance at his watch. Maybe if he served
dinner now, they'd be able to get through the hour and
twenty minutes until Sara's "all clear" phone call at nine.
He disengaged himself from Deanna.

"How about dinner?" he asked, standing up.

"Sounds marvelous," she said, again with that tiny extra pause that was beginning to rattle him. "Can I help?"

The last thing he wanted was for her to follow him into the
kitchen. He gritted his teeth and leaned over to kiss her. Her
lips were soft and yielding, the hand that took his narrow
and strong.

Ten minutes later, the delicately flavored Veal Oscar was
in front of them. Sam stood up to get the champagne from
the wine bucket.

"Let me," Deanna said, her eyes sparkling with what
seemed to him to be excessive delight. "To future pleasures."

She got up and took the bottle from the bed of ice and
walked over to Sam, who sat waiting, holding his glass up.
He noticed the way her right eyelid seemed to twitch slightly.

It was the last thing he remembered.

Maybe it was something a person got used to.

This was the second time in a few weeks that Sara had let
herself into another's apartment uninvited. Sure, her heart
was thumping a little more rapidly, and she was aware of her
heightened senses, but the extreme anxiety she'd experienced when she and Sam had "broken into" Paul's apartment was missing.

Of course, maybe part of the reason was that she was
more familiar with Deanna's place. Where Paul's had always been strictly off limits to visitors, Deanna and Neal

were always inviting her in for a drink or a talk, so Sara was in for no surprises as she made her way into the bedroom.

Well, maybe she was in for a minor surprise, she thought, as she approached Deanna's dresser. That enormous mirror suspended over the king-size bed was a relatively new addition, and she didn't care to pursue what kind of activity went on beneath it. It made her remember exactly why Deanna had gone over to Sam's, and that was not a thought Sara cared for at all.

The night before she'd made a list of the possible hiding places Deanna might have chosen for the diamond pendant and began her search with the most obvious of all: the jewelry case in the top drawer of Deanna's dresser. Deanna had a remarkably laissez-faire attitude toward jewelry. Sara could remember a beautiful eighteen-carat gold antique watch Deanna used to leave at the edge of the sink in the kitchen where it teetered over the garbage disposal. She was definitely not the kind of woman who would have a small safe hidden around somewhere.

The jewelry case yielded nothing. Neither did the desk drawers, the dresser or under the mattress. The only spot left was the unlocked file cabinet Sara knew she kept in the closet, and she was just sliding Deanna's coats and dresses aside when she heard the voice in the doorway.

"Can I help you with something, Sara?"

She spun around toward the sound, getting tangled in the sleeves of a score of silky dresses that surrounded her.

"What's the matter?" Deanna, a Valkyrie with flaming red hair, glided into the bedroom. "At a loss for words?"

Deanna approached her, blocking Sara so she could only hold her ground at the closet door. Deanna made as if to brush the silk dresses away from Sara, yet with one smooth, unthreatening motion, Deanna pulled the sleeves more tightly around Sara's throat.

"It feels beautiful against the skin, doesn't it?" Deanna asked.

Sara found her voice. "Yes, it does." She reached up and pulled the fabric away from her throat. She went to move past Deanna, but the other woman was not about to give up her ground. Sara could taste the bile rising in her throat.

Deanna watched her, her hazel eyes assessing.

"I'm surprised to see you back so soon." Sara moved to the right and stepped into the center of the bedroom. She forced herself to meet Deanna's gaze and not blink. "Was the Thalia closed?"

Deanna's chuckle was low, and it sent a thrill of fear along Sara's arms.

"Oh, Sara, Sara. Ever the polite lady of the manor." She reached into the pocket of her silky trousers and pulled out the diamond on the fine platinum chain. "Is this what you were looking for?"

Sara nodded. "Yes, it is." There was no point in lying. It was too late for that now. "Where is Sam?" *Please, let him be all right.* Fear for his safety swept over her, nearly drowning her.

Deanna smiled at her, the same high-wattage smile she'd always flashed at Sara. Why now did it seem to reveal the teeth of a predator? "Let's just say our Sam is quite a man."

"Where is he?" Her voice was getting shrill. She tried to force it lower. Deanna was a shark who would feed at the sound of Sara's fear.

"Forget him." Deanna's voice was hard despite the phony smile. She grabbed Sara's arm and shoved her down on top of the oversize bed in the center of the room. "You thought you were pretty clever, didn't you? Setting me up for a tryst with Maxwell so you could search my room—too bad your scheme didn't work."

"Maxwell?" What was she talking about? She started to get up, but Deanna, having a height and weight advantage, easily pushed Sara down once again.

"Did you really think you could come between us, little Sara? Did you really think all those years I loved him could be forgotten?"

"I don't know what you're talking about, Deanna. You just met Sam a few days ago."

Deanna looked confused for a moment. "Sam is gone," she said bluntly. "Forget him. You'll never see him again."

Rage and terror blossomed red and black before Sara's eyes. "You're lying," she said, slapping at the woman's restraining hand on her shoulder. "Let me go. I have to find Sam."

"You're too late." Deanna's shark smile flashed in the dim bedroom. "You won't be seeing him again."

Sara pushed Deanna away with a strength that came from beyond herself. "What do you mean, I won't be seeing him again?" She started for the door. She had to call Sam; she had to make sure he was alive, make sure—

Deanna grabbed Sara by the wrist and catapulted her body into the doorjamb. Sara's hipbone smashed into the lock plate, and pain radiated through her lower body. Blindly she swung out at the other woman but the size disadvantage made it useless. Deanna easily twisted her arm and flung her to the floor.

Sam was dead. That had to be what Deanna meant when she said she'd never see him again. *He can't be dead. I refuse to accept this.* If she let herself believe it, she wouldn't be able to go on. Grief would lead her to madness, the same madness that seemed to be destroying Deanna. A large scream of rage was filling her lungs, expanding them out against her rib cage and breastbone until she thought she would explode.

"You're sick," she said, looking up at the red-haired woman, who, even in her fury and torment, was still beautiful. "Let me help you," she said. "Let me get some professional help for you. Don't do anything you'll regret."

Deanna's laugh was the sound of fingernails on a blackboard. "The only thing I regret, little Sara, was letting Maxwell go." Sara's face must have registered profound shock, because Deanna laughed again. "Surely you knew your late lamented and I were lovers, didn't you?"

"I don't believe you." If there was one thing Sara was sure of, it was Max's love for her.

"Grow up, Sara. If I'd been smart, I never would have turned him down when he asked me to marry him." She looked at Sara, huddled on the floor, and drew the pointed toe of her boot closer to Sara's midsection. Sara could feel the barely contained violence, and she struggled to mask her fear by forcing herself to sit upright.

"You must have been teenagers," Sara said. "That was long before he met me."

Sara grunted as Deanna's foot found its mark in her rib cage. Nausea threatened to overtake her, but she fought it down. She couldn't lose control, couldn't give Deanna that satisfaction.

"You're more naive than I thought. I was stupid enough not to marry him," she said, "but no woman would be stupid enough to turn him out of her bed."

Pain, both physical and emotional, flooded Sara. "I don't believe you."

Deanna reached into the pocket of her trousers and pulled out the piece of coral Max had given Sara so long ago.

"Remember that little holiday in Greece?" Deanna fondled the shimmering coral, sliding its silky coolness along the skin of her cheek. Her sensuality was so pervasive, so overpowering, that for a moment Sara found herself drawn into her lie.

"Are you fool enough to think I joined you just for the sunshine?" Deanna slid the coral along the column of her throat. Her eyes were half-closed, pupils dilated with some obscenely personal memory that made Sara's skin crawl. "Max asked me to come. He said he needed some real excitement."

"I don't believe you."

"He said he needed a woman who knew how to make him tremble—"

"You're lying, Deanna." Sara was speaking over the other woman's voice, her own voice growing louder, more positive.

"He was sick of you. You bored him, Sara."

"That's not the way it happened, Deanna."

Deanna's grip on the coral tightened; Sara could see her knuckles whiten. "He wanted me, Sara. He couldn't have enough of me. Even that day you thought we went snorkeling off the reefs—" Again that horrifying laugh. "We were making love, little Sara, just fifty feet away from you. We were making love, and he was laughing at how easy you were to fool."

"Where did the scratches on his face come from? Passion?"

"Yes. Passion. Something you know nothing about." Deanna's beauty was beginning to twist into a parody of itself. The lovely features remained the same, but the rotting soul was becoming visible. "We were like two animals, two beautiful young animals who—"

"Enough!" Sara leaped to her feet, her body literally singing with power and anger. Too many lies. There had been too many lies, and they were going to stop. "That's not the way it happened, Deanna." Deanna stared at her blankly. "Nothing like that ever happened."

"Think what you want, Sara. I know the truth."

Sara moved closer to the woman, her anger overcoming her fear. "The truth is Max hated you. You came on to him, he turned you down, and you scratched his face. Isn't that the way it really happened?"

"Can't stand to think you weren't woman enough for him, can you? Can't stand the thought that I knew his body as well as you did, that I—"

"He called you a shark, Deanna."

"—lay beneath him and— What?"

Sara had inserted the knife, and now she twisted it. "He called you a shark."

Deanna's bravado was shredded away by Sara's words. "We had an argument," she said. "I said things I shouldn't have, and he lashed out at me. It meant nothing." She shook her head. "Nothing. If he'd stayed in Greece a little longer, we could have worked the whole thing out."

Deanna seemed to be retreating into some private fantasy world. Sara began to ease her way out the bedroom door and into the hall. If she could just get to the telephone and call the police—

"I heard you say all those things to him, you know." Deanna, fleet as a jungle cat, leaped in front of Sara and pushed her back into the bedroom.

As Sara fell onto the soft mattress, she caught their funhouse shapes reflected in the overhead mirror. To her horror, she saw the butt of a gun, clearly visible, tucked into Deanna's waistband near her left buttock. Her blood chilled even as sweat popped out on her brow and between her breasts. She tried to avert her eyes so that Deanna wouldn't realize Sara knew she was armed.

"I listened to all those conversations you had—'I love you, Maxwell.' 'Give me a break, Paisley.' 'I miss you so much.' 'How did we ever let five years slip away?'"

Deanna's voice slid up and down in imitation of both Sara's and Sam's voices. Sara listened, morbidly fascinated, as she realized Deanna had fused her memory of Maxwell with the reality of Sam. "How could you have heard us?" Sara asked. The walls between the two apartments had been soundproofed.

Deanna's monologue halted in midsentence. "Your cordless phone isn't the wonderful invention you think it is. A lot of your talks come through loud and clear on my radio."

There was no point in calling Deanna a liar, because her recitation of pieces from past conversations were too accurate to be denied.

Deanna approached the bed. Her hands were loosely clasped behind her, but in the overhead mirror Sara could see her fingers outstretched close to the butt of the gun.

"I must say you're smarter than I figured, Sara. The idea to lure me to Sam's apartment was a pretty good one. I had a better time than you know." Her left hand was almost grasping the gun.

Sara allowed herself to slump on the bed as if defeated, monitoring Deanna's movements in the mirror. "Max was unfaithful to me?" she asked, hoping Deanna could be lured back into that confused pattern of moments ago. She needed every advantage she could get.

"He would have been." Her slender fingers wrapped themselves around the gun. "I'm sorry I had to do that to him before we had a chance to start."

Do what to him? Oh, please, don't let him be dead. Sara's mind burned with pain, but she pushed on. It was only a matter of moments before Deanna would pull that gun out and turn it on Sara.

"I've lost him," she said, reclining now on the edge of the bed, her head drooping almost off the mattress as if her pain were too great to be borne. "You've won, Deanna." She looked up at the red-haired woman and took in the mirrored reflection at the same time. Deanna was inching the gun out in slow motion.

"Not yet," Deanna said. "I have to make sure you can't get him back. I have to make sure he can't change his mind again."

The flash of metal glittered in the mirror. Sara's body flew to life on pure instinct; her rational mind didn't have a chance to react before the visceral need to survive took charge. She rolled off the side of the bed and slipped to the floor as Deanna aimed the gun at the spot where Sara had been and fired into the mattress. The sound was deafening; Sara was sure she would hear it the rest of her life. Quickly, before Deanna could recover and shoot again, Sara grabbed the woman's ankle, and summoning up strength from somewhere deep in her soul, she knocked the taller woman off-balance and to the floor.

Sara linked her hands together in a double fist and smashed her hands down on Deanna's wrist. The woman's fingers flew open, and the gun fell out. Sara grabbed the gun and threw it toward the window where it shattered the glass and went crashing into the courtyard below.

"Great pitch, Mrs. Chance."

Sara's head shot up at the sound of the male voice at the bedroom door. Detective Lenihan watched her, a cigarette dangling from his lips and a .45 firmly gripped in his hand.

"We'll take over from here."

12

"Did you hear me?" Lenihan stepped into the room, followed by three uniformed officers.

Sara heard him, but she was frozen to the spot, with Deanna still pinned on the floor beneath her. Lenihan helped Sara to her feet, and she stared while two of the cops bent down and slapped cuffs on Deanna. She felt as if she were trapped in a surrealistic dream.

"I didn't call the police," she managed finally as a big dark-haired cop led her to a chair in the living room. "Excuse the language, but where in hell did you come from?"

"You have your pals Rollins and Farrell to thank."

Paul and that photographer? Now she knew she was hallucinating. She looked at Lenihan blankly.

Lenihan glanced toward the bedroom door where the youngest officer was reading Deanna her Miranda rights. "I don't have the details," he said, looking back at Sara, "but it seems they got to your friend Berenger's house just in time."

"Oh, no! He's been shot—"

"Not shot, but the redhead cracked him over the head with a bottle of champagne." He chuckled. "Good stuff, too. Left one hell of a mess."

Sam was alive. All the terror she'd been suppressing swept over her, and she lowered her head between her knees to keep from passing out.

"Drink this." Lenihan gave her an open bottle of whiskey from the bar, and she took a slug, shuddering as it burned its way down her throat.

She wiped her mouth with an index finger. "I don't understand any of this."

"I don't know the whole story, either," Lenihan answered, "but it seems Farrell and Rollins met up with each other in Philly. They compared notes, came to the same conclusions. Your phone was disconnected—"

"What?" She needed another stiff belt of whiskey.

Lenihan nodded. "Yep. The redhead cut your wires. Well, anyway, they went over to where Berenger was staying, and when he didn't answer the door, they got scared." He took a drag on his cigarette. "Your pal Farrell picked the lock."

Sara tried to stand, but her knees were still unable to support her. "Where is Sam? I have to see him."

"You'll see him. Right now he's getting stitched and X-rayed at St. Vincent's. We'll take you down there as soon as we get this squared away." He stubbed his cigarette out in a marble ashtray. "Consider it my way of saying I was wrong about you."

His backhand apology was something she would savor later. Right now there were other more important things to think about. The two uniforms were leading Deanna into the living room. The woman's beautiful silky pants were torn at the knee, and her blouse gaped open where a button had been ripped off during their fight.

"Sara? I don't understand what's going on." The hazel eyes were wide, and in them Sara read genuine confusion and fear. "Why are they taking me away?"

Lenihan looked at one of his men, who tapped a finger against his temple and rolled his eyes. He turned to Sara. "Did you know she was—"

Sara shook her head. "Not until tonight." The need for revenge suddenly evaporated. Looking at the woman in front of her, Sara knew that revenge seemed pointless.

Deanna had suffered—and would suffer—more than enough for one lifetime. "She needs help."

"You're not going to press criminal charges?"

"Not against her." She looked again at Deanna, who had disappeared within herself once more. "There was no real crime," she answered. "The only crime has been to the heart. I just want her to get the help she needs."

"What about Travis?"

Sara's face hardened. "That's another story entirely."

Lenihan nodded, then motioned to the officers. "Okay, boys, let's get the padded wagon out and get her over to Bellevue for observation."

They started to lead Deanna away.

"Wait." Sara rushed into the bedroom. The acrid smell of the gunshot filled her nostrils as she bent down to where both the diamond pendant and the piece of coral rested on the carpet. She slipped the necklace into her pocket. Tomorrow morning Alex Quieroz's son would dust it for the brand, but she already knew what he would find. This diamond was hers. She brought the coral into the living room.

Deanna, beautiful once again, watched as Sara approached and held out the lovely piece of coral.

"For you." Sara dropped it into the pocket of Deanna's trousers. "I want you to have it." The coral meant more to Deanna than it ever could to Sara. All Deanna had was the past, while Sara now stood at the threshold of her future.

"I loved him," Deanna said, her large eyes filling with tears. "I really did."

Sara looked away as the policemen led Deanna from the apartment. She was free at long last, yet the victory lay heavy on her shoulders. She turned back to Lenihan when the door closed behind the others. "You must have some questions," she said, meeting his eyes.

Detective Lenihan lightly touched her arm. "Come on," he said, his voice kinder than she could have imagined possible. "Let's get you to the hospital to see your boyfriend. I can ask my questions on the way."

Sam was bruised and stitched and would be confined to his hospital bed for a few days, thanks to a slight concussion, but he was alive, and for Sara that was a miracle of the first order.

"I thought I'd lost you." She buried her face against the side of his neck, her tears wetting the hospital gown draped over his torso.

Sam reached up and stroked her hair. "Not when we've come this far, Paisley," he managed, his voice low and slightly slurred. "I've waited too long to give up so easily."

She gazed into his eyes, which, to her, were still beautiful despite the rainbow of bruises encircling them. "I love you," she said softly. "I didn't realize exactly how much until I thought I'd lost you again."

She heard the sound of a heavy ring tapping at the hospital door. "Sorry to interrupt," Detective Lenihan said, "but we still have a few loose ends to tie up."

Sam cleared his throat. "Come on in," he said. "I want to hear about what I missed."

Lenihan took a last drag on his cigarette, then ground it out in an ashtray just inside the door to Sam's room. Sara got up to pull another chair near Sam's bed when Paul Rollins, looking pale with fatigue, came in just behind Lenihan. She had just picked up a folding metal chair and was starting to carry it across the room when Paul reached out with one hand to take it from her.

"Let me help you," he said.

She looked up into his hazel eyes and saw that they were nothing like his sister's at all. They held compassion and humanity, two attributes she'd never thought he possessed. "I think you already have," she answered.

Paul and Lenihan took their seats, and Sara perched on the edge of the bed, Sam's hand securely held between her own.

Sara looked at Paul. "Where's Jack Farrell?" she asked. "Is he here?"

"He's cooling his heels in the hall. I wouldn't be surprised if he has his ear pressed against the door." Detective

Lenihan answered for Paul. "We're gonna keep our eyes on him until we get Travis. Can't have the story broken before."

Sam muttered a mild oath against Farrell.

Paul laughed. "Don't be too hard on him," he said. "If he hadn't been able to pick that lock, you'd still be lying there in a pool of champagne."

"How will you keep Farrell quiet?" Sam asked.

"We have our ways," Lenihan answered with a grin. "But once Travis is arrested, Farrell's free to break the story. I can't stop him then." He pulled out a battered notebook and brought them all back to the story at hand: Deanna.

Deanna had indeed been in love with Maxwell Chance since she was fifteen. Her brother had brought his rich young friend home to their South Philly flat, and Deanna had experienced the phenomenon of love at first sight. Nothing had existed between them until their early twenties when they had a brief affair that apparently had meant much more to her than it had to Max.

"I'd never thought about it one way or the other," Paul explained, his long fingers laced in front of him as he leaned forward in his chair, "until she showed up in Greece. That's when I first realized she was carrying a torch."

"Why didn't you do something then?" Sam asked.

Paul shrugged. "She'd been going through some hard emotional times, and I chalked it up to that."

"Greece was over two years ago," Sara broke in. "What happened to make you suspicious now?"

"Those letters," Paul answered, referring to the abusive stream of letters Sara had received. "There was something about them, a certain phraseology, that made me start to wonder."

Lenihan was scribbling away furiously. "Does she have a history of mental problems?"

Paul hesitated. "She was a heavy drug user in the sixties. Hallucinogens, that type of thing. She'd been hospitalized twice—" he took a deep breath "—and she never really was the same again."

"Your husband never told you any of this?" Lenihan asked Sara, his pencil scratching across his notepad.

She shook her head. "Not one word."

"That's what made Max so special," Paul said, his voice cracking. "He would never hurt anyone he cared for."

Sara swiveled to face Paul. "You honestly loved Max, didn't you?"

"We fought like hell," Paul answered, "but I loved him like a brother."

Her next question popped out. "You never approved of me, did you?"

"I didn't think you were strong enough to handle him." His smile was slow and sad. "I was wrong, Sara. I'm sorry."

"You weren't wrong." She met his eyes. "Max and I were never right for each other. If I really had been strong, he might still be alive."

"Only Max could have kept Max alive," Paul said. "You couldn't have stopped him any more than I could have stopped Deanna. It's taken me two years to realize that neither of us are to blame."

With Lenihan's swift, efficient questioning, the puzzle pieces fit together in record time. Deanna had been shrewd enough to capitalize on the public's morbid interest in Sara and her life-style. She seeded vicious rumors in an all-too-willing press in an effort to discredit Sara in the eyes of Maxwell's fans and ultimately to establish herself as the source of all information on Maxwell Chance.

"It was Deanna who made the calls to the press when you were heading out to Quogue for the anniversary," Paul said. "She got Travis to call the TV station from a phone alongside the expressway to make sure they had camera crews stationed there. Getting you zonked on cold medicine was a gift from the gods. The media right away decided you were a junkie, and her plan was off and running."

"How do you know she made the calls?" Lenihan asked.

"I tracked down the limo driver," Paul said. "He distinctly remembered watching her legs while she got out and went to the phone booth."

That many of Sara's conversations on the cordless telephone came across loud and clear on Deanna's AM radio had made it easy for Deanna to trace Sam and Sara's budding relationship. Her extreme jealousy tipped her over the edge of reality, and she began to blur Sam with Maxwell, her ultimate undoing.

"What about Travis?" Sam asked. "Where does he fit in?"

"My sister has always held considerable charm for the opposite sex," Paul said dryly. "After she moved in with him and started working for Sara, she finagled it so Neal would be in charge of FAWN and gave him the idea to siphon the funds into their personal accounts. I caught on to it about three months ago, and I've been trying to accumulate the evidence to pin on them." He gestured toward the hallway waiting room where Jack sat, accompanied by a policeman. "We have our young friend out there to thank for that."

When Jack went up to Vancouver and discovered that FAWN existed in name only, he'd been convinced Paul Rollins was at the heart of it. When he and Paul collided in Philly on Christmas Eve, there had been a confrontation. The two men had faced one another like adversaries in the SALT talks, each convinced the other had his finger on the trigger. It took awhile but they finally consolidated information and found they had a solid case against Travis and, unfortunately, against Paul's sister, as well.

"What about the diamond?" Sam asked.

"I have it," Sara said. "We had the answer right in front of us all the time."

Both Lenihan and Paul turned to Sara, puzzled expressions on their faces.

She quickly explained her missing engagement ring and the coincidental appearance of Deanna's diamond pendant. "Here." She pulled it from her pocket and showed it to them. "I'll know tomorrow if it's mine or not." She briefly explained about the ion-implanted brand.

"Well, I guess that's it." Detective Lenihan got up to make a call to headquarters. An arrest warrant would be waiting for Neal Travis when he returned from his ski trip.

Once the detective left the room, Sara turned toward Paul and extended her right hand to him. "I owe you an enormous apology. I was wrong, and I'm sorry."

Paul shook her hand solemnly. "I gave you good reason to believe the worst. I knew you thought I was behind all of this, but I had to let you go on thinking it. I was too close to the answers to risk any foul-ups."

"Farrell told me about StopHunger while you called the cops," Sam said, his voice growing fainter with fatigue. "You've done one helluva job."

"That's what he wanted," Sara said softly, referring to Max and his dreams. "You accomplished the impossible."

Paul smiled. "If you remember, Max always said nothing was impossible."

Nothing could change the years of distrust that had existed between Sara and Paul Rollins, the years of suspicion and doubt. But they'd been through the worst and come through it on the same side. Sara's instincts told her he was the man to make her late husband's dreams come true, to help make the shadows disappear once and for all.

She hesitated. "Paul, I'll understand if you'd rather not, but would you consider getting FAWN on its feet? It would mean a—"

"Nothing would make me happier. I loved Max," he said simply. "It's the least I can do for him."

Sam, exhausted, had fallen into a light doze, his head resting against Sara's shoulder.

Paul lowered his voice. "You know, Farrell's going to make sure it's a big story, Sara." They both knew it was the kind of story that could make a career. "Do you think you'll be able to take seeing it spread all over the media?"

With Sam's body against hers, so warm and solid, Sara wondered if Jack Farrell would find fame to be not quite what he'd expected. "I can stand anything to set the record straight."

It would be lurid, she knew, for innocence was never as exciting as guilt. She could imagine the headlines: "Max's Ex-Lover Tries to Kill Sara! Everything She Did, She Did for Love." If the papers decided to jazz up the headlines— Well, that's what sold papers. She just wanted every person in New York to discover the truth about Sara Chance and remember it well, because after January first, Sara Chance was retiring from the public eye. She didn't need their love anymore; she only wanted their respect.

Sam moaned gently in his sleep, and Paul stood up to leave.

"Where will you be, Sara?" he asked as he gathered up his coat.

"In Maine," she answered, smiling at his curious glance. "I think I'll be in Maine."

Paul looked from Sara to the sleeping Sam, shrugged good-naturedly and left. Explanations could wait.

"I thought he'd never leave." Sam, sounding a little rocky, opened his eyes and looked up at Sara.

She smiled. "Alone at last." It was chilly in the hospital room, and she reached for the extra blanket at the foot of his bed and arranged it around both her shoulders and his.

Sam's eyes fluttered closed for a moment, then opened again. "Ah, Paisley," he said, his voice low. "It's cold as hell in Maine. How are you going to manage?"

She looked into his beautiful eyes and forgot about the snow outside and a world that very often played by rules she would never understand. A feeling of warmth spread through her, reaching all the way to her heart. "It's funny," she said, curling her body next to his and gently resting her head against his chest, "but I don't think I'll notice it at all."

He'd blown back into town like a

DUST DEVIL

REBECCA BRANDEWYNE

She was young and beautiful; he was the town's "Bad Boy." They shared one night of passion that turned Sarah Kincaid into a woman—and a mother. Yet Renzo Cassavettes never knew he had a child, because when blame for a murder fell on his shoulders, he vanished into thin air. Now Renzo is back, but his return sets off an explosive chain of events. Once again, there is a killer on the loose.

Is the man Sarah loves a cold-blooded murderer playing some diabolical game—or is he the only port in a seething storm of deception and desire?

Find out this March at your favorite retail outlet.

 MIRA The brightest star in women's fiction

MRBDD

Somewhere over the
MIDNIGHT RAINBOW
love is waiting

LINDA HOWARD

Priscilla Jane Hamilton Greer had always been given the best by her daddy—including the services of Grant Sullivan. Grant, one of the government's most effective, most desired agents, was given two orders—to find this high-society girl being held captive in Costa Rica, and to bring her home.

Alone in the jungle, fleeing armed gunmen, the two battle fear and find a love that teaches them to put the demons of the past to rest—in order to face the demons of the present.

Available at your favorite retail outlet this May.

Award-winning author!

They say opposites attract. Find out this March in

The Playboy

Cliff Howard drove an expensive sports car and was
on a first-name basis with every maître d' in town. A
confirmed bachelor, he wasn't prepared to trade in
the fast lane for car pools.

The Widow

Diana Collins drove a ten-year-old station wagon and
was on a first-name basis with teachers and ice-cream
vendors. A widow, she wasn't prepared to trade in her
nice safe life for high heels and small talk.

They had both become adept at playing their roles.
Until the playboy met the widow.

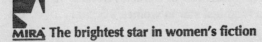

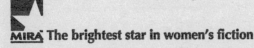